John Ryan

ALAN GLYNN is a graduate of Trinity College. His first novel, *Limitless* (originally published as *The Dark Fields*), was released as a film in March 2011 by Relativity Media and as a TV series in 2015 by CBS. He is also the author of *Winterland*; *Bloodland*, a finalist for the Edgar Award for Best Paperback Original; *Graveland*; and his most recent novel, *Paradime*, which is currently under option with ITV Studios America and One-Two Punch Productions. He lives in Ireland.

ALSO BY ALAN GLYNN

Paradime
Graveland
Bloodland
Winterland
Limitless (previously published as *The Dark Fields*)

RECEPTOR

RECEPTOR

ALAN GLYNN

PICADOR   NEW YORK

RECEPTOR. Copyright © 2018 by Alan Glynn. All rights reserved. Printed in the United States of America. For information, address Picador, 175 Fifth Avenue, New York, N.Y. 10010.

picadorusa.com • instagram.com/picador
twitter.com/picadorusa • facebook.com/picadorusa

Picador® is a U.S. registered trademark and is used by Macmillan Publishing Group, LLC, under license from Pan Books Limited.

For book club information, please visit facebook.com/picadorbookclub or email marketing@picadorusa.com.

Designed by Anna Gorovoy

Library of Congress Cataloging-in-Publication Data

Names: Glynn, Alan, 1960– author.
Title: Receptor / Alan Glynn.
Description: First U.S. edition. | New York : Picador, 2019.
Identifiers: LCCN 2018036692 | ISBN 9781250061805 (trade paperback) |
   ISBN 9781250061812 (ebook)
Subjects: | GSAFD: Suspense fiction.
Classification: LCC PR6107.L93 R43 2019 | DDC 823′.92—dc23
LC record available at https://lccn.loc.gov/2018036692

Our books may be purchased in bulk for promotional, educational, or business use. Please contact your local bookseller or the Macmillan Corporate and Premium Sales Department at 1-800-221-7945, extension 5442, or by email at MacmillanSpecialMarkets@macmillan.com.

Originally published in Great Britain by Faber and Faber Ltd as *Under the Night*

First U.S. Edition: January 2019

10 9 8 7 6 5 4 3 2 1

For the C-Dawg

He had come a long way to this blue lawn, and his dream must have seemed so close that he could hardly fail to grasp it. He did not know that it was already behind him, somewhere back in that vast obscurity beyond the city, where the dark fields of the republic rolled on under the night.

F. Scott Fitzgerald, *The Great Gatsby*

RECEPTOR

1

When Ned Sweeney leaves the apartment on West Fourth Street it's about 8:30 p.m. He's feeling distinctly weird, disorientated—not drunk exactly, he's only had three drinks in all, and over a period of hours—but not sober either, not normal. Is he coming down with something? A cold or the flu? There's a bug going around, at least so he heard at the office today—or maybe it was in the elevator, or at the newsstand, or sitting at the lunch counter at Sherri's. But isn't there always a bug going around? Isn't that one of those meaningless things people say to each other, everyone a doctor all of a sudden?

He huddles into his raincoat. The treetops and town house windows on West Fourth glisten in the orange wash of the streetlights. A taxi glides by . . . but it's less a car than a pulsating yellow daub, loosely streaked with a line of checkers, little marching heartbeats of black and white.

This isn't a cold.

He takes out his cigarettes, shivers, turns right and starts walking. After he crosses West Eleventh, he looks down at the pack of cigarettes in his hand, at the eponymous desert beast in profile, but it has the appearance of an alien object, something he's not familiar with, this small, solid, rectangular container. He squeezes it. It isn't solid. He squeezes it again, more tightly this time, crushing the cigarettes inside. He's aware that he's a smoker, and that he smokes a lot, but for some reason now the idea of smoking seems absurd to him.

He comes to a trash can on the sidewalk and tosses the pack.

For More Pure Pleasure.

That's the line on all the advertisements and billboards these days, in *The Saturday Evening Post,* and up in Times Square.

With the giant smoke rings.

He walks on, passing Perry Street, then Charles, remembering older slogans.

Smoke as many as you want . . .

He stops at West Tenth, at the curb.

More doctors smoke Camels than any other cigarette.

Traffic streams by. He watches it, and watches the flickering gaps between the cars as well—the asphalt, the small, oddly shaped pot-hole, the oily shimmer of a puddle left over from the earlier rain. In fact, he stands there at the curb for a good deal longer than is necessary. Longer than makes any sense.

He is thinking.

These ads—like all ads, really, like the ads his own agency comes up with—are lies. Smoke as many as you want? Someday people will laugh at this, because isn't it obvious that cigarette smoking *has* to be bad for you?

He looks around. People are passing by quickly now, in both directions—a man in a gray suit not unlike his own, a woman in furs, a tall, loose-limbed black man. Then a young couple. These last two are attractive in a fashionably scruffy sort of way, artist types. As they cross the street in front of him, the girl looks back, over her shoulder. She meets his gaze, and then looks away again. She is doe-eyed and willowy, anemic.

This is Greenwich Village, after all.

That fellow back in the apartment, Mike Sutton, he's an artist, too, or so he claimed. There weren't any signs of it, though, no canvases anywhere, or easels, or tubes of paint. Unlike this pair, he's clearly put his suffering days behind him.

Sweeney steps off the curb and crosses the street, trailing behind the young couple, not following them exactly . . . interested, though, curious. But then something strikes him out of the blue, and with considerable force. That Mike Sutton isn't an artist at all, is he?

Floating along the street now toward Seventh Avenue, colors stretching past, the sidewalk disappearing beneath him like a conveyor belt, Sweeney replays the previous few hours in his mind, leafs through the people and places as he would through the pages of a contract or a quarterly report. It becomes apparent to him pretty quickly that Mike Sutton is a fraud. His apartment, the furniture, the fittings, the overall feel of the place—none of it adds up. He visualizes the coral and gray living room they were in, pictures with crystal clarity the lounge chair, the ottoman, the lacquered drinks cart with the oval-shaped glass shelves and the smoothly rolling casters . . . also the well-ordered bookcases, packed with titles such as *A Pictorial History of American Ships* and *Fell's International Coin Book*. But it was all too neat, too deliberate, too much like a movie set.

He stops near the corner and closes his eyes.

There was that mirror, too. Something about it bothers him. It wasn't over the fireplace, where you'd expect it to be. It was on the wall to the left. And that just skewed the balance of the room, visually. But how had Sweeney found himself there in the first place?

He and Matt Drake had been downtown earlier, chasing an account. They were on Eighth Avenue afterward when Drake bumped into Sutton coming out of a coffee shop. Drake and Sutton had been in the same unit in the army together during World War II and apparently there was a good deal to catch up on. Sweeney would have preferred to head back to the office, as he had some correspondence to get through and was also hoping to make the 5:25—it *was* Friday, after all—but Drake was the boss, and under the circumstances he just wasn't confident enough to cut loose. So they made their way to the White Horse Tavern on Hudson Street for a quick drink, but one thing led to another and the three of them ended up going back to Sutton's place on West Fourth Street.

Sweeney had sat there for ages nursing a rather strong, or, at any rate, strange-tasting martini. He remembers glancing around the room, taking it in, half listening to Drake and Sutton shoot the breeze. Oddly enough, though, he's pretty sure that none of what's striking him about the room now, in such detail, struck him then, while he was in it. And another thing he's only now realizing—Matt Drake was scared of his own shadow.

On the face of it, this is ridiculous. Matt is his boss. He's forty years old, confident, charming, a shoo-in for account director some day. But all of a sudden, Sweeney can see him as he really is, can almost see inside him, like an X-ray, the guilt and anxiety and self-hatred sluicing through his system.

Opening his eyes again, Sweeney is met with an intense barrage of visual stimulation—streetlights, store windows, cabs, buses, everything shimmering brightly, and powered not just by electricity, but by some unknown source that seems to be emanating directly from himself. He crosses Seventh Avenue, makes his way over to Waverly Place, and turns left onto Sixth. He is aware of trying to remain calm, but then realizes he *is* calm. Which doesn't make any sense. St. Vincent's Hospital is a couple of blocks away, and if he were to go in there to get his stomach pumped, *that* would make sense. Because he now has a strong suspicion that the key to this whole business is the strange-tasting martini he was sipping earlier. But the idea of going into the hospital just doesn't interest him. Much more interesting, he thinks, would be to try to piece together what happened back in that apartment. Mike Sutton came across as someone who would pride himself on being able to make a good martini. He was a big man, chunky and muscular, but there was also something effete about him. He smoked du Mauriers. And he spent a lot of time with his back to the room, fussing at the drinks cart. He used Gordon's and Noilly Prat—four parts to one part, Sweeney calculates—and two olives. But unless something was up with the olives there was definitely another element in the mix. It wasn't brine, there was no cloudiness, or residue from the ice, or anything else you could identify. At the time, Sweeney was aware of only a slight oddness in the taste. Now he can almost see it, like a graphic superimposed on his retina, this fourth strand in the flavor spectrum. Then he revisualizes the sequence of Mike Sutton's actions at the drinks cart, each movement of each arm, each accompanying clink and glug, and it's soon clear to him that Sutton did something extra. He *put* something extra into at least one of the drinks—Sweeney can feel it, this substance, whatever it is, coursing through his bloodstream and lighting his brain up like a pinball machine.

But there is no fear, none at all, and there should be, because what Sutton did was highly irregular, not to say dangerous. What there is, again—shooting up simultaneously in a thousand little tendrils—is curiosity. What is this substance? Why did Sutton slip it to him? Who *is* Sutton anyway? Then there's Matt Drake. How does he keep the act up? He isn't a heavy drinker, he doesn't play around or anything, but it sort of seemed to Sweeney as if he was on the point of cracking up. And reviewing the guy's conversation with Sutton, their wartime catch-up, it's evident why. There were certain modulations in tone as Drake was speaking, variations in register, chromatic dips, which coincided with references to some "incident" they had both witnessed, or maybe participated in, when they were stationed in Italy.

For his part, Mike Sutton displayed a remarkably cool detachment. In fact, there were even a couple of chromatic upticks, indicating . . . what? Excitement? Arousal? Sweeney can't really say, but he has to wonder how many cases similar to Matt Drake's there might be out in the world, people walking around like ghosts, emotional time bombs who have no idea how long or short their own fuses might be. And not just ordinary people . . . those in positions of authority, as well. Take the new vice president, for instance, Dick Nixon. (*Please,* as Henny Youngman would say.) There's definitely something dark and twisted going on there—the rictus grin, the smarmy style, that business during the campaign with the funds and the dog. How short will *his* fuse turn out to be?

As Sweeney floats along the sidewalk, an answer forms in his mind. It's obvious, in a way. Nixon is a sort of political pathogen, and to release someone like that into the system is asking for trouble. Because patterns of behavior persist, they replicate . . . and sooner or later—maybe in '56, or in '60, if he decides to run his own ticket, or even some time beyond that—there will surely be another scandal, another newspaper headline leading to another television broadcast, only this time on a wider scale, and with much deeper repercussions for the country.

Sweeney slows down a bit and glances around—the city's electric swirl, on a millisecond delay, turning with him. He looks at his watch. What the hell is he *doing*? It's after nine o'clock and he hasn't called Laura yet to tell her he's going to be late. He'll be lucky to get the 9:45 now. He pictures his dinner in the oven, dried up and inedible, Tommy in bed, fast asleep, Laura in front of the TV, watching the *Philco Playhouse* or *Revlon Mirror Theater,* nervous, exasperated. Suddenly, this little picture of his domestic setup on Greenlake Avenue strikes him as profoundly strange. It's as though he's looking down on it from a great distance, from the sky, from another planet, no longer sure how any of it relates to him.

He crosses Twenty-Third Street. It's the same when he thinks about his job at Ridley Rogan Blanford. Anything he pictures about the place—his cluttered desk, a successful piece of artwork, the view from Jack Rogan's office—diminishes in significance almost immediately. It becomes small, irrelevant. But at the same time he feels amazing and is buzzing with energy.

It's all very confusing. For some unknown reason this guy back at the apartment on West Fourth slipped him a Mickey Finn. That usually means something like chloral hydrate, doesn't it? Something to incapacitate the target, so they can be assaulted or robbed or otherwise taken advantage of.

But Ned Sweeney is more in control, more aware, and more confident than he has ever felt in his entire life. Normally—and anyone who knows him would say this—Sweeney is a quiet, unassuming kind of guy. He's of average intelligence, works hard, and can be creative. But his ambitions are modest—to get ahead at the agency, to buy a bigger house some day, to keep Laura happy and send Tommy to college. Now all of that seems a bit dull, a bit limited. Sweeney is thirty-three years old. Is this supposed to be *it*?

Halfway along the next block, he spots a dingy bar and slips inside. He finds a pay phone at the rear. Normally, if he has to stay late in the city, if he's stuck with clients or finishing something up at the office, he'll be apprehensive about calling home, almost dreading the moment when Laura picks up. It isn't a regular occurrence— he's good about calling—it's just that everything seems to make her anxious these days. But dialing her now, considerably later than he has on any previous occasion, he doesn't feel the least bit apprehensive at all.

"*Hello?*"

"It's me."

"Oh my God, Ned, I've been worried sick."

"I'm sorry, I got delayed and couldn't call." Hearing himself say this, he stops. "Actually, you know what, that's not true. Of course I could have called. But I didn't. I must have *chosen* not to. There must be—"

"*What?*"

"Uh . . . sorry?"

"Ned? Are you all right?"

"Yes, strangely enough, I am."

"Are you *drunk?*"

"No, but I guess it must sound like I am, right? It's pretty much what I thought at first, too, but there's . . . there's just so much clarity, so much—"

"Clarity? You're in a bar, Ned, I can hear it in the background. Who are you with?"

"No one. But listen, Laura, it's all . . . I mean, there's . . ." He's aware now of a gathering speed and complexity to his thought processes that will make it difficult, if not impossible, to put comprehensible sentences together, to squeeze the words he wants to say down a phone line to his wife, especially with so much noise in the background here, voices, laughter, clinking glasses, the crack of balls colliding on a pool table.

"Ned? What is it? Ned?"

"I'll explain later, when I get home. Hug Tommy for me."

He hangs up.

Sweeney does feel apprehensive now, but this time it's at the thought of actually going home . . . because little by little, in his mind, 15 Greenlake Avenue is taking on the feel and dimensions of a doll's house—brittle, confining, prison-like. Which is what he wanted to explain to Laura: that he understands, that he can see the way her whole life is circumscribed by convention, that of course she feels perpetually anxious, not to mention frequently pissed off at him.

But if the prize here is an individual "identity," then how well is *he* doing—stuck every day, as he is, behind a desk on the fourteenth floor, in his gray flannel suit, a mere cog in the corporate machine? His sense of the absurdity of all this ripens to a point where he has to just block it out. Instead, he focuses on various snippets of conversation he overhears on his way to the exit, odd words and phrases—"Teamsters," "Cyd Charisse," "the roto-swirl agitator," "flight 723," "Mantle's home run." Instinctively, he extrapolates from these what each speaker is talking about, their point of view, possible gaps in their knowledge, flaws in their arguments—entire exchanges, in fact, all of it coming so thick and so fast that he gets a bit dizzy and brushes against a guy on the very last stool a few feet from the door.

"Hey, fella, watch it—"

"Sorry."

"Jesus."

"Oh, and by the way, it was five hundred sixty-five."

"What?"

Raising his hand to push the door open, Sweeney half turns back to look at the guy. "Mantle's home run?" he says. "In April? The tape-measure thing? It was *five* hundred sixty-five feet, not four hundred sixty-five . . ."

Back out on the sidewalk, he keeps moving, powered by the motor of his thoughts. But just how fast is he going? Because very soon— sooner than seems possible—he's all the way up at Forty-Second Street. He's also on the right side of the avenue now. He looks around, a little confused. When did he cross over? He has no recollection of doing so. None at all. This is alarming. He can conjure up long-forgotten details from when he was a kid, random stuff, anything . . . that small tin on his mother's dresser, for instance, Stein's Face Powder, with the weird list of colors on the back of it: Pink, Sallow, Olive, Cream, Othello, Indian, Lavender. But he can't recall crossing the street five or ten minutes ago?

And where is he headed anyway? Because if he doesn't want to go home, if that's too strange an option to even contemplate, what's left? Maybe more to the point, how long is this going to last? Not that he wants it to end or anything—he doesn't. What he wants, in fact, now that he thinks about it, is something to do. Or someone to talk to. But as more blocks flicker past, the lights of the city merging into a dense, multicolored plasma, he reckons he might be on the point of collapsing and actually dying right here on the sidewalk. Or perhaps he's already dead and this is just what it's like.

Though after a moment—after several moments probably, a rapid sequence of them—he finds himself somewhere else, indoors, at a bar. He's got a drink in his hand. It's a much fancier bar than the last one, and he's talking to someone, a guy in his forties. "So yeah," he's saying, "I work in advertising all right, but I can't help seeing it as this gigantic lie, because let's face it, here we are in 1953, eight years on from the war, and as a society we're already capable of producing whatever we need to survive, *more* than enough, in fact, and I mean for everyone—food, automobiles, TV sets, shirts, toothpaste, cigarettes, you name it. But you know what the problem is? It's not that we're not producing enough stuff—we are. It's that we're not consuming enough."

"But—"

"Our future as a democracy is contingent upon our ability to spend, to keep consumption in line with output, and we have to work harder at that, because there's no reversing this thing. The industrial output of goods and services is never going to stop, regardless of what we might need today and regardless of the fact that ten, twenty, fifty years from now, we'll inevitably have reached some outer limit of what it's even possible to consume. Plus, we'll have made ourselves sick in the process, actually poisoned ourselves, poisoned the planet, or blown ourselves up."

"So how—"

"Look around. Everyone's stalking the supermarket aisles, they're haunting the car dealerships, they're flicking through the Sears catalog, all in this hypnoidal trance. And who are the snake charmers?" Sweeney takes a mock bow. "The ad agencies up and down Madison Avenue, that's who. They're all—*we're* all—using new psychiatric probing techniques to chart the very fabric of the human mind. And we're not doing it to find out what people want, that's a dead end, we're doing it to find out how to *make* people want stuff."

"That's quite an extraordinary thesis you've got there, Mr. . . . uh?"

"Sweeney. Ned Sweeney. I'm with RRB, on Madison Avenue. What about you?" Extending his hand, he throws a surreptitious glance out over the room. However he's ended up here, he reckons the place is an upscale watering hole for Midtown executive types.

The guy shakes his hand. "Vance Packard," he says. "I work for *American Magazine*, over on Fifth, in the Crowell-Collier Building."

At the mention of this, a Technicolor blizzard of magazine covers flits across Sweeney's brain.

"You're a journalist?"

"Yes. I do features mainly." Packard then looks at his watch. "You know what, Ned, I'd love to continue this conversation, because I have a ton of questions I want to put to you, but I have to meet someone at the Waldorf. It won't take more than ten minutes. I don't suppose you'd like to tag along?"

At the entrance to the Waldorf, Packard engages briefly in some banter with the doormen, after which he and Sweeney skip up the short flight of stairs to the main foyer. As a New Yorker, Sweeney has passed the Waldorf many times, but he's never actually been inside it. Despite this, he seems to have accumulated a considerable knowledge of the place—mostly, he supposes, from magazine articles and movies. As they walk across the foyer, he notices everything in detail, the Rockwood-stone walls and columns, the travertine floors, the Louis Rigal frieze (an elaborate, thirteen-panel allegory about hunting, eating, drinking, and dancing), and that bizarre rug, with its central, six-part circular tapestry depicting the drama of human existence, the *Wheel of Life,* all of it stretching out before him now, oscillating, threatening to come alive and engulf him.

But he keeps walking, and follows Packard over to what is known as Peacock Alley. This wide, corridor-like affair leads through to the hotel's central lobby, but it is also a busy lounge area lined on either side with tables and chairs. Most of these are occupied, and more people are standing around in little groups, with the occasional staff member gliding past in one direction or another, carrying a tray of drinks or holding up a telegram.

A few feet ahead of him, Packard slows down, half turns, and indicates to Sweeney that he won't be long. He then approaches someone at a nearby table and joins him. Sweeney slows down, too, and makes a gentle turn, feeling slightly dizzy as he takes in the opulence of his surroundings—the French walnut paneling inlaid with ebony, the glass display cabinets showcasing expensive jewelry, the marble pilasters and nickel-bronze cornices. He starts to drift back toward the foyer, but in the next moment, and before he knows it, he's standing among a small group of men, everyone smoking, everyone having a drink, everyone listening . . . to him. "Consider it like this, gentlemen. A new highway opens, or a new expressway, or a new bridge, and a month later, however modest the projections might have been, it's already operating at full capacity, so simply building more of them is not the answer. It might actually be the problem. If we continue to churn out cars at this rate, followed by road networks to accommodate them, what do you think the city's going to look like in 1963? Or in 1973? By all means build roads, but you've got to expand the mass-transit system, too."

"Well, shoot," one of the men standing next to him, a fat guy in a silk suit, whispers loudly. "Don't let RM hear you say that."

The others laugh.

RM?

Glancing around, Sweeney quickly scans the room. Further back, Vance Packard is still sitting at that table talking to—or, rather, listening to—another man. Sweeney squints. The man is probably in his sixties. He's distinguished-looking and radiates a certain authority. It takes a couple of seconds, but of course . . . this is Robert Moses, the powerful city parks commissioner, and these guys here have to be his entourage.

Sweeney turns back to look at them again. He shakes his head. "RM isn't going to stop, is he? It's not in his nature. He's just going to keep doing the same thing over and over again, wave after wave of it, each phase bigger than the last, the Cross Bronx Expressway, the Horace Harding, this Lower Manhattan thing, whatever . . . he's chasing that elusive solution, the big fix—forty-five to sixty billion dollars over the next eight to twelve years, isn't that the figure I read somewhere recently?"

"Hey—"

"And no one'll say boo to him. *That's* the problem."

The men seem taken aback by this. One of them, a slim, nervous type in a bow tie, raises his eyebrows. "Do *you* want to give it a try?"

Sweeney shrugs. "Look, I don't have—"

But then the fat guy flinches and says, "Oh, shitsky." They all turn to see Moses striding toward them from the far end of the lounge area.

Is it possible to smell fear? With a fine spray of it in the air now, Sweeney certainly can.

"Time to ship out, fellas," Moses barks as he approaches. There's a rush to extinguish cigarettes. Drinks are abandoned on any available surface. As this is going on, Moses comes to a stop directly in front of Sweeney and just stands there.

"Who are you?" he says gruffly.

"Oh, I'm nobody, Mr. Moses," Sweeney answers, "just a regular schmo who comes into the city every day on the train, on the noisy, dirty Toonerville Trolley. You see, I live in the suburbs, but I don't own an automobile, so I guess I'm . . . what would you call me, a relic?"

Moses stares at him for a second, puzzled, processing what he's heard, or thinks he's heard. He moves his head slightly to the side. "Charlie? *Charlie?* Who is this clown?"

"Oh, Mr. Moses," the fat guy says, rushing over, "I don't actually—"

"Traffic will run *smoothly?*" Sweeney says, ignoring Charlie. "That's the prediction you keep making, year after year, like a . . . a mantra, but don't you see, it's never going to happen."

Moses's nostrils flare and a reddish, almost purple flush colors his cheeks. This isn't how people talk to him. He continues staring at Sweeney in disbelief but seems curiously unable to respond.

"It's the numbers," Sweeney goes on quietly, "they just don't stack up. They can't. They only go one way, and in terms of car ownership and daily commutes, the progression isn't even arithmetical, it's geometrical. It's like with everything else"—he takes a quick, deep breath—"in our society, in the economy, in the culture, all around us, it's just one big, ever-expanding, self-replicating fractal *pattern.*"

"Fractal?" Moses whispers. "Mantra? What the hell does that mean? What are you talking about?" Then, as though snapping awake from a trance, he turns to Fat Charlie and shakes his head. "What kind of liquor are they serving here?"

"Beats me, sir."

When Moses starts to move away, Sweeney leans in. "Uh, just one thing, Mr. Moses."

"What, goddammit? I'm *busy.*"

"Talk to Walter O'Malley, would you? Please."

Moses pulls back, as though to get a clearer look at Sweeney's face. "What did you say?"

"You heard me. If you don't let the O'Malley build his stadium on Atlantic Avenue, he'll move the Dodgers out of Brooklyn. Don't think he won't do it."

Fat Charlie makes a snorting sound. "That's ridiculous."

"You think?" Sweeney says. "The Boston Braves have just moved to Milwaukee."

"But that's—"

"Look, it'd be a business decision. Ebbets Field is crumbling, no one can get to it, and if they can, there's nowhere to park. The site O'Malley wants is right over by the Flatbush Terminal. People like me would come pouring in on the LIRR."

"All right," Moses barks, half lunging at him. "Who the hell *are* you?"

Fat Charlie and Skinny Bow Tie intervene. As they cajole a furious Moses away toward the Park Avenue foyer, Sweeney just stands there and watches. Then he glances back and sees that Packard, still at the table, is consulting his notepad. Was he interviewing

Moses? It seemed a bit short and informal for that, and anyway, Sweeney is pretty sure Moses doesn't actually give interviews. He's too important, or considers himself so, to endure the inconvenience. Nevertheless, Packard here is no hack. Didn't he spend a whole week the previous January with the Eisenhowers as they settled into the White House? Didn't he write about it for *American Magazine*?

Whichever it was, Sweeney is quickly losing interest. Robert Moses, for all his power and standing, strikes him as a fairly one-dimensional and transparent figure. Nor is Sweeney interested, for that matter, in answering any more of Vance Packard's questions about advertising. He's really said all he wants to say on the subject. So before the journalist happens to look up and spot him, he slips away. He doesn't go in the direction Moses went, but the other way, toward the hotel's bigger, busier central lobby. Here, as he moves about, voices slide in and out of his hearing, colors shift subtly, surfaces shimmer. Passing the registration desk, then a newsstand, then a cigar counter, he feels the strongest urge to stop and talk to someone, anyone. He needs to engage. But he also knows it can't be inconsequential, it can't just be small talk.

He keeps moving, and over the next couple of minutes wanders deeper into the hotel's maze of hallways and corridors, connecting galleries and side lobbies. But it may be longer than a couple of minutes, because once again he has the impression that time is skipping, jumping forward in barely perceptible increments, the missing beats like frames cut from a strip of film. He ends up at a bank of elevators near the Lexington Avenue exit and is staring at the elaborate bas-relief Art Deco design on one of the blue-steel doors when he becomes aware of people behind him, approaching—voices, one low and husky, mumbling, the other higher and sweeter, giggling.

"Going up?"

To his left, a tuxedo-sleeved arm reaches for the button, presses it, and withdraws.

He detects something—or, rather, many things, and all in an instant—cadence, pitch, inflection. Also, a scent, a fragrance. Without turning, he says, "Rose Geranium?"

There is a brief pause, and then, "I beg your pardon?"

"Floris," he says, turning slightly, but not making eye contact. "Rose Geranium by Floris? Your perfume?"

"Why, yes." Another brief pause, and a giggle. "Bet you couldn't do that, Mar."

The elevator door pings open. The attendant looks out and smiles. "Good evening." He steps aside to let them all in. "Please."

The ride in the elevator passes in a flash. Whatever happens in those few moments, and in the few after that, whatever is said—and it's probably plenty—Sweeney is hardly conscious of any of it. The space is too enclosed, the rush of sensory impressions too intense. In fact, the next time he feels any degree of control he is sitting in an armchair in a luxurious room, and Marilyn—in her black, pleated chiffon dress—is handing him a drink.

"I never heard it put that way before," she is saying.

He takes the drink. "Well, it serves our purposes to portray the Soviet system as evil, to portray Communism as a form of cancer, but to be honest, Joe Stalin was no Communist, and neither is this new fellow, Nikita Khrushchev, not really, not by any strict definition of the term. What these guys *are,* however, is autocrats, and to the bone. I mean, it's just how they roll over there. Look at the tsars, it was no different back then, either . . ." As Sweeney is speaking, he glances around the room. This is a residential suite in the Waldorf Towers. He didn't register where they were heading in the elevator, but glancing out the window now, and seeing a corner of what he takes to be Forty-Ninth Street, he reckons they are probably on the twenty-seventh or twenty-eighth floor. ". . . so what this is really about is control. They use the iron fist and the jackboot—we use soap powder and paranoia."

Marilyn is curled up on the couch opposite him now, listening intently. Brando, tie loosened, is pacing back and forth between them.

"But sooner or later," Sweeney continues, "if we're not careful, if we don't stand up to people like the senator from Wisconsin, that distinction will become blurred and will ultimately lose its meaning."

"Jesus, Ned," Brando says, "you're *killing* me with this stuff." He stops and turns toward Marilyn. "I mean . . . I see Gadge all the time now, every day, I gotta look him in the eye, and I . . . I . . ."

"Oh, Mar . . ."

It's a nice room, warm, clearly lived in. A bulletin board on the wall next to the door has some photos and cuttings pinned to it. There are books (*Invisible Man, Sister Carrie*) and magazines (*Popular Science, Modern Screen*) lying around. There is also a pile of typed pages bound with brass fasteners.

"Listen," Sweeney says, "I'm not just talking about the hearings, or about one guy giving names. It's bigger than that, it's about all of us . . . all of us capitulating at the most basic level, all of us being complicit in our own moral and aesthetic suffocation."

"All right, all right . . ." Brando says, turning around slowly, his fists clenched, a pained expression on his face. "Just who the hell *are* you, man?"

A bit later—ten minutes, twenty, an hour, it's hard to tell—Sweeney finds himself sitting on the other sofa, in quiet conclave with Marilyn. Brando is in another room, on a bed presumably, or maybe on the floor, snoring audibly.

"I don't mind being famous," Marilyn is whispering, "it's kind of fun, most of the time anyway, but then people can surprise you. They can be awfully cruel, you know. They can say things that just make you want to give it all up." She traces the line of a pleat on her dress with her finger. "But I think I'm probably going to do that anyway, sooner or later, you know? Give all this up, and retire." She pauses. "Into private life."

"Listen, Marilyn," Sweeney says, staring at her arm, her shoulder, her neck, tracing an imaginary line of his own. "That's not going to happen. There *is* no private life, not anymore, not for you, not for him in there either. You two are already so . . . so *imprinted* on the collective consciousness that I don't see . . . I don't . . ."

He feels a sudden ripple of exhaustion, of weakness almost.

"Don't see what, Ned?"

There is a hint of alarm in her voice.

"You're how old, Marilyn? Twenty-six, twenty-seven?" Sweeney glances in the direction of the other room. "He's twenty-nine?"

She nods.

"Okay, well, this level of fame you have now? It's not going away. Not ever." A pain starts throbbing behind his eyes. "Your career may peak at some point, then subside, and that could happen soon, next year, or the year after, or in 1960—or it may have happened already, who knows—but your actual fame? That will never see a peak, and therefore never subside. It can only ever expand, and widen, and fragment . . ."

Which is what Marilyn is doing now, fragmenting right there in front of him . . . multiple Marilyns in a grid, rapidly self-replicating, all bright colors at first, but then dimming, draining to a pallid gray . . .

At that point there is a shift, another jump cut. To the street.

Did he vomit in the elevator on the way down? He's not sure, but he has a really sour taste in his mouth as he walks up Lexington Avenue.

As he limps, actually.

He looks at his watch. It's late, after one, and much colder than before—so cold that his mind feels sort of numb. Approaching Fifty-Seventh Street, he slows down. Then he comes to a stop, right there in the middle of the sidewalk. Where was he just now? At the Waldorf Astoria? Inches from Marilyn Monroe? Gazing at her bare shoulders? Inhaling her perfume, her whispers?

Really?

And before that?

There were other people, other conversations, but he can't piece any of it together. He's confused, and tired. He hasn't eaten.

Will his dinner still be in the oven when he gets home? For that matter, will his *home* still be there when he gets off the train? Suddenly, more than anything else in the world, he needs to get to Greenlake Avenue. He starts walking again, in the opposite direction, moving fast, then faster. After a while, he throws his arm out and hails a passing yellow cab.

He piles into the backseat and tells the driver Penn Station. The driver flicks his flag down and hits the gas. Probably in the middle of his shift, the guy is fidgety, anxious to talk. Sweeney tunes in and out. ". . . that's where I saw it," the driver is saying at one point, "in that new magazine they're putting out, the *TV Guide* it's called, real neat little thing, fits right in your pocket. You ever see that, ever read it yourself, the *TV Guide*?"

Sweeney doesn't answer. He is staring out the window now, any shred of attention he has left consumed by the hypnotic pull of the city's lights as they flicker past.

2

"You really couldn't make any of this up." Congresswoman Stephanie Proctor flicks the newspaper in her lap with the back of her hand. "Am I right?"

"That's sort of the whole point, isn't it, Congresswoman? Now you *can*. Because it all is. Made up, I mean."

"Oh, come on, Ray."

"This is what it's come to." I lean forward. "And it's going to put everyone out of business. Those guys." I point at the newspaper in her lap. "Guys like *me*. What's the point of being a fact-checker if what you find out, if the facts you *check*, no longer have any value? If they're disposable?"

She shakes her head and sits back in the chair, her drink—a glass of Sancerre—left untouched.

We're in the Waldorf Astoria. The congresswoman has a dinner scheduled for nine with some big donors in a place across the street, but she wanted to run something by me first. Her assistant is hovering in the background, phone in hand. This person doesn't like me. She thinks I'm a bad influence on the congresswoman. She may well be right.

Proctor folds the newspaper and places it on the coffee table between us. A story from this morning's edition, clearly fake, has been burning a hole in the internet all day. Last night, Supreme Court Justice Darius Wilbur is supposed to have left a FedEx package in the backseat of a town car that was taking him to a D.C hotel—a FedEx package containing five hundred OxyContin pills and three blank prescription pads. In normal times, in the old days, in the *real* world—however you want to characterize it—a story like that wouldn't have made it into print that fast. A proper journalist, or someone who does what I do, would have chased it down, made a few calls, tracked some paperwork, and pretty quickly realized there was nothing there, and that would have been the end of it.

But not anymore. Now it gets published, regardless of how implausible or even preposterous it might seem, because people are going to read it anyway on their phones.

"I'd like your opinion on something, Ray."

I roll my eyes.

She widens hers. "What's that supposed to mean?"

"You know I don't do opinions, Congresswoman. Maybe that makes me a dinosaur, but what can I tell you?"

"You're a bit young to be a dinosaur. What are you, thirty-five?"

"Thirty-three."

"Pffh. I'm nearly sixty. In case you hadn't noticed. So what does that make me?"

I shrug. I know a conversational dead end when I meet one.

"You may not value your opinion, Ray, but I do." She stares at her untouched glass of wine. "They want me to bring in the old man."

I give this some thought. "They" means her team—the young woman standing behind us, and various advisors. The "old man" is her father, Clay Proctor. And by "bring in," I'm guessing she means haul in front of the cameras for an endorsement.

"Is that wise?"

"That's what I'm asking you."

"How would I know? I've never met him."

"No, but you could still form an opinion. Besides, I want you to meet him. There's a thing tomorrow night, he'll be at it, a book launch. Let me introduce you—five minutes, that's all. See what you think."

I don't know about this. Clay Proctor was defense secretary under Nixon. Later, he was an advisor to Reagan and the first Bush. He must be ninety years old, at least. So why do they want to use him? I'd have to look into it a bit before I could even guess what they're thinking.

But only if I cared, which I don't, not really.

I do like Stephanie Proctor, though. She's not insane. I remember once I found a box of LPs that belonged to my dad in the basement of the house I grew up in out in Westchester. One of them was by Lenny Bruce and was called *I Am Not A Nut, Elect Me!* That's Stephanie Proctor.

But without the Dilaudid and the jokes.

I shrug again. "I'm not sure I see the point, but . . . I'll check him out."

It's what I do. I screen people, usually election candidates. I dig into their backgrounds, trawl through their shit, my antennae up for anything that might derail a campaign. Opposition research is a neutral-sounding name for an essentially mean-spirited enterprise— get the other poor bastard before he gets you—but it's an inevitable part of the process and as old as the hills. I first did some work for Stephanie Proctor about a year and a half ago. I found out that one of her political opponents had serious gambling debts. These were subsequently dressed up as "ties to Chechen mobsters," and that was pretty much the end of that. I didn't make anything up, though. I didn't shape the "narrative." I simply uncovered some relevant facts.

A candidate wouldn't usually have direct contact with someone doing oppo, but before allowing her team to release the information I had provided, the congresswoman insisted on talking to me in person. We met in a coffee shop for fifteen minutes and hit it off.

I had an angle on things that she liked, which basically meant I was nonpartisan. I've done other work for her since, mostly background searches, voting-record sweeps, that kind of thing, and we've talked a few times on the phone—which she always insists I bill her for. Now, with the midterms looming, the pace is stepping up.

"Thanks, Ray," she says, reaching for her phone. "I'll have Molly send you the details."

I knock back what's left of my own drink, a seltzer water, then get up and leave.

Walking along Park Avenue, I call one of my research analysts and ask him to put together a short book on Clay Proctor—what he's been up to since he retired, board appointments, recent investments, public appearances, whatever.

"I assume this is urgent, Ray."

It probably wouldn't take me more than an hour to do the job myself, but I'm really tired, having just come off a two-day trawl through some financial-disclosure forms for an anxious client.

"Well, I . . ."

"Okay, don't worry, I'm on it."

"Thanks, Jerry."

I get dinner at a Korean place I like, after which I head home to my apartment on Sixty-Fourth for an early night. I flick through the channels for something to watch, but nothing takes. I could watch news, but that'd be too much like work. Plus, the idea of staying informed these days is an illusion—you pick whichever version of events you're going to believe and then block out anything that contradicts or undermines that view. Balanced reporting has gone the way of lunch. It's for wimps. What would you do with it, in any case? Yes, *this,* but on the other hand, *that.*

Fuck off. The real question is whose side are you on.

I get up off the couch and catch sight of myself in the mirror.

Shit.

I look away. My phone and laptop are over there on the counter, either one ready to devour me whole if I let it. When I'm at the office I can concentrate for hours on end, but lately, outside of work, my attention span seems to atomize within seconds—like now—and usually what I'm left with, all I'm left with, is an anxious thrumming in the pit of my stomach. How am I supposed to quell that? Gin or vodka tends to put a stop to it almost immediately—in seconds, like magic. But that only lasts about fifteen minutes. Then I'm in trouble again.

A few years ago, I had a bit of a heroin thing going on. It didn't last, but I skated on some *very* thin ice there for a while. I guess I got lucky in the end, if that's what you want to call it. The point is, though, heroin was made for the state of mind I'm currently in. Restive, fidgety, no off switch. I could go over to the counter right now, pick up the phone, call my dealer.

Or I could scale it back and just order some pills. It's a thought. It's always a thought.

Instead, I stick to my original plan. I have an early night. I go to bed.

Next morning, at the office, I have some calls and emails to get through before I can look at what Jerry sent me on Clay Proctor. But when I finally get to it, the file is a quick read. Nothing in it surprises me. After he retired, Proctor sat on the boards of Exxon-Mobil, American Express, the Uranium Mining Consortium, and Eiben-Chemcorp. He was named an emeritus member of the University of North Carolina's Kaplan Institute for Public Policy and set up the Clay Proctor Endowed Scholarship. He used to be an occasional guest on the Sunday morning talk shows, but not in the last couple of years. His most recent public sighting was about six months ago at a fund-raiser for the governor of Connecticut.

It's not clear to me why Stephanie Proctor's advisors would want her father to get involved in the campaign, or why she herself would want me to vet him. The old man is a revered Beltway veteran, without a hint of impropriety in his long career, so why hasn't the congresswoman pulled him out of the hat before, in her previous campaigns? I'd always assumed it was because Proctor was either too old or too sick. Maybe she just wants an independent assessment. Is the old man compos mentis? Would he be a liability? Maybe she thinks so, but is under a lot of pressure from her team, and is looking for a way to close this down, a second opinion. She knows I won't bullshit her, and I won't, but I'm also not happy about being put in the middle like this.

The launch is at 7:00 p.m. at an independent bookstore on Madison Avenue. Before then I have a ton of work to get through—a digitized archive of municipal records going back thirty years. I come up for air at about five, go home, take a shower, and change. The store isn't that far from where I live, so I decide to walk. The book being launched is a biography of Dr. Raoul Fursten, someone I've never heard of. As I wait for a light to change at Lexington Avenue, I do a quick search on my phone. Apparently, Fursten was an eminent scientist in the fifties and sixties, a chemist and later a clinical psychologist. He led various studies and has things named after him, but nothing that rings any bells. He died in 1973. I'm assuming that Fursten and Clay Proctor were contemporaries.

When I get to the bookstore, the event is already in full swing—if that's the right word, seeing as how, at a guess, the average age of attendees has to be north of seventy. I take a glass of water and scan the room for the congresswoman. I spot her in a corner with Molly and someone else who works on her team, a communications guy. My preference would be to avoid these two and to speak with the congresswoman alone, but that might not be possible.

I look around to see if I can identify the old man. Aside from a few overworked publishing and PR people, the room is mainly populated with old guys in tweeds and bow ties. For the most part, they're animated, shouting one another down, as if this might be their last outing, their final opportunity to catch up and reminisce about the old (now *very* old) days, when they all presumably ran things, institutions, departments, faculties, programs, who even knows what. But a smaller group of three, standing together, are quieter, meeker, as if the old days might just be too old, and what's actually interesting to them is yesterday, or this morning—what that dope on TV said, a ball game, the texture of the pastry in those croissants they serve at that place, where is it, you know, the one next to the other place.

In the middle of this group—I'm pretty sure—stands ninety-two-year-old Clay Proctor. He's especially small and frail looking, like a bird, with downy white hair and mottled skin, his frame stooped, his suit a size too big for him. He has what looks like a glass of wine in his hand and he seems pretty alert.

I glance over at the congresswoman. She hasn't seen me yet. She's still busy, switching her attention rapidly between a now stressed-looking Molly and her phone. At the top of the room, there is a podium and next to it a poster display of the book with an accompanying photo of the author. I turn back and walk toward Clay Proctor. His radar beeps at about ten feet and he looks up.

I hold out my hand. "Mr. Secretary."

He smiles. "No one's called me *that* in a while."

We shake, and he looks at me inquiringly.

"I'm sorry to intrude," I say, quickly making eye contact with each of the other two men, then returning to Proctor. "I'm a research analyst. I do some work with your daughter, who I admire greatly, by the way." I pause. "I just wanted to say hi."

"Well, what do you know?" Proctor says, addressing his compadres. "The kid's got manners. He's paying his respects. I like that." He looks at my glass. "What's that you're drinking? Water?"

"Yes."

He holds up his own glass. "It's probably better than this stuff."

"I know. The wine at these things is usually more trouble than it's worth."

"You're a practical man, too, I see."

"Oh, I wouldn't be so sure about practical, not really, but—"

"*Ray?*"

I feel a hand on my arm and turn around. "Congresswoman!"

"You snuck in!"

I hold up my free hand. "That's not how I'd describe it. You looked pretty busy over there on your phone."

Clay Proctor laughs at this.

"Don't encourage him, Dad." She sighs. "Anyway, I see you two have met."

"Yes, Stephanie, and we're having a perfectly nice time, so why don't you just skip back on over there with your phone."

"Very well."

As she glides away, the congresswoman catches my eye and emits a signal. But it's a bit crackly. I'm not sure if I'm being admonished or if she's telling me to be careful. She might have wanted to brief me on something before I met the old man, but if so, she should have done it last night. Anyway, I'm in control this way, and my impression of Proctor will be unfiltered—though I have to say I already like him.

"So . . . *Ray?* Is that what she called you?"

"Yes, I'm sorry. Of course. It's Ray . . . Ray Sweeney."

Proctor takes this in, as if it's something worth reflecting on. The other two old guys have broken away and are talking to a server holding a tray of canapés. "So tell me, did Stephanie put you up to this?"

I look back at him. No point in lying. Proctor is ninety-two years old, and what are the stakes here anyway? "Yes."

"It figures."

"I don't think it's anything nefarious."

He snorts. "I'll be the judge of that. So, are you supposed to try and rope me into attending some campaign event or something, is that it?"

"No, no, not at all. I don't work for your daughter, not in an official capacity." I am acutely uncomfortable now. In a couple of deft moves, he's made me show my hand. Because what do I say to that? I'm not sure. One thing I am sure of, though—there's no issue here with mental acuity. "She . . ."

"She asked you to check me out, right?"

I laugh, conceding defeat. "So I guess my work here is done. Sorry."

"Don't worry about it, Ray. Maybe you can relax now and have a proper drink."

At this point, chewed up and spat out, I expect to be dismissed, so Proctor can go back to jabbering with his cronies. But he stays where he is, and if his tone shifts at all I can't detect it.

"It's funny," he says, "I don't miss it."

"What, politics?"

"Yes, and you know, I was only what you'd call a politician for a relatively brief period of time. You just don't ever get to shake it off, no matter what else you do. Or *did*, beforehand."

"This was in the early seventies?"

"Yes."

I'm dying to ask him what it was like working for Nixon, but I don't want to push my luck.

He takes a sip from his glass. "Dick was always a challenge to be around, of course. You never knew what mood he'd be in."

"Oh."

"I've advised other presidents, too, from the private-sector side. I've seen them up close, and they were all weirdos in their own way, believe me, but Dick took the biscuit."

"I can't say I'm surprised to hear it."

"He was a Dilantin man. You know what that is?"

I make an appropriate face. "Remind me."

"It's an anticonvulsant, with a fairly impressive list of potential side effects, like suicidal ideation and psychosis. A couple of those bad boys, a glass of neat Scotch, and . . ." He shakes his head and makes a whistling sound. "It was hard on Pat, you know. She was a smart woman, and *sane*, too. At least at the outset."

He drains his glass and looks around.

I stare at him. How long have I known the man—five minutes? I could be anybody. I could be with the *National Enquirer* or BuzzFeed. I still like him, though, and would love to press him for more details, but . . . I get it. Stephanie's concern. Whether it's the filter-free joy of just being ninety-fucking-two or that *he's* on Dilantin, I don't know, but the campaign should clearly proceed with caution—which is obviously what Stephanie thinks anyway.

Whatever. Now I just need to get out of here.

And then Proctor says it.

"You said your name was Sweeney? Did I get that right?"

"Uh, yeah . . . Ray Sweeney."

"Funny."

Is it? I peer into my glass of nonalcoholic water and wait for more.

"I once knew a fellow called Sweeney. I wonder . . . Where are you from?"

"Oh, I'm sure a lot Sweeneys came over on the boat after the potato famine. It's a common enough name."

"You didn't answer my question."

"Long Island, originally. We moved up to Westchester when I was a kid."

"Oh." He pulls his head back a little. "Funny. The guy I knew was from Long Island."

"Really?"

"Yes." A pause. "His name was Ned Sweeney."

"Huh." I don't know what's going on here. I glance around for a second, wishing the congresswoman was nearby. But she's on the other side of the room. I turn back to Proctor. "That is funny."

He stares at me, but doesn't say anything. It's as if he's waiting for me to catch up.

Thankfully, there's some movement at the top of the room. A man is approaching the podium, and although he's clearly the author, he looks a lot older than he does on the poster. Someone else places a bottle of water on a small table next to him and starts fiddling with the microphone cable. If the event gets going soon, I should be able to inch away from Proctor and leave.

But it doesn't.

The author takes a call on his cell and begins pacing back and forth off to the side.

I have a tight knot in my stomach now. Proctor hasn't moved.

"Look," I say eventually, "I never met him, but I believe my grandfather was also a Ned. Actually, Edward, but he was known as Ned."

"Isn't that something. What did your grandfather do, Ray?"

"I don't really know. He died young." I swallow. "I think he was in advertising or something?"

Proctor nods along at this. "Yes, I reckon I knew him. Ned Sweeney." He takes a sip from his glass. Without looking at me directly, he adds, "He was one of the most extraordinary men I've ever met."

What?

The knot in my stomach tightens into a spasm. I lean forward slightly. "Excuse me?"

"I mean it. He was truly extraordinary." He pauses. "I can see that now."

Proctor looks away and seems lost in thought. This gives me a quick chance to reckon with a thought or two of my own. Am I being played here? Is this all a coincidence? How do I not know that my grandfather was *anything*, let alone extraordinary?

"To be honest, Mr. Secretary," I say in a loud whisper, drawing his gaze back to me, "the only thing I knew about my grandfather growing up was that he killed himself."

Someone taps the microphone, clears their throat. "Good evening, ladies and gentlemen, and thanks so much for coming . . ."

There's a general shuffling to attention and facing forward, but I don't move a muscle. I continue to stare at the old man.

Not moving either, Proctor just gives a gentle shake of his head. "No, son," he says, also in a whisper, but a barely audible one, "you've got it wrong. Ned Sweeney didn't kill himself."

3

When he opens his eyes, everything is gray and colorless, the ceiling, the walls, the drapes.

What time is it? What day?

He turns his head to look at the clock on the nightstand.

9:40.

What?

Please let it be Saturday, and not a workday. It *is* Saturday. It has to be. Laura wouldn't let him sleep in like this, not on a workday.

He stares up at the ceiling. His brain feels leaden. Thoughts start to form, then dissolve. His mouth is dry. His limbs ache. Was he at a party or something last night? Was he *drinking?* Because—

He closes his eyes.

Marilyn Monroe . . .

Her image overwhelms him, the intimacy of it, lingering like a strong fragrance. This is the power of dreams, he guesses, of the big screen, the way an image can lodge deep in your mind and hold fast there. He saw her in *How to Marry a Millionaire* recently, and before that in . . . what? It was probably *Monkey Business*, last year, with Cary Grant—

He opens his eyes.

But this *happened.*

He scrambles to get out of the bed, awkwardly kicking back the covers, as though under sudden attack from a swarm of insects. But then he just stands there, in his bare feet, facing the blank, gently rippling screen of the drapes, his mouth open in shock.

"Ned, are you all right?"

He turns and sees Laura. She's framed in the doorway. She looks worried, anxious even, but he doesn't answer. He has no idea what to say. He stares at the floral pattern on her quilted housecoat.

It must be Saturday.

Sweeney maintains his silence over eggs and coffee. He gazes vacantly at the wall, at his plate, avoiding eye contact with Laura. In the living room, Tommy is on the floor, busily muttering to himself, playing with his toy train set, surrounded by it—locomotives, passenger cars, freight cars, a signal box, loose sections of track. He's at that age where he can conjure up an entire world all on his own. Sweeney wants to engage with him—and Laura, too—but it's as if he has forgotten how. Every time he starts to say something it immediately strikes him as absurd and he can't proceed, or his mind just blanks over.

This continues all day, but Laura doesn't push him on it, there's no third degree. She probably assumes he's hungover. After all, he got in late last night and must have been in a pitiable condition. In the afternoon, he sits with Tommy and they play checkers. Tommy asks a seemingly endless series of questions: Who was Commodore Vanderbilt? Are we Presbyterians? Why do they call them TV dinners? Sweeney does his best to provide answers, but he finds it taxing.

"How do you know so much stuff, Dad?"

Sweeney smiles. "Oh, I wish, Tommy. Believe me, there's an awful lot I don't know."

"I bet you know more than Jim Sullivan's dad, and he's a scientist."

The way he feels now, Sweeney doubts he knows more than Jim Sullivan, let alone his dad. But he's not going to say that to Tommy.

When he doesn't appear to be any better over breakfast the following morning, Laura finally loses her cool.

"Jesus Christ, Ned, what's the matter with you?"

He looks at her, but doesn't say anything.

"You're beginning to scare me, you know that? Because I—" She stops suddenly. It's as if she's just realized something, and is trying to work it out. "Where are your cigarettes? You're not smoking. I knew there was something odd. I didn't see you smoking *once* yesterday . . ."

This is delivered like an accusation. But she's right. Sweeney would normally get through at least one pack of Camels over the course of a day, maybe a pack and a half, and he hasn't had one since . . .

"Ned?"

Since . . .

Staring past Laura, he struggles to form the memory. Not since he was sitting in that apartment on West Fourth Street with Matt Drake and . . . what was the guy's name? He can't remember. But he can visualize the scene clearly now.

"*Ned?*"

This has been eluding him since he woke up yesterday. He's had fleeting glimpses of it—and glimpses of other stuff, too, other people, other places, images both realistic and impossible, like photographs one second, and wisps of a dream the next. But that fucking apartment. *That's* where it started. He looks at Laura, the smoke from her own cigarette rising in a slow plume between them.

"I'm sorry," he whispers. "I'm feeling pretty lousy. I think I picked up a bug or something at work."

It's only half a lie, because the condition he's in now is a close enough approximation to being sick, to being infected with something, that once he's said it, it starts to feel true.

"You sure don't look well," Laura says. "Should you go back to bed?"

Sweeney thinks this is probably a good idea, though if he has to wait another twenty-four hours to see Matt Drake and compare notes with him, he's not sure how happy he'll feel lying on his back all day staring up at the ceiling.

As it turns out, he sleeps for most of it, and that evening there's a slight improvement. He and Laura have dinner and then watch Dean Martin and Jerry Lewis on *The Colgate Comedy Hour.* Sweeney normally finds these guys funny, but not tonight. Also, it's now been over forty-eight hours since his last cigarette and he can sense Laura staring at him.

He knows she's bewildered, but—in his own way—so is he. And all he's doing, or trying to do, is put a jigsaw puzzle together in his head. It's just that some of the pieces don't fit, they're too big . . . and the more he focuses on these, the bigger they seem to get. There are different locations, different bars, different drinks, and all of *that* makes sense, but Peacock Alley? Robert Moses? Marlon goddamned Brando? And the biggest piece by a long shot, the most vivid one— if he closes his eyes, even for a second—is still Marilyn Monroe . . .

On the train to work the next morning, Sweeney sits in his usual seat, but he doesn't read a newspaper or talk to anyone. He looks around, struck by the notion that after eight hours of desk-bound tedium in the city, every suit on the train here (himself included) will be yo-yoing right back to Long Island and a Sheetrock-and-plywood housing unit like the one he's just left. The subway ride from Penn Station to Forty-Second Street isn't much better. Sweeney has a rising sense of dread about what awaits him at the office—the meetings, the phone calls, the casual interactions that punctuate a working day. Out on the street, there's a chill in the air, and a strange quality to the light, and as he joins the torrents of people and traffic, a throbbing sensation takes hold in the pit of his stomach.

He doesn't know what's the matter with him. He's just going to work. He does it every day. There's no reason to be anxious like this. He's a rank-and-file executive. He has his clients and accounts. He gets along with people. He's not tortured, or driven by demons. He doesn't have secret ambitions, like a novel he wants to write. He's not an alcoholic or a hophead. He likes a pretty girl when he sees one, sure, but he's not one of those married guys who can't keep his pecker in his pants. If there is anything—and he can't even be sure he's not making this up on the spot—it's that he's maybe a little smarter than he allows himself to believe, and this is because he's afraid of what being smarter would involve, the things it might make him think.

As he rides the elevator to the fourteenth floor, he avoids making eye contact with anyone. This will be difficult to keep up. Ridley Rogan Blanford is a sizable outfit and at 9:00 a.m. the reception area looks a lot like the atrium at Grand Central Station.

"Good morning, Mr Sweeney."

"Hi, Phyllis."

He's able to meet her eye, but that's not so hard. She's the receptionist, the friendly face of the agency. It's her job to be nice.

"By the way," she adds, stopping him in his tracks. "Mr. Blanford would like to see you in his office."

"Oh." Sweeney gazes at her desk, at the neat pile of manila envelopes, the mimeographed pages, the coffee mug filled with ballpoint pens. He feels sick. He taps the edge of her desk. "Thanks, Phyllis."

With his head down, he walks past the bank of secretaries and typists, then along the row of writers' offices. He hears his name a few times but only grunts in reply. It's all too much, the din of voices, the clacking of typewriters, the harsh light from the fluorescent tubes in the ceiling. When he gets into his office, he shuts the door behind him and leans back against it. He stares over at the window. The blinds are drawn, not that there's anything to see. It's mostly brick, with just a sliver of a view on the left. The prized offices are all on the other side of the building. Or up on fifteen.

He'll pass Matt Drake's on the way to see Dick Blanford and can stop in for a moment. The sooner he talks to Matt the better, but how should he broach the subject? Matt was still in the apartment when he left. Or so he thinks, but how long did Matt stay? Did he have a similar experience to Sweeney's? And how much does he really know about this ex–army buddy of his? Mike Sutton. That was his name.

Sweeney takes off his coat and hangs it on the hat stand. He goes over and sits at his desk. He stares at the door.

The truth is he has no desire to speak to Matt Drake. At all. About anything. Or to speak to anyone else, if it comes to it. In fact, the thought of going back out through that door—or even picking up the telephone to make a simple call—fills him with dread.

He looks at the stack of memos and call reports in front of him and feels another ripple of nausea. How is he supposed to do his job? How is he supposed to function? He should have stayed at home today. He should have called in sick. But if he is sick, what's wrong with him? If he has a bug, what kind of a bug is it?

It's not a bug, though, because he's actually starting to remember stuff. This Mike Sutton guy, for instance. He put something in their drinks. Sweeney figured that out at some point, calculated it from how Sutton . . . from how he moved. At the drinks cart. With his *back* to them.

Is that even possible?

Sweeney realizes he has absolutely no choice now but to go upstairs and talk to Matt Drake. However awkward or embarrassing their conversation might be, he needs to know that he hasn't lost his mind. He gets up from the desk, goes over to a small cabinet in the corner, opens it, and takes out a bottle of vodka. As he unscrews the cap, he looks around, even though the door is closed and there's no one else in the room. He takes a quick swig from the bottle, then replaces the cap and puts the bottle back in the cabinet.

As he approaches Matt's office, Sweeney notices that the door is ajar. Next to it, Matt's secretary, Miss Bennett, is at her desk. She looks up.

"Is Matt free?" he says, nodding sideways at the door. "I need a minute with him."

"I'm sorry, but Mr. Drake isn't in yet."

"Oh." He looks at his watch. It's nine-twenty. "Isn't he normally here by now?"

She consults her own watch. "I guess . . ."

"Ned?"

He looks up. Further along the hallway, Dick Blanford is leaning out of his office. He raises a hand and makes a beckoning gesture, then disappears inside, leaving the door open.

Blanford is a legend in the business (aren't they all) and knows everyone from movie stars and baseball players to senators and cardinals. Despite this, he doesn't drink or smoke and has a reputation for being somewhat aloof. He's about sixty years old, tall, thin, and very distinguished looking. On any normal day, Sweeney would probably have jumped at the opportunity to go in there and impress him, or try to, but this doesn't feel like a normal day.

In any case, the first thing Sweeney notices when he steps into the office is that they're not alone. There's another man he doesn't recognize standing over to the left, by the window. The second thing is that the blinds are drawn. In his own office, that wouldn't matter. In here, it does. It's a corner office, and the view of Madison Avenue—if he remembers correctly—is fairly spectacular.

"Come in," Blanford says, "and close the door, would you?"

Sweeney does as instructed, then turns back to face the room, another knot forming in his stomach.

"Please, Ned, take a seat."

There are two olive-green leather chairs facing Blanford's desk. He goes over and sits in one of them. Blanford is behind the desk now, but he remains standing. He runs a couple of the agency's biggest accounts, and in front of him are the storyboards for various TV commercials.

As Sweeney looks up, waiting for Blanford to speak, something occurs to him. Maybe he's about to get fired.

Blanford clears his throat.

It sort of feels like it. Not that Sweeney can think of a valid reason. He hasn't screwed up any of his accounts, or insulted a client, or spilled coffee on some precious piece of artwork. Though the way he feels today, give him an hour or two and he probably will.

But Blanford doesn't know that. "Now, listen to me, Ned."

Sweeney straightens up in his chair.

"This gentleman here," Blanford says, indicating the guy standing over by the window, "is Detective Jim Ferguson. He's with the New York City Police Department." The knot in Sweeney's stomach tightens. He turns toward Ferguson and nods. Ferguson does the same. "Now here's the thing," Blanford continues. "What I'm about to tell you hasn't gotten out yet, and we need it to stay that way, at least until . . ." He pauses and Sweeney can see that Blanford is actually nervous. "At least until certain facts have been established." He pauses. "So look, I don't suppose there's any easy way to put this. Matt Drake is dead. He's been killed."

"*What?*"

"Yeah, it's awful, a tragedy. And I'm sorry to have to break it to you so suddenly, but I only just found out myself, about what"—he looks at his watch—"thirty, forty minutes ago."

"Oh my God."

"I know."

"What happened?"

"That's part of the problem," Blanford says. "It's not clear. Or, rather, what led up to it is not clear. What actually killed him is that he walked out in front of a passing car over on Broadway in the early hours of Saturday morning."

Sweeney leans forward in the chair. "*Saturday morning?* But that's . . . that's . . ."

"I know," Blanford says. "I know. The reason for the delay is that, well"—he nods in Ferguson's direction—"seemingly Matt had no identification on him and was . . . half naked."

Sweeney turns to look at Ferguson. He swallows loudly, and what feels like incriminatingly, before turning to face Blanford again. "My God," he whispers, "that's so weird."

"Yes." Blanford winces. "The body was only identified last night. Jessica's been told, and naturally she's devastated, but no one else knows." He waves a hand at the door. "Certainly no one out there."

In the brief silence that follows, the significance of this hits Sweeney. And it's obvious. Because why else is he here? It's not as if he's some kind of RRB insider. It's not as if he was actually friends with Matt Drake. Did he even know that Matt's wife's name was Jessica?

Sweeney knows there's only one reason Blanford called him up here. He stares at the surface of the desk, feeling as if he could throw up on it at any second—though unless he wants to get fired for real, he probably shouldn't do it all over these storyboards. He senses something to his left and turns slightly. Detective Ferguson is moving toward him. He stops by the side of Blanford's desk.

"So, Mr. Sweeney," he says, "it's my understanding that you're one of the last people who may have seen Matt Drake alive. Is that correct?"

"Uh . . ."

Sweeney feels like this is a trick question. But he and Matt left the office together on Friday afternoon to attend a meeting downtown, and neither of them returned, so quite clearly—

"Mr. Sweeney?"

"I suppose I could be, yes."

"You *could* be?"

"Well, it would depend on how many people he saw after me. I mean, how many people he saw between, uh . . ."

He's not sure what he's saying.

Maintaining eye contact with Sweeney, Detective Ferguson comes around to the front of the desk. He sits against the edge of it and folds his arms. In appearance, strangely, he's not unlike Dick Blanford. They're both tall and slim, and of a similar age, but if there's a fault line that divides them, it's the quality of their suits. Blanford's is bespoke, he's got the pocket square, the tie clip, the cuff links. Ferguson's, at a guess, is off the rack. It's plain and a little shabby.

But the quality of their suits, it turns out, has no bearing on the power dynamic in the room.

And that has definitely just shifted.

"Mr. Sweeney," Ferguson says. "Why don't you just run through Friday for me? The sequence of events. You left here with Mr. Drake at what time?"

Sweeney swallows again, self-consciously, hating that this makes him appear nervous or even, somehow, guilty. "We left at about two-thirty, I think. Our appointment was at three. We took a cab to West Houston."

"Who was the appointment with?"

Sweeney looks at Blanford for a second. "It was with Langhammer's, the furriers. We've worked with them before, and we were just pitching them some new ideas."

"I see. And how long did the meeting last?"

"About an hour."

"And how did Mr. Drake seem during this time?"

"How did he *seem*?" Sweeney considers the question. "Fine, I guess. He made the presentation and answered their questions."

"Did he seem in any way agitated?"

"No." Sweeney shakes his head. "Not that I noticed. He's always very professional. I mean, Matt's one of the best in the business." He swallows again. "Was."

"So the meeting ended at what time?"

"Uh . . ." He's acutely aware of what's ahead now, of where this sequence of questions is leading them, and in the swirl of nerves, uncertainty, and his continuing shock at the news, he finds himself making a very deliberate decision. "Just after four. I could check my diary, but yeah, it wasn't long after four."

"What happened then?"

"We walked around for a bit, comparing notes on the meeting, but given that it was Friday afternoon, and probably too late to come back here, we decided to go for a drink."

There's a pause. "Right."

What does that mean? Can Ferguson detect that Sweeney is already lying, or at least equivocating?

"Where did you go?"

"The White Horse Tavern."

"How long did you stay?"

"I don't know." Sweeney glances at Blanford again. "A couple of hours maybe."

"What did you talk about?"

"Everything. We spent a good while going over the meeting, but then, you know, stuff. It was a conversation." Ferguson seems to be waiting for more. Sweeney stares down at the carpet, at the geometric pattern, then looks up. "We talked about the Knicks, the Dodgers, Eisenhower, movies, whatever. I don't remember exactly."

"What did you drink?"

"Scotch. On the rocks. So did Matt. We had two or three. How is this relevant?"

Ferguson ignores the question.

"You and he get along?"

Sweeney shrugs. "Yes. Though we didn't socialize outside of work or anything, not usually. He was my boss."

"What does that mean? I thought Mr. Blanford here was your boss?"

"Yes, effectively. But I mean—"

"Detective Ferguson," Blanford says, cutting across Sweeney, "in an organization like this there is a certain hierarchy, a sort of chain of command, if you like. Matt Drake oversaw a lot of different accounts, he was a manager, and Mr. Sweeney here worked under him."

As Blanford continues, Sweeney reflects on the fact that by not mentioning Mike Sutton he has crossed a line. Because there's no going back on this, no reinserting him into the narrative.

How would it look?

Oh, by the way, I forgot, this other guy was there, too, and he was actually kind of creepy . . . He could say they bumped into Sutton after the White Horse, out on the street, and pick the story up from there. But he knows he's not going to.

"I see, yes," Ferguson says to Blanford, and then turns back to Sweeney. "So you were there for, what, two hours? Did you leave at the same time? Did you leave together?"

This is the crucial one. Sweeney has no clear idea what he's doing, or why he's doing it, but he suspects that if he takes a wrong turn at this juncture, none of that will matter.

"Yes, we left together," he says, "and talked for a few more minutes out on the street before going our separate ways."

His heart is thumping.

Ferguson hesitates, then fishes a notebook and pencil out of his jacket pocket. He starts writing. Sweeney watches each scratch of the pencil, each stroke and curl on the page, trying to decipher what these upside-down words could mean. He knows he's left a significant hostage to fortune with the White Horse Tavern story. Because what if Ferguson goes down there, speaks to the barman? *Oh yeah, Officer, sure, I remember.*

Without looking up from his notebook, Ferguson says, "Corner of Hudson and Eleventh, right? So which way did you go? Which way did he go?"

"I went east on Eleventh and I think he stayed on Hudson." Sweeney pauses. "Yes, he crossed the street and went north."

Ferguson looks up.

"Did he say where he was going? Did you discuss that?"

Sweeney shakes his head. "No."

He knows his answer feels a little abrupt. But what else can he say? Besides, he's too busy trying to chart a quick course for himself that will explain away the subsequent five or six hours of his own evening.

As it turns out, there's no need. Ferguson is not in the least bit interested.

"So, Mr. Sweeney, last question, and thank you for your cooperation. How did Mr. Drake *seem* when he left you?"

This again.

"He seemed fine. I don't know what to tell you, Detective. He was a stand-up guy, even-tempered, always friendly. He didn't seem any different on Friday."

Ferguson pulls a pained expression, as if to say, *I know, I know.* He slips the notebook back into his pocket, pushes away from the desk, and stands up straight.

"Thank you, Ned," Blanford says. "And remember, we'd appreciate it if you'd keep this, you know, under your hat, so to speak. For now."

Ferguson nods in agreement.

It's clear that Sweeney is being dismissed. He gets up out of the chair, mumbles a quick "Thank you," and leaves.

He returns to his office, closes the door, and sits at his desk. He stares vacantly out over the room. There's plenty of work he could be doing, some of it urgent, but he's too agitated to even think about reading ad copy or picking up one of these call reports. Plus, he's tired. Going up there took a lot out of him, having to lie like that, and not just to one of the senior partners, but to the police.

The hour or so he and Matt Drake spent in that apartment on Friday evening is the key to this thing. It could explain what subsequently happened to Sweeney himself—which now, though still unclear, doesn't seem all that bad. More important, it could explain what happened to Matt. It could explain how and why he died. Which is an event Sweeney didn't witness and had nothing to do with. So why did he feel compelled to lie about it?

He doesn't know.

At the time, it felt like an act of self-preservation. He didn't even have to think about it. What he suspects now is that it was fear of embarrassment. If Matt Drake were still alive, and in the hospital, say, it would be different, but did Sweeney really want to tell the police—and, possibly, through them, some newspaper reporter—that a guy he'd just met had slipped something into his drink? That he'd then wandered the streets of the city for a few hours like a fool, having strange visions, convinced he was meeting Robert Moses and Marilyn Monroe? And that the same thing must have happened to poor Matt Drake? Who hadn't handled it so well? Who must have lost control, and then his mind, and ended up running out into traffic to his *death*?

How would that play? How would it affect, for example, Sweeney's chances of promotion here at Ridley Rogan Blanford? Or, if they found out, how would the board at Tommy's school look at it? How would they look at him?

How would he explain any of this to Laura?

He moves some papers around on his desk, barely aware of what they are, hoping the telephone stays quiet, hoping no one comes through the door with a question, or with art that needs to be approved, or just to shoot the Monday-morning breeze. Because right now his brain is a mess, a flickering kaleidoscope of emotions—first relief that he didn't have to tell Ferguson the truth about what happened, then fear that the account he did give had serious holes in it, then curiosity, a sort of queasy, distracted longing for how he actually felt the other night, all of this followed quickly by shock, as he remembers once again that Matt Drake is dead, and that it could just as easily have been him.

But as it has to, time marches on, the phone does ring, people do come through the door, and he makes an effort to get some work done. He's aware that his mood and behavior this morning—downcast, sullen, difficult even—are uncharacteristic, and are being perceived as such by his secretary and by the colleagues he interacts with, but he also knows it'll all make sense in retrospect, or it will simply be forgotten, when the news about Matt Drake finally gets out.

And that happens just after lunch.

The background noise in a place like RRB is constant, and any variation in volume, any disturbance, is hard to miss. It starts with a single, startled syllable. This is followed by a cluster of voices raised in anguish. Then someone starts sobbing loudly. Before long Sweeney's door is open, and people are floating in and out. Soon enough, all the doors are open, on both floors, and as the afternoon passes, bewilderment and grief merge into a sort of collective numbness.

Sweeney still can't believe the news himself, but any feelings he might have are filtered through a thickening haze of confusion—because the more clearly he recalls what happened on Friday night, and there's no doubt the details are coming back to him, the less about it he understands.

At five o'clock, as Sweeney is getting ready to leave for the day, there is a light tap on his open door. He looks up.

"Hi, Ned," Dick Blanford says. "A quick word?"

"Sure, please, come in."

Sweeney stands and indicates the free chair in front of his desk. Blanford closes the door behind him, as though declaring an official end to the public mourning.

"That was quite a day," he says, shaking his head.

"Yes. It was."

What else can he say? Nothing, except that maybe it still is. And that his current mood—dark, unsettled, and, yes, mournful—shows no signs of lifting either.

Blanford sits down with a weary sigh. He crosses his legs and flicks away a speck of lint. "People are upset," he says, "and understandably so, but I wonder how they'd feel if they knew the real circumstances here."

Sweeney looks at him. "Do *we* know the real circumstances?"

And did he just say *we*?

"Without going into too much detail," Blanford says, but clearly about to, "not only was Matt half naked when they found him, he had marks on his back, as if he'd recently been, well . . . whipped." He lets *that* sink in. "And apparently he was wearing red lipstick. And rouge."

"Holy shit."

"Who knew, right? But the police are looking into it. They say there are some underground clubs, places he may have frequented."

"I . . . don't know what to say."

Blanford sighs. "You learn something new every day." Then he leans forward and taps the edge of Sweeney's desk with his finger. "Anyway, listen, I know I probably shouldn't be bringing this up now, it's too soon and all, but the fact is, there's a lot happening at the moment, so we're going to need someone to replace Matt, and more or less immediately. I've had a look at your record and a quick look at the numbers and I think we could make this worth your while. What do you say?"

Sweeney stares at him in silence for a few seconds. Blanford has always been a remote figure to him, reserved and patrician, the ad-agency equivalent of an Olympian god. But he finds this shocking of him, almost indecent.

"Oh, I don't know, Mr. Blanford," he says. "I mean, don't you think—"

"Sure, Ned. I know." He stands up. "I'm a heartless prick. But what do you want? Life goes on." He glances at his watch. "And *someone* has to look after the shop." He moves toward the door. "Do me a favor, Ned, go home and think about it. We'll talk tomorrow. And in the meantime, let's keep this whips and rouge stuff hush-hush, okay?"

Sweeney lingers at his desk for another few minutes, staring into space, but then gets up, puts on his coat, and leaves. On the way down in the elevator, he feels a little nauseous and headachy. It's as if he has a permanent hangover now. Everything seems bleak to him, even stuff that shouldn't, like the glittering store windows out on Madison, the lively pulse of the sidewalk, the gentle dimming of the afternoon light.

It's understandable, though. He's upset about what happened to Matt Drake. They were colleagues. They sat in meetings together.

Sweeney turns at Forty-Second Street and heads west into a chill wind.

At the same time, he didn't know the guy, not really, and Dick Blanford is right, life has to go on. So shouldn't he be excited, even a little bit, at this prospect of a promotion? He's on thirteen thousand a year, and a managerial position would probably bring him up to seventeen or eighteen, maybe more. Laura would be over the moon. They could think about moving to a bigger house.

Except that . . .

He's not excited.

And it's got nothing to do with timing, with what is or isn't appropriate. It's got nothing to do with Dick Blanford being a heartless prick. It's a new way of seeing things—or, rather, the memory of one. Because although he's fairly certain that the Ned Sweeney of Friday night would consider this promotion a bad idea, the Ned Sweeney of right now can't conjure up a sublime storm of words and logic to explain why. Not the way Friday-night Ned no doubt could.

And that's a more exciting prospect than literally anything else he can think of. So despite the phantom hangover, despite all the stomach-churning confusion about what may or may not have happened the other night, and despite the near panic about how things turned out in the end for Matt Drake, he's got only one thing on his mind.

It's how to get back there. It's how to be *that* Ned Sweeney again.

4

As the author of *Raoul Fursten: A Life* starts talking, I turn to face the podium. But I'm unable to focus. I stare ahead, calculating how long this will take, how long it'll be before I can engage with Clay Proctor again. I want to ask him more questions. I want to get him to explain what he said.

Ned Sweeney didn't kill himself.

As the voice from the podium drones on, I become more and more anxious. This whole thing could just be a coincidence. Or maybe someone engineered it. But why? Every now and again, I glance sideways at Proctor, who appears to be listening intently. I tune in for a moment. ". . . it was a time of great rivalries and intense competition, but also, let's not forget, a time of discovery and innovation . . ."

The author reads a couple of passages from the book and then there's an interminable Q&A session, with most of the questions inaudible and most of the answers incomprehensible. To be fair, I'm not really paying attention. I've been blindsided. And I'm not used to thinking about my family, certainly not being forced into doing so by a virtual stranger. This was meant to be a quick favor for the congresswoman, in and out in five minutes, tops.

The Q&A ends and there's a round of applause. People start talking again, turning, moving about. I'm positioned behind Proctor now and am on the point of sidling around to try to get his attention when someone else leans over to him and whispers a few words in his ear. This becomes a conversation, a couple of other people join in, then the author himself makes his way over. I see my opportunity receding and have to fight an impulse to elbow my way through the crowd. But say I get back in front of Clay Proctor, what then? *Tell me about my grandfather?* A raw plea like that with all of these people listening?

I don't think so.

More minutes pass and I decide to leave. But when I turn toward the exit, Stephanie Proctor is standing there, directly in front of me. She's alone.

"Well?"

"He's . . . charming. And very alert, as I'm sure you know."

"Yes."

I really need more time for something like this. "Look, he was on to me in under a minute, so if there's a cat in this equation, and a bag, they're no longer . . ."

"Okay."

"What I will say, though—"

"Yes?"

"He might just be *too* alert. And too relaxed. I mean, how many fucks has he got left to give? Not that many, I'd say, if any at all, and that could be dangerous."

The congresswoman doesn't react to this at first. She studies me closely for a moment or two. She seems to be weighing something. "You're rattled," she says eventually. "What did he do? What did he *say* to you?"

I don't like this.

"What makes you think he—"

"Because I know him, Ray."

"Then what the hell do you need *my* two cents for?"

"Aw . . ." The congresswoman turns her head to one side and extends a hand to stroke my arm. Then she gives it a gentle squeeze. "Are we fighting, Ray?"

"*What?*"

Behind her, I spot her father and a couple of his cronies shuffling toward the exit. Do I go after them, tap Proctor on the shoulder, make some kind of a scene? I look back at the congresswoman.

"No, we're not fighting. I'm just a bit—"

"I know. He does that to people, Ray. He says stuff, he turns things around, so you don't know if you're coming or going. It's a technique. I don't notice it anymore. In fact, I reckon I'm immune. And that's why I wanted this little reality check." She pauses. "I don't suppose you'd like to come and run my campaign, would you?" She seems to mean this, and I wonder if she hasn't had a glass or two of the local vino. "If you think good candidates are hard to find," she goes on, "believe me, good campaign managers are even harder."

Standing there in front of the congresswoman, the room thinning out around us, Clay Proctor gone, I'm no longer sure what's happening.

"I'm not a campaign manager," I say. "It's not what I do."

"But it *could* be."

"Is that a job offer?"

"Nah. You'd turn me down. But a girl can dream, can't she?"

Why do I feel as if this is another setup? As if Stephanie Proctor is playing an angle here? I guess if she's just as much of an operator as her father, it wouldn't be a surprise.

Shaking my head, I look down at the floor. "I'm tired, Congresswoman. Is there anything else I can do for you?"

"No. But what you have done was a great help. It really was. I hear myself telling people what he's like sometimes and then it's *me* who ends up sounding like the monster."

"I think I said he was charming."

"Yes, you did, but . . ." She studies me closely again. "He pressed a button, didn't he? And I just don't know how he does it." She pauses. "Aren't you going to tell me what he said to you?"

I consider playing dumb here—and I'd do it, too, if it wasn't how I already felt. Besides, she's right. The old man did press a button.

But it's also none of her business.

I move away and wish her good night.

Outside, on Madison Avenue, I call Jerry Cronin again and ask him if he wouldn't mind digging a little deeper into Clay Proctor.

"A little deeper?"

"And a lot further back. All the way to the 1950s, in fact."

"What is this, Ray? I mean, we're swamped at the moment."

"I know, but let me switch a few things around. This is important, Jerry, and there's no one else I'd trust it with."

"Sure." There's a pause. "Am I looking for anything specific?"

"Not yet. Just cover the basics, then we'll talk. And thanks."

The company I run is called Park Row Research. I set it up because I couldn't do all the work on my own. Making money was never a serious motivation, although it hasn't hurt. By the time I was fourteen I had overheard plenty of people call me the weird kid, or the geek (today they'd say I was on the spectrum), but I didn't really mind, because I knew what they meant, or at least what they were referring to—my obsession with data and with facts. I wasn't into computers for their own sake, I wasn't a coder or a programmer— it was more than that. I loved information, I loved patterns. I never saw the internet as a highway, super or otherwise—rather, from the get-go, I saw it for what it was, an ocean, vast and heaving, maybe not bottomless, but deep enough to contain more multitudes than we could imagine or ever hope to hold in our minds at any one time. It was where all the secrets lay, many of them just scattered on the silent floor, waiting to be discovered.

In college, I did my thesis on political plagiarism and spent endless hours going through thousands of pages, cross-referencing, comparing, analyzing. Later on, sophisticated algorithms would be developed for this, but at the time it was enough to get me hooked, because not only were there thousands—in fact, hundreds of thousands, millions—of pages out there to trawl through for secrets, there were just as many hours of audio and video, too. So, after interning for a couple of political campaigns, where I ended up doing basic oppo work, I branched out on my own, offering my skills to whoever wanted them.

And my key skill, as it turned out, was pretty rare. It wasn't even a skill so much as an old-fashioned virtue: patience. Very few people were willing to do what I did, to put in the endless, mind-numbing hours—until, that is, I produced some nuggets of pure gold and it became obvious what we were all sitting on. Now most of the big oppo companies have backroom sweatshops—rows and rows of twentysomething researchers sitting at terminals, with headsets on, combing the internet for shiny baubles of telltale info.

I cross Seventy-Second and keep going. It's a bit desolate up here at this time of night. I gaze around. There's passing traffic, sure, but never that much. Everyone is always somewhere else. The glitzy store windows are lit up, and well populated, but even the mannequins—in their carefully arranged tableaux, with their Barbour jackets, riding crops, filigree lingerie, and one-thousand-thread-count bedsheets—all seem lost somehow and hopelessly lonesome.

One of the most extraordinary men I've ever met.

Did Proctor just say that to mess with my head? I don't know. Maybe the "extraordinary" part was just something an old guy like him would say, as he peers back through the dimming years, locating memories, picking them up to examine like smooth pebbles on a beach.

I turn left at Sixty-fourth.

It doesn't matter, though, because the damage has been done. There's no way my head won't be flooded with unwanted thoughts now—about my mother and my father, about my sister, about growing up, about the houses we lived in, all of it. When this happens, it never ends well. That's because driving it, pumping it, is the monolithic fact of my father's deep misery, and at the back of that was whatever went on with his father. Which didn't end well either, of course. But not—it now seems, out of the blue, and according to Clay Proctor—the way we all thought.

I arrive at my building. I slowly walk over to the elevators, press the button, and wait.

Ned Sweeney didn't kill himself.

The elevator door slides open.

It's so easy for someone to just throw a thing like that out there, like a grenade. But why would they say it if it wasn't true?

By the time I'm getting out on five, I feel dizzy. I move unsteadily along the hallway. I have two neighbors on this floor, an old lady who used to be a TV actress, and a young couple in IT with small kids. It's a nice place, and I like living here, but as I approach the door to my apartment, I feel a queasy sense of insecurity, as if the building itself might turn out to be an elaborate movie set that a crew of technicians could come along and dismantle at a moment's notice, and then remove.

Once inside, I calm down a little. I have a shower and order up some dinner. No men in overalls with crowbars and wooden crates arrive to take my world apart and pack it away. Just the young delivery guy, who knows me well by now, and always has a word to say about this or that—the weather, a new show on Netflix.

I have a beer with my food and it steadies me. Also, instead of flicking the TV on, I flip open my laptop. My hand hovers for a while over the keyboard, I could go anywhere, but I eventually just do it. I type in the name. There's nothing there, of course—nothing obvious anyway. I'd have to go a lot deeper, and I will, probably . . . but not now.

I consider giving my sister a call.

She's in Boston, married to a real estate guy. But what would I say to her? *Remember that toxic strain that ran through our child-*

hoods? Where there were certain things we half knew, or half un-
derstood, snippets of conversation we overheard, stuff we went out
of our way not to talk about? Well . . .

She wouldn't have any patience with it. Or with me, really. We
always got on, but we were very different. Younger by a year and a
half, Jill was less guarded. She had a mouth on her, too. I was quiet
and tended to stay in the background. We never made a formal
agreement about not discussing stuff, it was more that what passed
between us—uncomfortable looks, awkward glances—seemed, at
the time, to be enough. In fact, I have always assumed that what I
pieced together in my head was the same as what she pieced together in hers—that our partial understanding of events was the
same. In any case, we've never talked about it as adults, either. Our
dad died of liver cancer—another good conversation stopper—when
I was twenty-three and she was twenty-one, and since then we've
lived in different parts of the country, with different things going
on in our lives. Our mom died five years later.

When I'm done with the food, I tidy up. I crave a sugar hit and
struggle with this for a bit. Then, almost to distract myself, I pick
up my phone and call Jill—because why not?—and ask her directly
if she remembers it the way I do. Dad's old man? He killed himself,
right? That was the story.

"Seriously, Ray?"

I close my eyes. "I'm asking for a friend."

"Are you high? I'm trying to put the kids to bed, I've got work to
catch up on, and Jim is in Buenos Aires, plus I've got a lousy cold,
and what, you want to chat about . . . *what* exactly?"

"Never mind."

"Nope. *You* called *me*. You don't get to do that."

"I know. But look . . . you heard me. I'm just asking."

She sighs loudly. Then there's the unmistakable sound of ice
cubes clinking in a glass. "Did he kill himself? Sure. I mean, I don't
remember being told about it in so many words or anything. As a
kid, you just absorb stuff, right? We never talked about it, but that's

what I always understood. And then . . . *Wait.*" She sneezes loudly.
"Sorry, shit. And then before Mom died I had a few conversations
with her about it all."

"You did?"

"Yeah, and man, *that* was weird."

"Why?"

"Well, she said . . . actually, she said a lot of stuff, which I'll have
to tell you about some day, but this one thing she came out with
really surprised me at the time, the word she used. She said Ned
Sweeney's suicide was the *crucible*. That's what she called it." Without telling me to wait, she sneezes again, then takes a clearly audible sip from her drink. "I think what she was talking about was
Dad, and the effect it had on him. Or maybe she was talking about
us, and how it all trickled down to us, who knows? But remember,
Dad was a kid at the time, when it happened. That had to have
fucked him up pretty bad. It'd explain a lot. I mean, *I* have kids
and, Jesus, if Jim, for all his faults, if he were to go and do that, it
would destroy Ellie and Josh, they'd never get over it. My God,
even the thought."

Our partial understanding, it seems, was the same. And with reason. But what do I say now? I can't mention Clay Proctor, not without having something to back it up. It wouldn't be fair.

"How is Jim?" I say. This is an awkward shift, but I don't want
Jill asking me awkward questions either.

"He's good. He's finalizing a deal. It's some apartment complex,
I think. He'll be back on Thursday."

"Good. Listen, I'm sorry I bothered you with this, Jill. Tell Ellie
and Josh their uncle says hi. And look after yourself, okay?"

Standing at the counter, I stare out over the apartment.

That senile old *fuck.*

Who does he think he is? And how would he have known about
Ned Sweeney anyway? Back in the fifties, Clay Proctor was probably a dime-a-dozen young lawyer working at the State Department
in Washington.

It's ridiculous.

Nothing to see here. Time to move on.

I go over and open the fridge, then hunker down at the freezer unit. There's some Ben & Jerry's in here somewhere—Strawberry Cheesecake, if I remember correctly.

It's been there for a while.

But at least if I eat it now, it'll no longer be a temptation, right?

As I'm scooping out the last spoonful, my phone vibrates on the counter. I pick it up and look at the screen. It's a text from Jerry Cronin: *Don't know if this is what you had in mind, and more tomorrow, but apparently in the mid-1950s Clay Proctor worked for the CIA.*

5

Approaching the subway entrance at Times Square, Sweeney slows down, then keeps walking.

Why? Because he's not going to get the train to Penn Station and then the 6:13 out to Long Island feeling like this. What use would he be to Laura, or to Tommy? It's only after another block or two that his real intention becomes clear to him. He's not just wandering aimlessly here.

He takes a left at Eighth Avenue.

What he's doing is heading down to Greenwich Village.

He starts moving faster now and more efficiently. Within a few minutes, he's slipping down into a subway station and then getting on an A train. A few minutes after that, the train is pulling into West Fourth Street. Then he's making his way over to Sheridan Square and on toward Charles and Perry. He's retracing his steps, getting ever closer to Mike Sutton's apartment. It's on the next block, between Eleventh and Bank.

He moves slowly along the tree-lined street—everything solid now, fixed in its place, sleepy and quiet. This is not how it was on Friday night, not how he remembers it. A yellow cab passes, as one did then, but it's just a yellow cab. It's not kinetic, not *alive*.

He comes to Sutton's building, passes it, walks on. At the corner, he stops and looks back. A minute goes by. The other night a minute felt like a second. This minute, by contrast, feels like an hour, each of its seconds a slow, ponderous thud.

There are no lights on in the building—though he does seem to remember that the apartment was at the back. He tries to picture it now, the layout, the furniture, but he can't conjure up as much detail as he could earlier. It merges with other apartments he's been in, other rooms. Standing here on the corner, he's not sure what to do next. He could go and see if Sutton's name is on the doorbell, but if it isn't, what then? Sit on the stoop and wait for Sutton to show up? Because he's not walking away from this. He has too many questions that need to be answered.

But a few minutes later, when he spots Sutton approaching from Waverly Place, Sweeney is reminded of what an intimidating presence the guy was on Friday evening and all of a sudden the idea of confronting him doesn't seem so smart.

But it's too late. Sutton has seen him.

What did Sweeney have in mind anyway, a direct accusation? That might be a little foolish without anything concrete to back it up.

"Hey . . ." Sutton gets closer, bobbing his head in recognition. "You're . . ." He stops directly in front of Sweeney, clicking his fingers. "The other evening, am I right?"

"Yes."

He's a big man, thickset and imposing. There are alcohol fumes on his breath and he's sweating profusely. He's also not so steady on his feet. But his eyes are intense, alert and unblinking.

"*Sweeney*," he says after the longest time. "Ned Sweeney."

"Yes." Sweeney nods, and follows it with a nervous, audible swallow.

Sutton smiles, clearly pleased with himself, and then starts going through the pockets of his overcoat. "So, Ned, what can I do you for?"

"Uh, I . . ."

Producing a latchkey, Sutton holds it up between his thumb and index finger like a piece of evidence in court. "Aha!"

Sutton clearly remembers who Sweeney is, but he doesn't seem in the least bit alarmed. He's certainly not acting as if he knows that Matt Drake is dead. Plus, he's drunk. Sweeney has to make a little calculation here. "I lost something the other night," he says. "A fountain pen. It's engraved. It must have fallen out of my pocket somewhere, or, I don't know . . . I must have dropped it."

"And you got to thinking that maybe I have it? That it's maybe up there?" He points in the direction of his building. First floor.

At the back.

That weirdly laid out room.

"Yeah, maybe."

Sutton holds Sweeney's gaze, an enigmatic look in his eyes that could mean anything. *Nice, well played,* or just, *I'm so drunk right now.* He gives the key a little shake. "Let's go take a look, shall we?"

They go inside and up to the first floor, where Sutton fumbles again with his key. Stepping into the apartment feels strange to Sweeney. It's like reentering a dream state, only this time fully awake. The air is stale, probably due to a combination of body odor and cigarette smoke, but it's also pungent—an extra element in the mix that Sweeney can't identify. Sutton turns the light on and it's a shock to see how untidy the place is—empty bottles everywhere, dirty glasses, full ashtrays, items of clothing strewn about, a pile of newspapers on the floor next to the coffee table.

"Oops," Sutton mutters, "you'll have to excuse the mess."

"Looks like you had quite a weekend," Sweeney says, shaking his head.

"This is Greenwich Village, my friend." Sutton's speech is definitely slurred. "A lot of strays and hobos out there, drifters, artists, you name it, and I like to keep what you might call an open-door policy. It gets like this pretty often, and not just on the weekends."

"Place was really tidy when Matt and I were here on Friday evening."

Does this sound pushy? Like an accusation? Sweeney's not sure.

"Well, my housekeeper usually comes in Friday afternoons." Sutton turns around. "So I guess you were just lucky."

"Matt Drake wasn't so lucky," Sweeney says. "As it happens."

"Really?" Sutton looks interested all of a sudden. "How so?"

"You haven't heard?"

"Would I be *asking*?"

Sweeney pauses. "He was killed, Friday night, late. Very late. In the early hours."

"You're kidding me. What happened?"

"Uh, it's not clear—"

"He was *killed,* you say?"

"Yes . . . by a car, on Broadway, Midtown somewhere, up in the Forties." Sweeney waits a moment, then asks, "Did he stay late?"

"Huh?"

"Here, I mean. With you. On Friday night."

Sutton makes a snorting sound. "What are you, a detective now? You come here asking questions? I thought you lost your fucking pen." He extends an arm. "You want to look for it, be my guest, but I gotta take a leak." He turns, still a little unsteady on his feet. He walks over to a narrow corridor on the left and disappears through a door.

Sweeney is unsure what to make of this. Was Sutton being callous just now or was he not really listening before? Whatever. It doesn't matter. The guy may be drunk, but when he comes out, Sweeney's going to have to confront him.

He surveys the room. The mess is awful. He steps forward to inspect the drinks cart. He doesn't see anything out of the ordinary—just liquor bottles, a soda siphon, a cocktail shaker, an ice bucket. But then something catches his eye—on the floor, next to the fireplace. It's a pile of magazines. He leans down to get a closer look. The top one is called *Bizarre* and the image on the cover is of a nearly naked woman who appears to be chained to a wall.

Holy shit.

Sweeney hears a sound, which he can't identify, and straightens up. When he turns, he catches his reflection in the mirror. After a second, it dawns on him. This is a *two*-way mirror, isn't it? He stands there motionless for a while, staring at himself, in shock—and with the growing conviction that Sutton is staring right back at him.

Sweeney is out of his depth here. It feels as though he's been caught in a spider's web. He tries to remember some of the things Sutton said on Friday—what it was about the man that he found so creepy and intimidating. But it's all a blur, a dizzy flicker of images and half-remembered phrases.

When Sutton reappears in the room a moment later, Sweeney quickly gets the impression that he's not as drunk as earlier, that he's more sure-footed somehow, more alert.

"No sign of the holy fountain pen?" Sutton says. There's a crisper tone to his voice as well.

"Look, Mr. Sutton," Sweeney says, feeling his heart starting to race. "I didn't lose any pen. I came back here because of Matt. Because of what happened on Friday night. Because of—"

The doorbell rings.

Damn.

Sutton rolls his eyes and goes over to answer it. From where Sweeney is standing, he can't see who's there. Sutton holds the door open and half leans out, not allowing the person to come in. Sweeney can't hear what's being said either, not at first, but then Sutton raises his voice.

"That was never a part of the arrangement, never, now get out of here."

"Oh yes it was. *Oh yes it was!*"

The voice is female. And angry.

Sweeney wonders what the arrangement is.

"No, it *wasn't*, and how many times do I have to deal with this? Look, you want me to call the cops, is that it? Because I will."

"Oh no, you don't call the cops, mister, I call the cops. I *call the cops. You hear me?*"

Sutton pokes his head back into the room and looks at Sweeney, exasperated. "Sorry about this. Give me a few minutes, will you?" He points at the drinks cart. "Make yourself at home."

He slips out into the hallway and pulls the door closed behind him. Sweeney stands and listens intently as Sutton and the woman continue arguing, but then their voices begin to recede. Where are they going? Downstairs? After another moment or two, Sweeney hears the front door of the building slam shut. The voices stop altogether. He waits. Is Sutton coming back up? Nothing happens.

He listens as hard as he can. After a couple of seconds, he hears a sound. It's the woman's voice again, though muffled this time. She's still shouting, but he can't make out any words. They're clearly outside the building now, either on the stoop or on the sidewalk.

In the next second, and almost without thinking, Sweeney goes over and opens the door Sutton went through earlier. He feels for a light switch and turns it on. The room is small and very narrow. It's definitely not a bathroom. For a second, he doesn't know what it is, a recess or a cubbyhole or some sort of a walk-in closet. And when he focuses properly, he realizes he was right—on the wall to the left is the other side of a two-way mirror. He takes a step forward and peers through it into the living room. This is insane. Even more insane is what else Sutton has in this custom-fitted little room of his. There's a long single-sided bench table running along the wall beneath the mirror and on it sits an eight-millimeter cine-camera. It's set up on a small tripod, facing out.

Sweeney tries to make sense of this. What? The guy drugs people and then *films* them? What kind of a sick son of a bitch is this?

He stops for a second, remains completely still, and listens for any sounds. There's nothing. He glances around again. There are papers and notebooks spread out on either side of the camera, as well as a full ashtray and some empty candy wrappers. At the far end of the table, he spots another pile of magazines. The top one is called *Exotique* and the cover features a woman in a leather corset, fishnet stockings, and high heels. She's wielding what looks like a bullwhip.

Holy *fuck*.

Sweeney picks up one of the notebooks next to the camera and flicks through the pages. There are lists, charts, symbols—lines and lines of scrawled handwriting. It could be anything. The next one he picks up is almost empty, but he examines the first few pages. It seems to be a diary. The entries are dated. He reads a couple, and doesn't understand them, but then he spots his own name, and Matt Drake's, and it's like a punch to the gut.

> *Friday, 18.45 administered 75 mcg of MDT-48 to Ned Sweeney. No apparent effect, disappointing. But Sweeney left early, so can't be sure. Also administered 50 mcg of LSD-25 to Matt Drake. Delayed reaction, but oh boy. A dose of the horrors, mitigated by generous quantities of bourbon.*

He drops the notebook, feeling a little dizzy.

A dose of the horrors?

What does that mean? What is MDT-48? What is LSD-25? And who *is* this guy?

He pokes around some more. There are pull-out drawers under the bench table. He flicks some of these open and finds more notebooks, packs of cigarettes, loose pills, razor blades, small canisters of film, and dozens of photographs—none of which he can bring himself to look at. Besides, he's been in here way too long. What if Sutton comes back?

That's when Sweeney realizes what's delaying him. It's not just this discovery—which is awful—it's that he's looking for something.

It's the reason he came back down to West Fourth Street in the first place.

He stays in the room for another couple of minutes. It frustrates him that he doesn't know what the thing he's searching for even looks like. Eventually, he has to give up. He's tempted to take the diary with him—as what, evidence?—but he leaves it. He flicks the light switch, closes the door, and goes back into the living room.

He doesn't hear the muffled shouting anymore. He doesn't hear anything. He tries to figure out what he's going to say when Sutton shows up again. Then he looks around, surveying the room for any clue as to where the stuff might be kept. He goes over and checks out the drinks cart again. It's the same as earlier, but this time he decides he could probably use a shot of something. He examines what's on offer. There's a bottle of Old Fitzgerald but Sweeney instinctively avoids it and picks up a bottle of Wolfschmidt instead. He finds a clean glass and pours himself a decent measure. The ice bucket has a pool of cloudy water at the bottom of it. He hesitates, not sure he wants to drink neat vodka.

He turns and puts the glass down on the coffee table. Maybe it's to distract himself from what he's just seen, he doesn't know, but he decides to go and look for some ice. He finds the kitchen over to the right. The mess in here could go pound for pound with the one in the living room—piles of old newspapers, dirty dishes on every surface, empty milk bottles. He opens the refrigerator, hoping that what he finds won't be too disgusting. To his surprise, it's almost empty—a few eggs, some cold cuts, and half a watermelon. He opens the freezer section. Right there, he sees a tray of ice cubes, one of those new lever-operated aluminum ones.

Bingo.

But . . .

It's a double bingo, because behind the tray of ice cubes is a different metal tray that contains up to maybe twenty glass vials or apothecary bottles, each with a little cork top. Sweeney looks over his shoulder and listens for a second. Nothing. He turns back and eases the container forward a bit. Each of the glass bottles has a label on it and he quickly checks all of them. None of the names means anything to him—except two, LSD-25 and MDT-48.

He hesitates and then removes the bottle marked MDT-48. He slips it into his jacket pocket. He pushes the container back to the rear of the freezer. He forgets about the ice cubes, closes the refrigerator, and heads back out to the living room.

There's still no sign of Sutton.

Sweeney sits on the couch and picks up the glass of vodka from the coffee table. He takes a sip. And then another. He looks at his watch. Sutton has been gone nearly ten minutes.

As the clear liquid burns its way down to Sweeney's stomach, he reflects on what he's just done. It seems barely believable to him. His behavior. He hasn't actually stolen anything since he was a kid.

He swirls the vodka in the glass and takes another sip.

This is different, though. He has to believe that. And Sutton is guilty of a far more heinous crime. Whatever this LSD is that he slipped to Matt Drake, it clearly caused, or was instrumental in causing, his death.

A dose of the horrors. Sweeney shudders and takes another sip from the glass.

Then he hears a loud banging sound. His heart jumps. It's downstairs, the front door of the building.

He straightens up and clears his throat.

He thinks of the drugs, the dirty magazines, the camera, the two-way mirror. He thinks of poor Matt Drake losing his mind and rushing out into traffic to his death.

But that's not all he's thinking about. That's not even mainly what he's thinking about.

The key rattles in the latch, the door opens, and Sutton spills into the apartment.

"Holy fuck," he says, shaking his head. "Is there no end to the shit I have to take from these people?" He's addressing himself more than Sweeney. He makes his way over to the drinks cart, pours a shot of something into a glass, and knocks it back in one go. Then he turns around. He looks flustered. There's a small scratch just under his right eye. He sees Sweeney noticing it and lifts a hand up to feel it. "Little bitch," he says, then smiles. "So, Mr. Ned Sweeney, where were we?"

Sweeney takes a sip from his glass. This is to make it clear that he took Sutton at his word and made himself at home. But he wonders how obvious it is that his hand is shaking.

"Matt Drake," he says eventually.

"Oh yes, of course."

"I felt you should know about what happened to him. Because it occurred to me that you might not have heard. Seeing as how before Friday, you and he hadn't seen each other since . . . the war?"

Sutton stares at him. "Yeah, yeah, that's right. And thank you."

"It's a terrible business. We're all cut up about it at the office."

"I can imagine. Terrible." Sutton seems distracted, idly feeling the scratch under his eye again, tracing a finger across it. "He was a stand-up guy, all right."

"Yes, Mr. Sutton, he sure was." Sweeney is trying so hard to sound normal that it's easy to forget just how twisted this whole situation is. But he can't backtrack now. It was the same earlier on in Blanford's office, with Detective Ferguson—once he'd started lying, there was only one direction to go in. "It's such a waste, such a tragedy." He looks down into his drink.

"Yes, I know, I know. And call me Mike, would you?" Sutton clears his throat loudly. "Look, he stayed here awhile after you left, maybe an hour, we had a couple more drinks, then he skedaddled."

Sweeney's impulse is to ask him if Matt said where he was going, but he resists. What would be the point? Besides, Sutton was right. Sweeney is not a detective. He's a grieving colleague, letting an old friend of the deceased's know what happened.

"Thanks," he whispers. He takes a last sip from the glass and puts it down. "So, Mike . . . I guess I'll be on my way, then."

"Yeah, sure."

But as Sweeney is getting off the couch, Sutton adds, "You know, Ned, I was just wondering . . . that business with the fountain pen?" He shakes his head, the conciliatory tone gone. "What was that about?"

Sweeney tries not to freeze. It's a reasonable question, the kind an actual detective might ask. Sutton is staring right at him. This is so weird. Is it really just the pen thing? Or is it the fact that he seemed to change his story after Sutton came back? Either way, it occurs to Sweeney that if he wants to push this, he could make a lot of trouble for Sutton—the magazines, the drugs, the camera, not to mention whatever involvement he had in Matt's death.

But really, all Sweeney wants to do is get out of here.

"Look . . . uh . . ."

"Yes?"

"To be honest, I was a little intimidated by you the other night. I still am."

"*What?* That's ridiculous."

Sweeney doesn't know if the surprise is genuine, but the smile that accompanies it sure is. Sutton *likes* the idea.

"If you remember, I didn't say much when I was here. You and Matt, telling your war stories . . . I was sort of overwhelmed. And then, when it came to approaching you today, with what I had to tell you, this awful news . . . I guess I just blurted it out. About the pen, I mean. To buy a little time. I'm sorry."

Sutton considers this, continuing to stare at Sweeney—which by now feels like a deliberate technique, something he's trained in.

Is he a detective?

Sweeney swallows, and then breaks eye contact—two very obvious tells, he's sure, at least for any professional interrogator.

"Don't worry about it," Sutton says, finally. "And I appreciate you dropping by to tell me the news."

Sweeney acknowledges this and moves toward the door. Convinced now that Sutton *is* in some branch of law enforcement, he can't get out of the apartment fast enough.

He walks a few blocks on West Fourth Street and then hails a passing cab. He gets in the back and sits there, his heart still pounding. The driver looks at him in the rearview mirror.

"Sorry," Sweeney says. "Penn Station."

The cab moves off.

He takes the glass vial out of his jacket pocket and examines it. As he considers all the possible ways he may come to regret this, he also detects a hint of anticipation.

6

I lie awake for most of the night, moving the various pieces around in my head—the former cabinet secretary, Madison Avenue, the State Department, the CIA, my own grandfather—but I can never quite get them all to click neatly into place. Proctor working for the CIA is no big deal—plenty of people were recruited by the Agency back in those days—but here's what I can't figure out: Even if Proctor was Agency, and also knew Ned Sweeney . . . so what? The implication (still only in my head at this point) is that there's a connection there, that something shady was going on.

But where's the evidence for it? A throwaway remark by an old man at a book party?

It's not enough.

I wouldn't include it in a report for a client, not without further investigation.

And yet—at 2:00 a.m., at 4:00 a.m.—it continues to bug me.

I found out a few things about my grandfather last night—very basic stuff, but more than I'd ever known before—and it barely took me twenty minutes. After I got the text from Jerry Cronin, I opened my laptop again and did some more digging. Ned Sweeney was born in Poughkeepsie in 1920. He had a heart murmur and didn't see active service during the war. The ad agency he worked at in the early 1950s was called Ridley Rogan Blanford.

I also found this in the *New York Times* archive:

On Tuesday evening, a man plunged to his death from the fourteenth-floor window of the Fairbrook Hotel in Midtown Manhattan. He has been identified as Ned Sweeney, 34, from Long Island. Police say Sweeney was found on the sidewalk by passersby at approximately 9:00 p.m.

Later, in a follow-up report, the death was ruled a suicide.

That was sixty years ago.

So why did Ned do it? There was no real context provided in the report—no background, nothing to work with. Was he depressed for some reason? Did he have financial troubles? Was he a Communist? It could have been anything. I'm certainly not going to find out what it was in the archives of *The New York Times*. Or anywhere else for that matter. Because no one involved with Ned back then, no one who knew him—relatives, friends, nobody—is still alive.

I gaze up at the ceiling.

Nobody except, it seems, Clay Proctor.

At seven, I roll out of bed. I have a shower and get dressed. I'm never hungry first thing in the morning—I just knock back a couple of espressos. Then, with a rising sense of dread, I scroll through various news and social-media feeds on my laptop, followed by a quick look at email. But by then I usually am hungry, and that's when the struggle begins.

Before I had my brush with heroin—which only lasted about six months—I had a problem with food. Heroin you can kick, and it's not easy. But food? Forget about it. According to the latest studies, it's not even a question of willpower anymore. It's all about controlling your environment—clear your cupboards of the wrong foods, don't have stuff in the house you shouldn't be eating. Fine. But I don't have food in the house. My environment is New York City, so try clearing those cupboards of inappropriate food choices and see how it goes. It's not as if I work out either. I do have a gym membership, but where am I supposed to find the time to go? Or the motivation. Which is another depletable resource, apparently. It's all about establishing micro-habits and incrementally adjusting your behavior patterns.

I'll put it on my to-do list.

At the diner on the corner, I have a bowl of muesli and some orange juice. I get a coffee to go and sip it outside on the street as I decide what to do.

I know what I should do. Park Row Research currently has about fifty clients on its books—a range of Congress members, labor unions, and various Fortune 500 companies. We have three full-time staffers and two interns, as well as half a dozen operatives who work either remotely or in the field, visiting libraries, scouring through archives, filing Freedom of Information requests. So it isn't as if I don't have plenty to do. But I'm distracted. And it's not idle distraction. This business with Clay Proctor, this anomaly, is very unsettling, and I want to clear it up.

The office would be the best place to do that, but I know if I go in I'll just get caught up in other stuff, so I send a text to my assistant, Rosie, and tell her I won't be in today, that I'll be working from home.

I head back to the apartment.

For about an hour, I do nothing. Work is always easy to put off, but I have to start sometime, so I sit at my desk and do a review of what I found out last night.

After a while, I hear the ping of an incoming email. It's Jerry Cronin's preliminary file on Clay Proctor—preliminary, but still substantial. Turns out that Proctor wasn't a lawyer at the State Department in Washington in the mid-1950s, as I had guessed. He

worked as a statistician at the RAND Corporation on their campus
in Santa Monica.

Which would make it even less likely that he had known Ned
Sweeney.

But whatever . . .

The more I think about this, the crazier it seems. It was clearly
a mistake. I misheard Proctor, or Proctor misheard me, we got our
wires crossed, and now, as a result, there's this thing in my head that
I can't let go of.

But I have to.

Because there's nothing in the file that puts Proctor anywhere
near Ned Sweeney. There's no evidence that their paths ever crossed.
There's no evidence of anything at all, really. And what other route
is there back to that time, what wormhole or rip in the continuum
can I resort to if I want to resolve this? The CIA stuff doesn't even
help. Proctor was originally hired at RAND to do statistical analysis of data on the prevalence of mental illness among draft-age men
and then found himself teamed up with a university research program that was bankrolled by the Agency. The next step was the cre-
ation of a special 'medical intelligence unit' within the CIA itself
and Proctor seems to have been involved in that.

But again, so what?

A little frustrated, I call Jerry, who works remotely from Philadelphia. Jerry's reports are always extremely dense, and while this
isn't usually a problem for me, right now I need clarity.

"Well, I haven't gone through everything myself yet, Ray—I
mean, obviously, you only gave it to me last night. All I did was a
quick trawl to gather up relevant material for later, but when I saw
the Agency stuff, I figured I should put a red flag on it."

"Sure. And thanks." The problem—and it's only occurring to me
now—is that I haven't mentioned Ned Sweeney's name. And I don't
intend to, at least not yet, so if there's going to be any connecting of
dots here, I'm going to be the one who needs to do it. "Look, Jerry,
what I'm wondering is . . . does the work Proctor did for the CIA

translate into anything?" I'm aware of how maddeningly vague this must sound.

"Uh . . ."

"Did it *lead* to anything?"

"Oh, for sure. Did you come across that bit yet where it says the Agency wanted to set up a medical intelligence unit?"

"Yes."

"They certainly went ahead with *that,* because what it turned into, and pretty quickly, was MK-Ultra."

"Oh." I look down at the notes on my legal pad, as distant alarm bells start ringing inside my head. *"Oh . . ."*

"Yeah."

I whistle. "Proctor was involved in *MK-Ultra*?"

"Looks that way. I haven't worked out to what extent, though. Do you *want* me to?"

I think about this. "You know what? No. Leave it there. This was just a hunch. Anyway, as you said, we're pretty swamped at the moment, so . . . go back to whatever you were working on before."

"Fine." There's a pause. "If you're sure."

"Yeah, Jerry, I'm sure. And thanks."

I put the phone down, lean back in my chair, and stare up at the ceiling.

It *is* weird, of course. There's no question about that.

In fact, it doesn't get much weirder.

Project MK-Ultra was a notorious CIA mind-control program that started in the early fifties. I actually have a book about it. I sit up now and look over at the shelves on the other side of the room. I trace a line, row by row, until my eye rests on a familiar dark blue spine. I read this book a few years ago, and while it was long and densely researched, certain details really jumped off the page.

One of these comes back to me now. It's sudden and vivid, like an electric shock. I don't even need to go over and check the reference.

But I stand up anyway, my pulse quickening.

Because I remember.

It was 1953, a notorious case . . .

This isn't dots connecting, exactly, or pieces clicking into place, but it's *something*. There are echoes here, and I can't just dismiss them. I have an urge to get on the phone again with Jill. She's my only family, the only person in the world who might hear these echoes and be affected by them. Yet it wouldn't be fair to call her, because there's no way I could explain everything without sounding unhinged.

Which is how I'm beginning to feel.

I walk over to the bookshelves, and gaze down again at the blue spine.

The facts here are simple.

Clay Proctor said that he knew Ned Sweeney. He also said that Ned Sweeney—who died after falling from a fourteenth-floor window in 1954—did not commit suicide. As a young man in the early 1950s, Clay Proctor was involved at some level with MK-Ultra. One of the most infamous casualties of that program—as detailed in the book I am now staring at—died from a similar fall, but was declared, many years later, after a second autopsy, to have been murdered.

I start to feel a little sick.

It appears—after a brief search—that Clay Proctor doesn't have any contact info that is public, or an office where he can be reached. He is no longer affiliated with any foundations or educational institutions. He has no online presence. Clearly, the quickest way around this would be for me to pick up my phone and call the congresswoman.

But I'm reluctant to do that.

Asking her to set up a meeting with her father would mean stepping outside the parameters of our relationship, which up to now has strictly been a professional one. It would also mean admitting that she was right—that Proctor had rattled me in some way. She'd want to know how and might even make me spill the beans.

I know I have a tendency to overthink these things. But I also know when I'm cornered. I decide I'll just show up and take her by surprise.

I take a cab to her office, which is on Third Avenue at Forty-Sixth Street. I enter the building and make my way over to reception. I ask to see Congresswoman Proctor. The woman at the desk calls up and announces me.

"I'm sorry," she then says, shaking her head. "Congresswoman Proctor is not here today, but what did you say your name was again, sir?"

I tell her and she repeats it into her headset.

"Hold on a moment, sir," she says.

I look around. I've never been here before, never been to her offices. We've always spoken on the phone or met briefly in bars or coffee shops.

"A Ms. Boyd would like to speak with you, sir, if you'd like to go on up."

"Thank you."

I walk over to the elevators.

Ms. Boyd? I think that's Stephanie's assistant, Molly. What does she want? To take this opportunity to tell me to fuck off and stop bending the congresswoman's ear? She might want to, but it seems unlikely that this is how she'd go about it. Maybe she has a message for me from her boss.

When I get out on the third floor, it's immediately apparent that something is up. There's a hint of panic in the air. Voices are a shade too loud, most of them unloading into phones. Out of the kinetic blur, Molly Boyd herself emerges, striding toward me, a phone in each hand.

"Hi," she says, her jaw clenched.

"Hi . . . Molly, isn't it?"

"Yes."

She's about twenty-eight and has the harried look of someone barely clinging to whatever idealistic notion it was that brought her into this job in the first place. She's intense, though, with dark hair in a bob, blue eyes, and black-rimmed glasses.

"I'm Ray Sweeney," I say, "but you already know that. I was looking for the congresswoman."

"She's not here."

"So I gathered. What's going on?"

"Um . . ." One of her phones releases a plaintive ping. Half glancing at it, she rolls her eyes. "So, yeah . . . there's a bit of a crisis." She takes a sharp breath, then pushes it out, and hard, as if it's either this or tears. "And I'm not sure what to do."

"What is it?"

She looks at me, her expression uncertain, questioning. *Am I supposed to just tell you?* But there must be something in my demeanor.

"We heard about an hour ago that Rise & Unite has some dirt on Stephanie, ethics violations, I don't know, something to do with rental income and tax breaks. We're trying to work it out, but it's messy as fuck and I mean . . . she's *on* the goddamned Ways and Means Committee."

Rise & Unite is the super PAC of Proctor's chief opponent in the District, Howard Noakes, and if this stuff is true they'll soon have ads up everywhere. It'll be a bloodbath.

"Where did you hear about this? Or *who* did you hear it from?"

She looks behind her, as if to check that no one is listening. "I got a heads-up from someone I know who works for Jason Becker."

Rise & Unite's main oppo guy.

"How much do you trust this person?"

Her brow furrows. "What do you mean?"

"I have to *explain*?"

"No, but—"

"These allegations, are they true? Partly? A little bit?"

"We don't . . . we don't know, because—"

"—because the congresswoman's not here and for some reason you haven't spoken to her yet today, am I right? Where is she?"

Molly hesitates. "She's having a dental procedure done, she'll be out of commission for the whole day."

"Which you maybe mentioned in passing last week to this friend of yours who works for Jason fucking Becker, yeah?"

"But—"

She's confused now, and angry. I feel bad for her.

"Look, Molly, here's my best guess. Congresswoman Proctor is too smart to allow herself to be compromised in such an obvious way. These people are just fucking with you. It's what they do. They knew she'd be off the grid today, so they dropped this little bomb through a back channel and are waiting to see if you guys panic and maybe *deny* it, which would then put you in an endless loop of denying it. It's a trap. I may be wrong, but I know Jason, and he's a prick."

"Fuck."

"This hasn't gotten out yet, has it? From *here,* I mean."

She shakes her head.

"Good. Keep it that way. And listen . . ." I gaze over her shoulder, considering something.

But she's fidgety, impatient.

I look back at her. "Okay, talk to your person at Rise and tell them not only are they full of shit, but that Howard Noakes is being catfished by a hacker in Dagestan. Tell them we're eighty-five percent sure."

"Is that true?"

"It doesn't matter." I wave a hand in the air. "I'm maybe *sixty* percent sure. Whatever. It's a thing I'm working on for another client. But we can use it." I pause. "This is a onetime offer. Just say the words. There'll be no need to follow up. It'll be a surgical strike, and believe me, it'll help shut this thing down."

"Oh my God, Ray." She can barely contain her relief. "*Thank* you."

"It's okay."

We stand there looking at each other, and for longer than seems necessary.

"So, Molly Boyd," I say eventually. "You'd better get on the case, then, no? Before it blows up."

"Right."

She turns to go, holding up the phone in her left hand to check the screen.

"Oh, by the way," I say.

She turns back.

"Her father? Clay Proctor?"

"Yes?"

"How do I get in touch with him? Do you know where he is, where he lives?"

Molly holds my gaze for a moment. She seems torn. Is she walking into more trouble here? Can she trust me now? But then, as though snapping out of a trance, she says, "Of course. He's at Beekman Place, an apartment building there." She gives me the address.

"Thanks."

I smile. So does she.

7

When he gets home, the first thing Sweeney does is hide the vial in
an old shoe box on top of the wardrobe in the bedroom. It occurs
to him that he should probably put it in the refrigerator. But then
Laura would inevitably find it and he'd have to tell her what it was.

Or lie to her.

He's done this already, though, hasn't he? As well as lie to the
police. And withheld evidence. And stolen.

Is this really *him*?

For a while, he thinks about little else. Then he gets used to the
idea. It's not as if he doesn't understand the reason for his behavior.
With a full vial of MDT now in his possession, he starts obsessing
about when and where and how he might be able to administer another dose. Naturally, he worries about safety. Is it dangerous? Will
it damage his brain? How much exactly *is* seventy-five micrograms?
He was tempted to sample it immediately, as he sat in the back of
that cab, but something held him back.

In the office the next morning he has so much to do that he can't
even think about it. The phone won't stop ringing and the pile of
correspondence on his desk keeps getting bigger. Matt Drake's funeral arrangements are all anyone seems to be talking about, though

he suspects that in the general chatter there's an undercurrent of speculation about who'll be replacing him.

At one point—and for the second time in two days—Dick Blanford drops by his office. He only stays a couple of seconds, and could have easily said what he needed to say through their secretaries, but it's pretty obvious what he's up to: his appearance down here on fourteen is intended to add fuel to the speculation.

As well as pressure on Sweeney.

"When you have a minute," Blanford says, and nods toward the ceiling.

Then he's gone.

Sweeney has given a lot of thought to Blanford's offer, and really, what choice does he have? The salary increase would be welcome and getting to manage Matt's accounts would certainly look good on his résumé. Why is he so reluctant to accept it, then? The obvious answer has to do with how the whole thing came his way in the first place. If a promotion is contingent on the death of a colleague, then someone else can have it, he's not interested.

But something else is playing on his mind. If he accepts the offer, he'll be busy all the time—there'll be more meetings, more client dinners, more late nights at the office. He might have to travel. He might have to play *golf*. Why should any of this be a surprise, though? Or a problem? Doesn't it come with the territory?

As he leaves the office and makes his way up to fifteen, Sweeney begins to see what the real issue is here: he's only interested in one thing now, and that's MDT-48. He doesn't want to be distracted from it, not even by work, or money, or the prospect of advancement.

But Dick Blanford is a formidable character, and he'll be hard to say no to. When Sweeney enters his office, he sees that Jack Rogan is there as well, standing over by the window, and it's then that he understands he's effectively already said yes. Because in their minds there's no other possible answer. Why else would he have shown up for work this morning?

"Ned, Ned, come in." Rogan walks toward him, extending his hand. He's a small man, stocky and balding, maybe fifty years old, but he's got boundless energy and is really the heart of the agency. "I wish the circumstances were different," he says. "That's a given. But let me extend my congratulations to you anyway."

They shake and Rogan indicates for Sweeney to sit down in the same olive-green chair that he sat in yesterday. Dick Blanford is behind his desk, leaning back, arms folded. Sweeney glances around. The blinds are open and there's a bright, airy feel to the office. It's sunny outside and the city is humming busily below.

"It's a terrible business," Rogan says, shaking his head. "Just terrible."

Sweeney doesn't say anything. There may be an inevitability to all this, to his promotion—it suits them, too—but he's not in the mood to play along.

Rogan offers him a cigarette. He declines. Rogan seems surprised by this, but lights one for himself anyway. After an awkward silence, Dick Blanford launches into what sounds like a prepared speech. Sweeney hears things like "client accounts," "half a million in billings," "dividends and profit-sharing." He meets Blanford's eye at one point, and Blanford stops talking.

"When is the funeral?" Sweeney says.

After another awkward silence, Rogan says, "Thursday morning."

"Thursday," Sweeney says, half to himself. "Day after tomorrow. Fine."

He notices a quick look of concern passing between the two men.

"You know what, Ned?" Blanford says. "This stuff can wait. We're just glad to have you on board."

"We're also glad," Rogan adds, "that *someone* around here has the decency to put the brakes on once in a while. I mean, in a situation like this—"

Sweeney stands up, cutting him off. "So, we'll talk on Friday, then?"

"Yes. Absolutely." Rogan nods vigorously.

Blanford does likewise. "Friday."

Sweeney turns and leaves.

Although the official announcement will come later, it's generally understood around the office now that Sweeney will take Matt's place. One or two of his clients call and he deals with them as best he can. There's also a ripple of discord he picks up on—it's between the secretaries, it's about who'll be doing what and for whom, but he avoids getting involved.

At home, Laura is still really puzzled about why Sweeney seems to have stopped smoking. It bugs her in a way she can't bring herself to express. She knows she should be jumping for joy at his salary increase and flicking through catalogs to decide which drapes to get for the new house they'll be able to move into . . . but no, he sees it in her eyes every time she looks at him. Something is different. But since she doesn't bring up the issue, he doesn't either. His not smoking *is* a big deal, however. He's always been a smoker, a heavy one, and, quite frankly, he's puzzled about this, too. It's connected to the MDT, he knows that much, but he can't explain how or why.

The funeral is a nightmare, as most funerals are. It rains incessantly and the small chapel in Brooklyn is packed. Everywhere he turns, Sweeney sees faces he recognizes, mostly from the office, or from the wider world of advertising. Matt's family is understandably paralyzed with grief, and there's nothing anyone can say or do that will ease their pain. Behind a mourning veil, Laura is stifling tears, and every few seconds she reaches over and squeezes Sweeney's hand. It's the seeming randomness of Matt's death that has floored everyone.

Apart from Sweeney, that is.

Because he's the only person here who knows what really happened. Unless, of course, Mike Sutton shows up.

The possibility has crossed Sweeney's mind several times since Monday. In fact, as he sits here, facing Matt Drake's open casket, not paying attention to the service, not listening to the eulogies, it's entirely possible that Mike Sutton is sitting directly behind him, or two or three rows behind him, or that he's standing in the doorway of the chapel—or hunched at the wheel of his car outside, watching, waiting.

Sweeney is actually surprised Sutton didn't show up at the office on Tuesday morning. It couldn't have taken him long to notice that one of the vials was missing from his freezer, and since it was obviously Sweeney who took it, why would he even think twice about heading up to where he knew Matt and Sweeney worked?

But he didn't, and there was no sign of him here this morning, either, when Sweeney arrived at the funeral home with Laura, or later, when they were all filing into the chapel. Maybe Sutton hasn't looked in his fridge yet. Or maybe he thought better of attending the funeral of someone whose death he actually caused. Sweeney has tried imagining what he'd say to him if he were to show up, but it's complicated—guilt and indignation don't go well together.

The cemetery is a choppy sea of raincoats and umbrellas. Sweeney is standing a few feet away from Laura, who is talking to Jack Rogan's wife, when it happens. Seemingly out of nowhere, Sutton materializes.

"You're some prick, you know that?"

"Jesus." Sweeney flinches. "Jesus *Christ*."

"Don't raise your voice."

"What?"

"Don't make a scene."

"I'm not going to unless you *make* me," Sweeney says, turning to look at Sutton. He's wearing an open trench coat and a homburg. His complexion is gray and pasty, and the beads of sweat from the other day have been replaced by raindrops. "You know, there are plenty of people here who'd be very interested to talk to you. Matt's widow, for one." Sweeney's insides constrict as he says this.

"Oh, think you're a tough guy? Think you can threaten me?" Sutton laughs. "What are you going to do, scratch my face?"

Shit.

"Listen," he says, his voice quiet but controlled. "You took something that belongs to me, and I want it back."

Sweeney squirms. What is he going to tell him? "I . . . I don't have it anymore."

"What do you mean? Where the fuck is it?"

"Look, I *dropped* it," he says. "The damn thing was so small. When I opened it, the bottle just slipped out of my hand. It fell on the kitchen floor and cracked. The stuff spilled out." He swallows. "So I mopped it up and threw everything away."

Sutton sighs. "Jesus H. Christ, you're shitting me, right?"

"No."

He shakes his head. "I've got a dilemma here. Either I choose to believe you." He turns to look at Sweeney. "Or I don't. For your sake, my friend, you'd better hope it's the first."

Sweeney holds his gaze. "Who *are* you? We're at a funeral here, of a man *you* helped to kill."

Sutton looks away. "Oh, please."

"What was that stuff you put in his drink, then? It wasn't the same as what you put in mine, that's for sure."

Sutton takes ahold of Sweeney's arm suddenly, grips it. "How do you know that?"

"*Hey.*"

"Describe it to me," he says, tightening his grip for a second, then loosening it, a new urgency in his voice. "The stuff in *your* drink. The effect of it. What did it make you feel?"

Looking out over the rainswept cemetery, at the rolling hillside, at the rows and rows of gravestones, Sweeney remembers the entry in Sutton's diary: *No apparent effect, disappointing. But Sweeney left early, so can't be sure.*

Sutton doesn't know. He's conducting experiments with these different substances and recording the results, but he doesn't even know what he's dealing with.

"I felt dizzy at first," Sweeney says, as an idea forms in his head.

"Then just a little nauseous. That's why I left when I did. A weird thing, though . . ."

"What?"

"It appeared to kill any desire I have to smoke."

"To *smoke*?"

"Yes, I used to smoke a pack a day, at least."

Sutton seems puzzled, waits for more, then looks at Sweeney impatiently. "And?"

Sweeney shrugs. "I haven't smoked since last Friday. In your apartment."

"So what? I don't understand."

"That stuff, whatever the hell it is, it had the effect of making me not want to smoke."

"That's *it*? That's all you felt?"

"Yeah, but that's not nothing. I mean, I'm happy to stop smoking. I saw this thing recently in the *Journal of the American Medical Association* that said men with a history of regular cigarette smoking have higher death rates from lung can—"

"Shut up." Sutton exhales loudly.

"I was just *saying*."

"You felt nauseous, you didn't want to smoke. Great. Then why did you come back for more?"

"I don't know. In case it wore off? In case I wanted to start smoking again?"

Sutton stares at him.

"Look, I didn't know what you'd done. I was guessing. If that martini hadn't tasted so weird, I probably wouldn't have made the connection. But with Matt dead and all, and then you leaving me in your goddamned apartment, alone, just sitting there, what did you expect?"

"Yeah, well."

Sutton takes something out of his coat pocket. It's a small notebook and pencil. He huddles forward a bit to get more cover from the rain. Sweeney glances sideways and down. Sutton flicks the notebook open to a page with a column on it of what look like letters and numbers. Some of these are crossed out. With the stubby pencil, he draws a straight line through another one. Sweeney only catches a glimpse of it, but he's fairly certain it says "MDT-48."

Sutton puts the notebook and pencil away. Then he takes a handkerchief out of his other pocket and blows his nose.

Sweeney guesses he's made his choice.

But he doesn't feel like leaving it there.

"So, I was just lucky?" he says. "Is that it? Matt drew the short straw?"

"Watch it, buddy."

"Watch it? We're at his *funeral,* for Chrissake. You slipped something into his drink that made him go crazy and he ended up dead. What gives you the right—"

"Put a sock in it, okay? Otherwise I'll break your fucking jaw. Now, you want to know who I am? I'll tell you. I'm a federal narcotics agent and that means I've got jurisdiction over your skinny ass. Because you know what? That little bottle you stole? It was government property, and believe me when I tell you, taking it was a *very* serious offense. I could have you arrested and charged. In fact, I could do it myself, right here, right now." He clicks his tongue. "And think about this—when you're sharing a cell up in Attica with some three-hundred-pound hophead from Harlem, who's going to be taking care of that pretty little wife of yours over there?"

How does Sutton know who his wife is? Has he been watching him? Or did he just see them coming out of the chapel together? Sweeney's stomach turns.

"Not such a tough guy now, eh?"

No, not so much, and as a result his mind starts racing, looking for a way out of this, a route back. But then Sutton turns and says, "Relax, you dope. We're at a funeral. Besides, maybe you caught a break."

What does he mean by that? Sweeney stares at the ground and waits for Sutton to explain.

"Well, well, what have we here?"

Sweeney looks up. Laura has turned away from Jack Rogan's wife and is walking toward them, holding up her umbrella.

"Ned?"

Before Sweeney can say anything, Sutton extends his hand. "Mike Sutton."

They shake.

"Laura, Mike here is an old friend of Matt's." Sweeney can barely believe this is happening. "Mike, this is my wife, Laura."

"Charmed, I'm sure."

Charmed? Sweeney can see from the way Sutton is looking at her that he's more than charmed. Laura *is* pretty, and she looks particularly good today, in her camel-hair coat, her black chiffon dress and high heels. She smiles politely at Sutton and then turns to Sweeney. "Ned, are you coming? I think Jack and Susie are ready."

They came with the Rogans in their car and are going with them to the post-funeral reception at the Grenada Hotel.

"Honey, I'll be with you in a minute, okay?"

"Fine."

As she's walking away, Sutton looks down at her bare legs, and then catches Sweeney watching him. "Oh, keep your hair on."

There's nothing Sweeney would like more right now than to break Sutton's jaw, but he can't see it working out. He's not really the fighting type. Anyway, Sutton says he's a federal agent, and even if Sweeney is not sure he believes him, he wants as little to do with the guy as possible.

"What did you mean before," he says, "when you said I maybe caught a break?"

"Ha." Sutton glances at his watch, then adjusts his hat. "I'm not going to be here for much longer, that's what I meant. I'm being transferred to San Francisco. I'm taking over the Bureau's office there next month, so as much as I might have enjoyed having you around to torment, it looks like you might be off the hook."

"Off the hook?"

"Well, it depends."

Sweeney waits for more. Is he supposed to guess?

"It depends on you keeping your trap shut about anything you think you saw in my apartment, or anything you think might have happened there. It's that simple." He clicks his tongue again. "Don't be a pain-in-the-ass concerned citizen, Ned. Don't be a loose end I have to come back and tie up."

Sutton starts buttoning his coat. "Look, I'm sorry about what happened to Matt. I really am. I liked him, he actually was a friend of mine, but the amount of liquor the guy had in his system, it could have stopped an elephant in its tracks."

"It wasn't just liquor."

"You see? There you go." Sutton turns quickly and stands in front of Sweeney, his face too close for comfort now, his rank breath almost overpowering. "You keep on with these unfounded claims of yours, these ridiculous allegations, and I'll come down on you like a ton of fucking bricks. Do I make myself clear?"

Sweeney hesitates, but there's no point in pushing him. If he really is a federal narc, then Sweeney is way out of his depth here. And the shoe box is still at home on top of his wardrobe. "Yes, crystal clear."

"Good." Looking around, Suttons straightens his hat. "Rain is easing off."

Sweeney rolls his eyes. "Looks like it."

"I'm going to leave now," Sutton says, but then remains standing there. He reaches into his coat pocket and takes out his cigarettes— du Mauriers, the distinctive red box—and a lighter. Smiling, he extends the box and offers Sweeney one.

Sweeney shakes his head. "No, thanks."

"Really? That's something else." He lights one up himself and takes a deep drag from it. "That's really something else." He looks at Sweeney. "And all it took was one dose?"

8

On my way over to Beekman Place, I try to work out a strategy. I should simply ask Proctor to explain what he meant last night. Let *him* do all the talking.

But at what point, if answers aren't forthcoming, do I intervene? At what point do I mention the CIA? Or even MK-Ultra?

That connection still seems unreal to me.

It sounds ludicrous now, but during the early days of the Cold War—from what I remember reading—the CIA actually believed they could harness the power of a drug like LSD and use it as a truth serum, or as a method for reprogramming the brain, or for wiping memories, or . . . they didn't *know* what. But things certainly got out of hand, because over a twenty-year period the program ballooned into a vast, drug-fueled apparatus of mind control and behavior modification. It also pretty blatantly crossed every known ethical boundary. Because the fact is, operatives recklessly and surreptitiously administered doses of LSD—an unknown substance at the time—to unsuspecting victims who then had no idea what was happening to them. It must have been devastating, an eruption of unimaginable chaos and disorder into their lives. Some of these people became psychotic and died in "accidents." Others never recovered from the psychological trauma of the experience.

And the worst part is, there was no real accountability. Many of these victims, along with their families, remained in the dark for the rest of their lives. And so, a couple of blocks from Beekman Place now, I have to wonder—was Ned Sweeney one of them? Is that what happened to him? And was Clay Proctor actually involved in some way?

I must be out of my mind to even be thinking this. At the same time, I can't ignore it as a possibility. Because the damage caused by my grandfather's suicide was incalculable. It seeped down through two generations, into my DNA, into Jill's. And as for our drunk, shouty, sweary, frequently teary dad—well, in his case, the damage probably was calculable. It's just that no one ever bothered to stop and add it all up. Jill and I certainly never did, and for good reason— we were too busy either deflecting or absorbing our own share of it.

Nestled between First Avenue and the East River, Beekman Place is an unspoiled two-block oasis of prewar co-op buildings. It's like a mirage of old Manhattan, and as I walk along Fiftieth Street, I feel as if I could indeed be in another era. I've never had a taste for nostalgia, or been intrigued by the notion of time travel, but right now I'd like nothing more than to be able to turn around and have it be 1954, have it be that other Manhattan, the city in soft pastel greens and yellows, all laid out before me, Saul Leiter–style, so I could pound its sidewalks, ride its checkered cabs, drink coffee in its chrome luncheonettes, and then burrow into it, to look for and find Ned Sweeney, before his fall.

With my luck, I'd probably run into Clay Proctor instead, the dapper young thirtysomething RAND Corporation whiz kid, fresh in for the weekend from Santa Monica, who'd spin me a line of beautiful bullshit—all the bright angles, all the proto–New Frontier gobbledygook. It would be a trip, no doubt about that, but it'd also be a distraction, and frustrating, like in a dream where you keep moving but never quite get to where you want to be.

Knowing I'll have to settle for this Manhattan, and for Clay Proctor six decades on, I don't even bother to turn around. Besides, not even Beekman Place can hide from the passing helicopters and the jagged skyline across the river. I locate the address and decide to just waltz into the lobby and take my chances.

"Mr. Sweeney here to see Mr. Proctor."

The doorman reaches for his phone.

I look around. The spacious, polished lobby has a marble floor and wood-paneled walls, gilt-framed mirrors and leather couches. It's that kind of building. I fully expect that the ninety-two-year-old, up on whatever floor he's on, will have no recollection whatsoever of any conversation he had last night with a Mr. Sweeney.

I will be asked, politely, to leave.

The doorman turns, holding the phone against his chest. "Mr. Proctor needs ten minutes, sir, and then he'll be down to see you."

I'm surprised by this, but I nod. "Of course. Thank you."

The doorman says something into the phone and hangs up. He extends an arm, indicating the area with the leather couches. "Please, have a seat."

I wander over and sit down, choosing a spot facing the elevator. I take out my phone to check email and Twitter. Work is piling up, but I can't concentrate on any of it. Why is Proctor coming down to the lobby to see me? Why not have me go up to the apartment? That's about my current bandwidth in terms of what I can pay attention to.

The elevator has an old-style semicircular floor indicator and its dial kicks to life now, scaling down slowly from seven to one. I stand up.

The door opens and Clay Proctor emerges. He's holding a dog leash. On the other end of it is a pudgy King Charles Spaniel. Behind him is a thickset guy wearing a black trench coat and shades.

Proctor has a security detail?

"Ray Sweeney!" he declares, as though introducing a guest on a game show. He holds out his free hand. "Thanks. I'm glad you could come."

This makes it sound like I was invited. I reach out to shake his hand and nearly answer with a reflexive *Not at all* or *My pleasure,* but stop myself short. I decide to stick with objective reality. "Thanks for agreeing to see me."

"Yes, yes. Now, let's take a walk. Mitzi here needs to get out for a bit. We'll go to the park."

Proctor heads for the exit, I follow, and the security guy, at a discreet distance, follows me.

We make our way over to Peter Detmold Park, which runs along the East River from Forty-Ninth Street to Fifty-Second. The main entrance is a steep brownstone staircase at the end of Fifty-First. Proctor takes his time negotiating the steps and insists on holding Mitzi under his arm. The security guy gets out in front of them and seems quietly attentive to the old man's needs.

"You ever been to this park?" Proctor asks.

"No, but I've read about it."

"It's terrific. I come here every day."

There is silence for a moment, as Proctor puts Mitzi down. Then the three of us stand there awkwardly, waiting.

"Come on, Mitzi," Proctor says. "Make! Make!"

The dog looks back up at him, and Proctor sighs. "Okay, Dean," he says, handing the leash over to the security guy. "You take her, will you? I gotta sit down. Come on, Ray."

Dean silently takes the leash and wanders off with Mitzi. Proctor and I go a few yards farther along the walkway by the railings and find a bench under the cover of some trees. Facing the East River, we sit down, the traffic humming as it passes below us on the FDR Drive. It's a nice day, and this is a relatively peaceful setting, but I'm nervous. I don't have my bearings. There's a strange, skewed quality to the situation—again, almost like that of a dream—and I'm not sure where it goes from here.

We sit without speaking for maybe a minute.

Then Proctor begins. "It's a funny thing, you know."

"What is?"

"Being in your nineties. There are a few of us—me, Kissinger, 41, Andrew Marshall. I was just seven years old when the Wall Street Crash happened. And I remember it. Think about that. People my age have witnessed more rapid change than any other generation in the whole history of the human race. It's quite something."

"I guess."

"Oh, really? Well, wait till *you're* ninety-two. Maybe they'll finally have flying cars by then. But the point is, it's a long time to be alive." He raises a finger and taps the side of his head. "It's a long time up here."

He pauses, and I wait.

"You know, for the longest time the world seems one way, it's got fixed parameters, American exceptionalism, us versus them"—he holds a hand up and starts checking things off—"containment, capitalism as the least worst option, ditto democracy, all the tenets, and then it's like you wake up one day and everything has changed, it's all different. I mean, not everyone agrees. Look at Henry—there he is, still trying to map out the world order, still operating as if there's some Grand Strategy that will keep us out in front. He'll never let go. But I already have."

Let go of what exactly? I'm thinking. "That must be . . . a relief?"

Proctor turns to look at me, his eyes deep and rheumy. "No, there's no relief, Ray. Just confusion and regret. You see, I've lived long enough to understand that maybe we've blown it. And I don't just mean my generation, the so-called best and the brightest. I mean *humanity*." He pauses. "Oh, but listen to me, going on." He stops and claps his hands together. "So. Ray Sweeney. What do you think happened to your grandfather?"

I didn't expect this to loop around so fast. "I really don't know. I grew up hearing that he'd killed himself." There's a tremor in my voice. "It was just common knowledge. No one in our family talked about it."

"Well, that's not surprising."

I continue and keep my gaze straight ahead, "You said last night that he didn't kill himself. What did you mean by that?"

Proctor hunches forward on the bench. "What do you know about me, Ray? About my background. You run an oppo shop, you must have done some research."

I glance to the right. Twenty yards away Dean is busy scooping up Mitzi's poop into a bag. "Well, in the fifties you worked at the RAND Corporation, and at some point you were recruited by the CIA, where you got involved in MK-Ultra."

"Yes. And what conclusion did you draw from that?"

"I didn't draw any conclusion. I'm seeing a lot of dots, but I don't have any reason to connect them. That's why I'm here."

"You're here because I wanted you here."

"Excuse me?"

"Stephanie's campaign people aren't interested in me. I asked her to set something up so I could meet with you."

I close my eyes for a second. I should have known. None of this ever made sense. "She doesn't know *why*, though, right?"

"No."

"I think it might be driving her crazy."

"She'll survive. Look, Ray, I've had my eye on you for quite some time. It was me who steered Stephanie in your direction in the first place. That was nearly two years ago."

I lean back and gaze up at the sky. Little wisps of cloud drift past. I don't have anything to lose now, do I? "I did draw *one* conclusion," I say. "It was more of a supposition, really. Not based on anything concrete. And I didn't believe it for a second. Now I don't know."

"What was it?"

I sit forward again. Dean is on his phone. Mitzi is next to him, panting busily. "I wondered something," I say quietly. "I wondered if Ned Sweeney might have been a casualty of MK-Ultra, one of its guinea pigs. I wondered if someone—*you* maybe—might have slipped him some LSD, the way it appears you guys used to do back then. And after that, who knows. All bets would have been off, right? So . . . he freaked out, he got depressed, he jumped. Or, for some reason, he was pushed."

Proctor slumps back. "I'm sorry I got you to say all of that, Ray. I really am. It should have been me saying it."

"Why?"

He turns to look at me. "Because what you just described? It's essentially what happened."

"*What?*"

"Except for a couple of important details. One, it wasn't me, I wasn't there, and two—"

"Sir!"

We both look up. Dean is approaching, Mitzi in tow. He seems agitated.

Proctor raises a hand.

Dean stops in his tracks, but stands there, waiting.

"What is it, Dean?"

"I have instructions to take you back to the apartment, sir. Immediately."

"All right, all right."

Proctor stands up. So do I.

"What's going on?"

"Oh, don't worry about it." The old man pulls back the sleeve of his jacket and shows me a thick black band on his wrist. "I'm being monitored remotely. So I'm guessing that my blood pressure has shot up, or my pulse is going haywire. Who knows. This hasn't been easy."

"Sir!"

"I'm coming." He turns to me. "We'll talk again."

I don't need a wearable monitor to know what's going on with my own blood pressure.

"When?" I ask.

Readjusting his sleeve, Proctor says, "When what?" After a second, he adds, "Oh. Yes." He reaches out and takes Mitzi's leash from Dean. "Soon, soon."

Feeling the opportunity slip away, I lean in toward him. I also half turn my back on Dean—though I'm acutely aware of his physical presence, his watchful eye, his cologne, even. "What were you saying there? What was the second thing?"

With his free hand, Proctor takes me by the elbow. "It wasn't LSD," he says, in a whisper. "Not in Ned's case. Look it up. It was called MDT-48."

9

It takes Sweeney a few more days.

He keeps making excuses, or finding them—urgent telephone calls, meetings with clients, commitments at home. But if he's going to administer another dose of this stuff he needs to carve out an appropriate chunk of time in which to do it. The most obvious one is Friday evening after work, like that first time, but on Friday they have dinner with the Rogans, their new best friends, so that's out. The weekend is a possibility, he supposes. It's just that he's nervous. He remembers being in control the whole time, and it was a level of control he'd never experienced. But experiencing it from this perspective? That's a little scary. Plus, he's unsure about how much, or how little, he should take.

He spends his lunchtime on Friday at the New York Public Library and does a bit of research on units of measurement and dosage calculations. He reads about active ingredients and oral solutions and half-life cycles, but it's all too technical and he comes away understanding less than when he started. The one thing he does get is that seventy-five micrograms is a tiny amount and that without specialist equipment it might be next to impossible for him to administer with any degree of accuracy.

What gets him in the end, though, is a mixture of curiosity and impatience—as well as a tincture of boredom. When he wakes up on Monday morning, he lies in bed for a while, thinking. The prospect of going to work, of what's on his desk at the office, the grind of it all, just kills him. Before this, he would have been excited to work on new accounts, bigger ones, with major clients.

But not anymore.

While Laura is in the bathroom, he gets the old shoe box down from the top of the wardrobe and takes out the small bottle. He sits on the edge of the bed and examines it. He removes the tiny cork top and gives it a quick sniff. There's a faint scent. Or odor. He's not sure if it's his imagination, but this immediately brings to mind, Proust-style, the taste of that martini he had in Mike Sutton's apartment. He looks at the bottle again. It's full. So what does he do? Or what does he *take*? A drop in some water? Two drops? More? Less? After a moment's hesitation, he puts the bottle down. He rummages around in the drawer of his bedside table and finds a safety pin. He dips the pin into the bottle and withdraws it. On the head of the pin, barely visible, there's a glisten of something, a tiny residue. He then dips the pin into the glass of water on the table and shakes it around. He puts the pin down, takes up the glass of water and drinks it. He replaces the small bottle in the shoe box and puts the box back on top of the wardrobe.

What has he done? Is he insane?

He really has no idea. He does feel slightly better, though.

He's no longer waiting.

Sweeney's early morning routine follows its normal course— shower, coffee, a few minutes with Tommy, a peck on the cheek for Laura, and then he's out the door. Since nothing happens, he almost forgets that he expects something to happen, and as he gets on the train and sits down, newspaper in hand, he concludes that he has erred on the side of caution. He has underestimated the dose. But this is okay. He'll try again tomorrow. He's happier to proceed slowly rather than jump in at the deep end and maybe lose his bearings, or worse.

With the clapboard houses and lawn sprinklers of the new sub-urbs gliding past, he settles down and starts to read the paper.

The first story he looks at is a call for "ailing" British Prime Minister Winston Churchill to resign. Opposition leader Aneurin Bevan made the call at a Labour Party conference in Margate amid growing concerns that because of Churchill, East–West re-lations could be compromised. It doesn't say in the article, but just how old *is* Churchill? He was born in 1874, so that must make him seventy-eight or seventy-nine.

And Margate. That's an English seaside town. On the east coast. In Kent.

Isn't it?

The next story that catches Sweeney's eye is about the Millinery Workers International Union and their strike against the Hat Cor-poration of America. The union has seemingly issued $500,000 in three-cent bonds to be sold to its beleaguered members, all 35,000 of them. Then there's a report on the project to plug weep holes in the spandrels of the United Nations Secretariat Building. He reads about how the Iranian government hasn't settled on a date yet for the trial of ousted premier Mossadegh, about how Senator Richard Russell Jr. of Georgia hopes that Spain can become a "full and complete" member of the North Atlantic Treaty Organization, and about how President Tito of Yugoslavia has condemned so-called "priest-baiting"—violence carried out by Communist-led mobs against certain Roman Catholic bishops.

He reads through *all* of the sections, Editorial, Financial, Soci-ety, Sports, Obituaries, Weather, even the classifieds. He doesn't feel any different from normal—not physically, not like he did coming out of Sutton's apartment that night, his senses tingling at first, then on fire—but when the train pulls in at Penn Station, he does real-ize something significant: he's read the entire *New York Times*, from cover to cover, every word. Which he's never done before, mainly because it's not really possible, certainly not in forty minutes, plus who'd want to do that anyway?

Still, he wonders how much of it he's retained.

On the subway ride to Forty-Second Street, he tries to call up ads, anything that might have caught his eye. There was one for the Executone Intercom System ("Just push a button and talk!"), another for the latest Dale Carnegie course in Leadership Training ("Sessions start at 6.30 p.m., air-conditioned rooms, no dinner"), and another for Howard Johnson's ("The Landmark for Hungry Americans: Chicken Fricassee on Toast Points, $1.65"); others for Bonwit Teller, for De Pinna on Fifth Avenue, for North American. This may seem random and useless, and it is (he could just as easily be scrolling through the death notices: "Abernathy, Norville J., loving husband to Dorothy Cartwright, father to Philip, Janis, and Grace"), but he also has to believe that if the situation demanded it he could apply some sort of a selection filter here. Otherwise, he doesn't get the point of being able to retain this much information. And all he did was read a newspaper.

As he passes along the platform now and makes his way up to street level, he notices *everything*—signs, transit maps, magazine covers, buttons, window displays, faces. It's intense, close to overwhelming, but he quickly discovers that with a little effort he can put the brakes on, slow it down, redirect his attention. In this respect, he guesses, it's a little less intense than the first time. But it's still extraordinary. Which must mean he got the dose right after all.

Or maybe it's too soon to tell. There's no way to know.

In the elevator, two guys in front of him are talking about Morton Sobell, a co-conspirator in the Rosenberg espionage case, and one of them mentions that as far as he knows Sobell is currently doing life in Sing Sing. Okay, not that it matters or anything, but it's *thirty* years and it's *Alcatraz*, so naturally he's tempted to point this out to the guy, tempted to tap him on the shoulder and . . . well, who knows where that might go. In any event, he resists. Then, as he's walking through reception, past desks and open doors, he picks up on other conversations, snatches of phone calls, snippets of gossip—it's like being caught in a blizzard of different radio frequencies—and he resists here, too, but as he arrives at the door of his own office, he catches a quick exchange between two copywriters standing a few feet away and he can't help getting involved.

"A one-bedroom . . . anything. Even a studio."

"Jeff, don't panic, let me ask around."

Sweeney stops and turns toward them. "Where are you thinking of, Jeff?" he says. "Where are you living now?"

They both look over, a little surprised. Jeff's about twenty-one, tall, with a crew cut and horn-rimmed glasses. The other guy, Al—or Abe, *Al*—is thirtyish, also tall, but heavyset and kind of tired-looking.

"Oh, hi, Mr. Sweeney," Jeff says. "Upper West Side?"

Al's brow is furrowed.

"Let's see," Sweeney says. "There's a furnished one-bedroom on West Seventy-Third. Kitchenette, tile bath, elevator, seventy dollars a month."

They both stare at him.

"Or, on Eighty-Second Street, there's an immaculate two-room apartment, utilities included, for twenty-six dollars a week. I can give you the numbers, but . . . *what?*" He indicates the folded paper under his arm. "I just saw the listings."

"Oh, sure," Jeff says. "Thanks."

Al seems impressed now.

Sweeney extracts the paper with his free hand and flings it in Jeff's direction. "Take a look."

Once inside his office, coat off and at his desk, Sweeney feels a real sense of urgency. There's a lot to do, as there always is, but his impulse is to burn through it, to clear it all away, to get out ahead of it. Within about an hour, he's reduced the pile of memos and carbon copies on his desk to nothing and his new secretary to a state of near nervous exhaustion. He sends out a bunch of copy leads to be typed up, and some reworked headlines to the art department. Then he gets on the phone to call a couple of clients whose accounts he has concerns about. He feels that RRB is doing both Hamble Carpets and Paradise Royal Pet Foods all wrong, and he quickly outlines some new approaches that he thinks might work. In talking to his counterparts he soon comes to the conclusion that Matt Drake was actually on shaky ground with these accounts and may well have been on the point of losing them. But now, after a few minutes on the phone with Sweeney, their executives are all fired up again and want to make appointments to come in and talk or have lunch. He says sure and bounces them back to Miss Bennett.

Just before noon, Dick Blanford appears in the doorway of Sweeney's office. Sweeney looks up from a notepad where he's sketching out a strategy for G. C. Barrett's girdles and corsets.

"Slow down there, cowboy," Blanford says, with a big smile on his face. "You're not getting *my* job, not yet at least."

"Sorry." Sweeney puts his pen down. "What?"

"I just got off the phone with Bud Hamble. It seems you suggested to someone over there that they restructure their entire advertising budget, is that right?"

"Well, I—"

"It's okay. He likes your ideas. In fact, I've never heard the guy more excited in fifteen years of working with him."

"Oh . . . good." Sweeney is not sure he can add anything here that won't reflect badly on Matt Drake, so he just shrugs. He glances down at his notes, eager to get back to them.

"Come on," Blanford says, rapping the door with his knuckles. "Let's go to lunch. I want you to meet someone."

Initially, Sweeney is reluctant, frustrated, but he snaps out of this pretty quickly and by the time they're downstairs and hitting the sidewalk, he's puzzled by how wrapped up he got in all of that *stuff*.

Carpets? Pet food? Girdles? It suddenly seems insane to him that so much time and energy could go into devising an ad campaign for any of these things. *Girdles?* He gazes upward, at the side of the building they've just come out of—twenty floors of frenetic activity in various ad agencies, law offices, accounting firms, with most of it, he has to think, being utterly inconsequential.

Listen to him. Is he going to repeat any of this to Dick Blanford? And over lunch at 21 Club? He doesn't think so. Though he suspects that if he'd taken even a slightly stronger dose of MDT this morning he already would have. There was an ineluctable forward momentum that first time, something reckless and immune to reason that he's not detecting now. Which is probably a good thing, because he needs this job. He can't just throw it away. Nevertheless, in the cab on the way to 21, as Blanford talks in detailed, almost rhapsodic terms about the future of television and advertising (the guy they're meeting for lunch, apparently, is a big-shot producer at CBS), Sweeney stares out the window and silently formulates elaborate counterarguments to every single point Blanford is making.

At 21, they're greeted like movie stars. It's clear that Blanford is a regular here and they're shown to what Sweeney assumes is his usual corner booth. As they're settling in, Mr. CBS shows up.

"Hey!" Blanford says, stretching out his hand.

"Dick!"

"Bob, I want you to meet Ned Sweeney, he's taking over for Matt."

"Ned, Bob Saunders."

They shake hands.

"Pleased to meet you," Saunders says. "We were all cut up over what happened. It was so . . . senseless."

There's a bit of business with the waiter. Blanford orders a fruit juice, Saunders a martini, and Sweeney gets a seltzer water. Then the two big shots get into some small talk about their wives.

"You got kids, Ned?" Saunders asks after a few moments, turning to Sweeney.

"A boy, Tommy. He's six."

"Ah. You're lucky. I got three girls."

Sweeney is about to ask him why that makes him lucky when the waiter arrives with their drinks and the conversation moves on. Saunders is fortyish, slim, and of medium height. He has the looks of a slightly shop-soiled matinee idol, but his eyes are alert and he has an easy, confident way about him. He takes out a cigarette case, flicks it open, and offers Sweeney a smoke. Sweeney tells him no thanks, that he's quit. Saunders lights one up himself and takes a deep drag from it.

"So, what am I dealing with here," he says, waving his free hand in the air, "a couple of goddamned choirboys? No one drinks or smokes anymore?"

"I can't speak for Ned," Blanford says, "but there *are* other vices, you know. Slim ones, blond ones."

Surprised by this, Sweeney studies Blanford for a moment.

Of *course*.

Patrician, aloof Dick Blanford—he's actually an old dog who chases secretaries, typists, and hat-check girls, just like any other old dog of his vintage or privileged position. In fact, in a disconcerting flash, Sweeney can suddenly account for three recent employees, now ex-employees, of Ridley Rogan Blanford, two secretaries and a junior copywriter, whose brief sojourns at the company, whose trajectories there (he sees these mapped out like flight paths on graph paper), must each have ended as a result of unwanted contact with Blanford—disastrous collisions they certainly wouldn't have seen coming. It then occurs to Sweeney that in different—in other words, normal—circumstances, he'd be pretty intimidated right now himself. He'd be out of his depth and trying to come up with a good line, just to fit in with these guys. But as it turns out, Sweeney is not intimidated. If anything, he's bored.

"You bet," Saunders says, as if on cue, and holding up his martini, "and don't forget those fiery little redheads, either."

"Ned?"

And it's showing.

"Yes?"

Blanford shoots him a look.

"Oh . . . right."

What Sweeney should probably chime in with at this point is something like, *I'm strictly a brunette man myself,* but the actual words that come out of his mouth are, "So, Bob, Dick tells me you're putting a new show together at the network, a playhouse theater kind of a deal, and you need a sponsor. That's great, but as I see it, there's a fundamental problem here, and if we're going to collaborate on one of these things, it really needs to be cleared up in advance."

Saunders looks puzzled.

"Let me explain," Sweeney goes on, avoiding eye contact with Blanford. "Because it's very simple. All the dramas we're seeing on TV these days, on *Philco Playhouse,* on *Kraft Television Theatre,* on the *U.S. Steel Hour,* they're great. I mean, *Marty?* Oh my God. *My Brother's Keeper?* Fantastic. But you know what? In a way, they're too good. They examine why people fail in life or can't find love, why they're lonely or alcoholics. And whatever the issue is, they drill down on it, they expose it, but they don't provide solutions, they don't offer any hope. And here's the problem. Then the commercials come on and what happens? *We* show up with more solutions than you can shake a stick at—a shiny new pill or hair tonic, a better toothpaste, a bigger car, and none of it adds up. The contrast is too stark. People are going to notice that. Then they're going to resent it."

Saunders leans forward. "Oh, now hold on a minute, I don't accept—"

"Ned—"

"Listen to me, Bob, all I'm saying is that you'll need to be on the same page as us when the inevitable happens, when some writer who should be aiming for Broadway turns in a script that we're uncomfortable with. Maybe it has a story line that's too overtly political or it deals with a controversial social issue, whatever, but one way or another it's going to have an effect, it's going to start making our ads look fraudulent—"

"Oh, that's—"

"What? I'm *wrong*? People enjoy having their noses rubbed in it? Being reminded of how shitty their lives are? I don't think so, Bob—and Dick here agrees with me. Right, Dick?"

Blanford looks annoyed. He does agree, because he's smart, but this isn't how he saw lunch turning out.

"I might have taken a different approach, Ned," he says quietly, an edge to his voice. "I might have gone at it a bit more diplomatically, and chosen a better time, but yes, it's not an incorrect analysis."

"Jeez, fellas," Saunders says, taking a long sip from his martini. "Take it easy. What is this, an ambush?"

"We're just thinking ahead, Bob," Sweeney says, adopting Blanford's quiet tone. "We're being realistic. This will eventually become a problem, so doesn't it make sense to head it off at the pass? I mean, we're not saying every show has to be *I Love Lucy* or *You Bet Your Life*, but the picture has to fit the frame, so to speak, and like it or not, we're the frame."

Sweeney is aware that Blanford's growing unease here may be more than that, it may be actual panic. He's about to say something when Saunders holds a finger up to silence him.

"How long has it been, Dick," he says, "you and me, here at 21?" He gives a little wave of his hand to indicate their surroundings. "How many lunches? How many meetings? Quite a few, I'd say, and yet, never once have I been spoken to this way."

Blanford almost audibly deflates.

Sweeney stares at his glass of seltzer water.

"But you know what?" Saunders continues. "It's *very* damned refreshing. People these days are too afraid to speak their minds, in case the other fellow disagrees with them or they somehow get it wrong." He looks at Sweeney. "So I appreciate how frank you've been about all of this, Ned, and I . . . I guess you might actually have a point. I'm certainly open to discussing it."

By the time they're heading back to the office, Blanford has not only come around to Sweeney's "way of seeing things," as he calls it, he's talking about instigating a new "honesty is the best policy" policy at RRB.

Though, to be *really* honest about it, this is not Sweeney's way of seeing things at all, and he doesn't understand why he said what he did to Saunders. He certainly doesn't believe any of it. The more difficult and controversial a TV drama can be the better, as far as he's concerned—and to hell with the sponsorship and advertising. He thinks he just got caught up in the rhythm and flow of that particular argument and could have been equally persuasive making the opposite case.

On reflection, this is somewhat alarming. Over a four-hour period a tiny dose of MDT has given him the energy and confidence to sway the opinions of three major clients, to plan meetings with several others that could conceivably yield similar results, and to inject a new enthusiasm into the very veins of the company. The only problem is, he's not in the least bit interested in any of this— in client meetings, in the company, in advertising, in his *job*. He can fake it, very clearly, and could go on doing so, but is there any compelling reason why he should?

By mid-afternoon, an oppressive cloud has settled over him. If he stays here in the office, he'll have no choice but to attend to whatever work comes his way, and any work that does he'll no doubt attend to with extreme diligence and pinpoint focus. But his impulse is simply to leave, to go and engage in whatever random way he can with the world outside.

What he's beginning to realize is that he actually shouldn't have come to work in the first place—because his suspicion is that whatever energy MDT releases in the brain, it needs to feed on what it's exposed to, and so far all he has exposed it to are the mundane and the pedestrian. So what did he expect?

And it's not as if the day is over. Just after three o'clock, he gets a call from Jack Rogan asking him to swing by his office if he has a minute. Rogan would like him to sit in on something—a pitch he and his art director are putting together for a big presentation tomorrow.

Sweeney tells him sure, and immediately heads down the hall to his office. Rogan is one of the few account executives in the business who works closely with his art director and has the personal confidence to share credit on a project—something that should be automatic, but isn't. Art directors and copywriters have their place in the hierarchy, like in a rigid class system, but it's obvious that that's bullshit and can't last—just as the exclusive, WASP-y nature of the major Madison Avenue firms can't last either. What about all those talented Jews out there, all the Italians, the Greeks, the Armenians, this great tidal wave of résumés and portfolios, this persistent—

"Ned?"

"Huh?"

He needs to focus. He's standing in the doorway of Rogan's office. "Sorry, Jack," he says, giving his head a little shake. "Midafternoon slump."

He steps inside and Rogan closes the door behind him.

"I think you've earned it, Ned. You want a drink?"

"No, thanks. I'm fine."

He glances around. The venetian blinds are closed and the atmosphere is dense with smoke. Rogan's art director, Dale Porter, is sitting back on a couch with a glass in his hand, and next to him, looking a little uncomfortable, are two copywriters. Sweeney nods at everyone.

"We're pretty much done," Rogan says, "but I'd love to hear any thoughts you have."

It's a pitch for Kokomatic Electrics and their new line of "bigger, better" refrigerators. The main artwork is set up on a stand next to Rogan's desk. Sweeney walks over to take a closer look. The illustration is of a spacious, sparkling suburban kitchen, at the center of which stands the Kokomatic 2000. This enormous refrigerator has been left wide open, its green and gold interior proudly displaying a multicolored treasure trove of enticing foodstuff—a gallon carton of milk, two dozen eggs, items of fresh produce, a chicken, a casserole dish, bottles of beer, some chocolate cake, Jell-O molds, strawberry salads, and, at the bottom, a pull-out section stacked with frozen TV dinners. Visually, the ad is rich, almost garish, but it gets its point across. The copy is simple and strives to be clever: "The Kokomatic 2000—Abundance, in Abundance."

Without looking away, he takes a few steps back.

"Well?" Rogan asks.

Sweeney turns around. Everyone is staring at him. He gets the impression that he's been talked about quite a bit today, and he can't pretend he doesn't know why. But he's starting to feel tired and a little less sure he can meet what now seems to be a palpable sense of expectation. Still, there's something about this artwork that's not right, and it's bugging him.

Then he sees what it is.

He looks over at Rogan and shakes his head.

Rogan flinches. "What?"

"That's not going to work," Sweeney say. "Not as it is."

Dale Porter sits up straight on the couch. "What's wrong with it?"

"Well, it's because . . ." Sweeney hesitates to point out what now seems so obvious to him. "There's no one there. The kitchen is empty."

"Oh my God, that's *deliberate*. Foreground, background, the contrast, the pure lines—it's a statement."

"I get that, Dale, but your average housewife is going to look at this and be appalled. You leave the refrigerator door *open*? With all that food exposed? You walk *away*? It's what she's going to think.

It's *all* she's going to think. It's a distraction. She's not going to see any statement." He pauses. "But it's an easy fix. You just need to drop her in there. In a housedress and apron, her long, slim, bare arm *holding* the door open."

Dale Porter is ashen.

Jack Rogan looks at Sweeney in disbelief, his brain almost audibly processing what he's just heard. Then he looks back at Porter. "Holy shit, Dale, he's right."

A while later, sitting on the train, his mind slowing down, Sweeney starts to feel anxious again. This substance, whatever it is, and however it works, seems to make you smarter. Is that possible? He was more efficient and creative at work today than he's ever been, and he's not stupid to start with. He can *do* his job. But this was ridiculous. And it wasn't just being able to race through paperwork and influence clients. The job itself was almost beside the point. His mind was on fire with ideas. He could remember stuff he'd read in a book maybe ten years earlier and then make a connection with some article he saw in a magazine last week. He understood concepts he hadn't even been aware of before. He had insights. Who has insights on a Monday morning?

Sweeney doesn't know whether to be excited by this or afraid of it. Because he doesn't know what it means. He doesn't know what it's going to make him do. At one point he finds himself thinking about how beneficial MDT could be for Tommy. It could help him with his grades at school and boost his prospects for the future. And then he's thinking, *really?* He's going to give his six-year-old son a powerful drug he knows absolutely nothing about, a drug that may even, at this very moment, be causing permanent and irreversible damage to his own brain?

How irresponsible would he have to be to do that?

Then he thinks about Laura. Couldn't she benefit in some way from MDT? Maybe find a route back to the energy and ambition she had when she first came to New York?

He stares out the window of the train.

Laura would think he was out of his mind for even suggesting such a thing. Also, and not unreasonably, she'd want to know where he got this stuff in the first place. Who he got it from. How would he explain that to her?

By the time he gets home, the effects of the MDT have worn off and he's exhausted. He helps Tommy with a little bit of homework, but it's a struggle to concentrate. Over dinner, Laura is keen to talk through her day, and he listens, but again, it's a struggle.

Lying awake in bed later, Sweeney wonders if he's going to be tired like this at work tomorrow, making mistakes, firing creative blanks. Are Jack Rogan and Dick Blanford going to be scratching their heads and wondering if *they've* made a mistake?

10

On my way back to the apartment, I stop at a coffee shop and scribble down a few notes. There are too many weird angles here and I don't want to forget any of them—that little jeremiad Proctor delivered, for example, the thing about Stephanie, the qualified confession . . . then Dean, the wristband, and, of course, MDT-48, whatever the hell that turns out to be.

It hasn't escaped my notice that Proctor's behavior in general is fairly eccentric. There's a real possibility the old man is nuts and that out of some dark stew of experience and information, accumulated over so many years in secret, he has conjured up a twisted, alternative version of the past and is now imposing it on people around him.

Still, I'm not buying it, and for a few reasons. One is that Proctor's actual past was sufficiently dark and twisted all on its own. Another is the elaborate pretext for our meeting. Another is simply my gut. I believe Proctor. There's something authentic in the old man's tone, a sense of guilt, of torment, even.

And I want it to be true. I sense there's something here, a long-buried version of events struggling to find some light—an alternative version certainly, but not a twisted one, maybe the right one.

Back at my desk, I open the file on Clay Proctor that Jerry Cronin

sent me, most of which is a tedious catalog of the various positions
Proctor has held in his career, from his days at RAND, then at the
Pentagon, to his time in government, and later in the corporate
sector. Next, I start my own search, using my own methods, and
soon I'm building up a picture of Proctor's personal life—his three
marriages, his health, his finances, his investments, his real estate
portfolio. It's all fairly bland and gray, though—this life of a civil
servant, a politician, a businessman. Proctor was a public figure
during the Nixon administration, but only briefly, and he was never
a "celebrity." There are no interviews or biographies, he hasn't written any memoirs, there's no gossip. And yet, he *has* been around for
all of these decades, around and presumably doing stuff. So there
must be something—unexpected alliances maybe, secret intrigues,
boardroom dust-ups. At the very least, those three marriages must
have generated a fair amount of drama.

But none of it shows up in the records.

Nevertheless, I persist. I know from experience that unexpected
patterns usually emerge after I've pushed my way through a certain
tedium threshold.

And, sure enough, one does.

Scanning the material I've accumulated on Proctor, I keep coming across references to Eiben-Chemcorp. They were there at the
beginning—as Eiben Laboratories—when that CIA-led "medical
intelligence unit" was being set up. They were there in the 1960s
collaborating on various research projects with the RAND Corporation. In the early seventies, when Proctor was defense secretary,
they signed a major biotech deal with the Pentagon. Later, in the
eighties—how did I not know this?—Proctor served as CEO of
Eiben for five years. And, in retirement, he sat on the board as a
member emeritus. But really, the details here, the sliding con-
tours, are unimportant—the point is that the man's very close association with Eiben-Chemcorp, the third largest producer and
distributor of pharmaceuticals in the world, spans more than half
a century.

But in all of that time . . . no gossip, no stories, no anomalies, no weird shit.

I order up pizza around four-thirty, call it a late lunch. For dinner, some time after midnight, I cook pasta—olive oil, garlic, and jalapeños—and open a bottle of wine. I pour a glass, but end up not drinking it. When I hit a certain level of focus, food is fuel, but anything else is trouble in the making. Music is somewhere in the middle. I can't have lyrics, or showing off, but if it's down tempo, minimalist, repetitive, I'm fine with it. There's the usual noise from outside, too, traffic and sirens and stray voices. But along with the shifting gradations of light, it's all just texture, familiar and reassuring—perfect for work.

And, at around 2:00 a.m., there it is—the anomaly, the weird shit.

I'm looking at clips of Proctor's appearances on *Meet the Press* from a couple of years ago, and one of these—what turned out to be his last appearance on television—strikes me as pretty odd. In the lead-up to the 2012 election, David Gregory is conducting a roundtable discussion with Proctor, David Axelrod, and Marco Rubio, when Proctor appears to lose track of what he's saying and goes off on a tangent that no one can follow and that Gregory eventually has to interrupt. For the remainder of the segment, Proctor sits in silence, looking a little confused, with Gregory skillfully directing the rest of his questions to Axelrod and Rubio. Proctor looks really old—older, in fact, to my eyes, than he looked this morning in Peter Detmold Park.

But how is that possible?

I watch the clip again. It was recorded more than two years ago.

Curious, I start checking and it seems there was even something of a minor controversy around the incident. Or at any rate, there was a general consensus that the poor old bastard was probably suffering from some early form of dementia.

He *was* nearly ninety, after all.

But I push further into the deep Web and worm my way through a dense nexus of electronic health-care records and soon find what appears to be a preliminary diagnosis of Alzheimer's, linked to the name of Clay Proctor.

At this point, I just sit there, bewildered, staring at the screen. As I understand it, Proctor's next public appearance—actually the next reference to him that I can find anywhere—is eighteen months later, at a fund-raiser for the governor of Connecticut.

But eighteen months? With Alzheimer's the decline in cognitive function is progressive and irreversible. There's no cure for it, no effective treatment. You don't *go* into remission.

I stay at my desk, slumped in the chair, for another half an hour—thinking, or trying to, sliding into what feels like a cognitive decline of my own.

Then I sit up straight again and take a few sips of water from the bottle next to my laptop. I can't put this off any longer.

I look up MDT-48.

A few minutes after 9:00 a.m., my phone buzzes and jolts me awake. I'm still at my desk. I answer the call with a grunt.

"Ray, *hi*. Are you coming in today?"

"Uh . . . Rosie." I look around, trying to rewind the last few hours in my head, unsure of when to press *play*. There's a mug of cold coffee and a banana peel on my desk, as well as a few printed-out pages, some marked up in red pen, others stained with coffee rings. My laptop is open, but the screen is dead. It needs to be charged.

"Ray? Are you okay?"

"I'm . . . fine." Then I remember what I was doing. "But not *that* fine. Look, I'm probably not going to make it in today." I make a run at some damage control, but Rosie doesn't seem too convinced. It's not that she can't handle the extra work—Rosie could handle anything—it's that she's not used to me going AWOL like this. I never call in sick, and she knows I'm not sick now, so what the fuck is up with me? Not that she asks directly—or at all, really, because what would be the point?

"I'm here if you need anything, Ray."

"Thanks, Rosie. And I might."

I put my phone down. Really? *I might*? Like what? I don't have a clue what I'm doing at the moment and even less about what I'm supposed to do next. This is unlike anything I've ever had to deal with.

None of it makes sense.

Clay Proctor's being spry and alert two years after a diagnosis of Alzheimer's doesn't make sense. Nor do any of the references to MDT-48, a drug or pharmaceutical product that in all probability doesn't even exist. Most of the relevant "information" I tracked down was on extreme, conspiracy-theory websites, and very little of it was credible. I started with reputable scientific and medical sites, but drew blank after blank. Then I moved on to the world of underground pharmacology and nootropics. Here, MDT was alluded to in what seemed like hushed tones, as though it were a sort of lost elixir, a mythical compound of the gods. There were plenty of substitutes on offer, so-called brain supplements with science-y sounding names such as Cerebral Max and MetaCog 50. Most of these claimed to be the "real" version of a fictional smart drug that had been featured in a recent movie. Finally, I hit sites like reddit and 4chan. MDT narratives occasionally popped up, but hard facts about it were thin on the ground, and there was little or no agreement about its origins.

Although everyone identified MDT as a smart drug, and an extraordinarily powerful one, no one seemed to have any direct experience of it. It's also doesn't seem possible to buy it anywhere, not even in the shadiest corners of the dark Web. So I can't shake the suspicion that the whole thing is bogus, that it's little more than an urban legend.

But I can't really dismiss it, either. Not yet. Because if you ask me what my job is, I won't say I run a business, or conduct opposition research, I'll tell you I'm a fact-checker. And so far, most of the "facts" here remain unchecked. Up until last night they weren't really even facts, they were assumptions, and there were enough of them to draw down the deadly swish of Occam's razor—the notion that the least complicated version of events is probably the right one, i.e., in this case, the conclusion that Clay Proctor is simply out of his mind.

But I know a little more now than I did last night, and some facts I've checked have only led to further assumptions—so many that I wonder what the opposite of Occam's razor might be, and if it would accommodate a maximal version of events, like the one I'm currently being forced to consider: that MDT-48 is real, that it is produced by Eiben-Chemcorp, and that Clay Proctor is taking it.

The next time I talk to Proctor, I'll clearly have to be better prepared, and with this in mind I contact a source I sometimes use when I hit a wall.

I have little or no patience with people who trade in extreme conspiracy theories, but occasionally they have their uses—and they're not all the same. Some are essentially entertainers, carnival barkers, while others are true believers. The first group cynically foment discord and paranoia, whereas the second group draw you in with apparent logic and then proceed to suffocate you with their conviction. Kasper Higgs belongs in the second group. His breadth of knowledge is impressive, but this is offset by an utter lack of discrimination. Moon landings? Check. Crop circles? Check. Chemtrails? Check. The Federal Reserve? Check. Big Pharma? Check. Vince Foster, Princess Diana, Andrew Breitbart? Check, check, check. The fatal tendency here is that if you believe one of these theories, you'll end up believing all of them.

Kasper is a structural engineer who works for a construction company in Brooklyn. The batshit-crazy stuff—long Twitter threads, contentious blog posts, guesting on fringe podcasts—he does on the side. I met him a few years ago at a political event in Washington, liked him, and have used him as an occasional backup source ever since. Kasper looks and sounds like a corporate executive, and you can have several perfectly rational conversations with him before it becomes apparent that he's a certifiable nutjob. So I'm wary of dealing with him. But Kasper sees more dots out there than almost anyone else, and he does a good job of connecting them, too. Admittedly, most of his conclusions are easy to dismiss, but now and again he'll stumble onto something significant.

I send him a text using an encrypted messaging app—Kasper won't talk on the phone—and we arrange to meet at a bar in Carroll Gardens at seven. I then go to bed for a few hours to catch up on the sleep I lost last night.

Duma is a retro dive bar on Smith Street that serves a bewildering array of vodkas, as well as a selection of dumplings, blinis, and dried fish. Kasper is in a booth at the back. He's fortyish and wiry, with dark eyes and thinning brown hair. He's wearing a gray suit. There's a cocktail and a small plate of pickled green tomatoes waiting for me as I sit down.

"I hope you don't mind," he says, a slight Southern twang to his accent. "I went ahead and ordered."

"Not at all."

The accent thing has always puzzled me, because I know that Kasper is originally from North Dakota. The ordering thing, I reckon—because who does *that*—is some form of behavioral compulsion, a need to control his environment.

"The vodka?" Kasper indicates my drink. "It's Beluga."

"Oh."

"With horseradish, pepper, and honey."

I take a sip. "Nice."

It isn't.

"Siberian." Kasper raises his own glass. "It's the best."

"I'm sure. So. Look. Thanks for agreeing to see me."

"Sure."

"Uh . . ." I'm not being cagey. I'm apprehensive. Any time I've used Kasper as a source it's been for something grounded in trace-able fact—a pattern of transactions I know no one else had seen, say, or some undisclosed intel connection that needed an unofficial confirmation. This is different. This doesn't have that kind of a safety net. "I wanted to run something by you."

Kasper nods.

"How much do you know about the company Eiben-Chemcorp?"

"Some, I guess. It depends." He makes a face.

"What?"

"I'm just surprised is all. Big Pharma isn't exactly your beat, is it?"

"No, I suppose not." I've had dealings with pharmaceutical com-panies in the past, but mostly over personnel issues. "I have this client *now*, though . . . and . . ."

I want to groan. This is harder than I thought it would be.

Kasper takes a sip from his drink. "Well, would you care to elab-orate?"

There's no point in putting it off any longer. "Have you ever heard of a drug called MDT-48?"

"Whoa."

I lean forward. "You have?"

"Sure."

"And?"

Kasper laughs. "Jesus. Who's your *client*?"

This is a fairly obvious question that I should have anticipated. I need to be careful here. "Oh, it's nobody. I mean . . . it's just a guy. He worked at Eiben years ago, twenty years ago. I was doing a rou-tine background check and came across a reference to MDT. It was in a letter. I asked him what it was and he couldn't tell me. He was actually kind of weird about it. So I got curious and looked it up. Then I got more curious."

Is that going to be enough? I'm not sure, but I catch a flicker of disappointment in Kasper's expression. It was probably the twenty-years-ago part that did the trick.

"As far as I know," Kasper says, "it dates back to the seventies. It's what we'd now call a smart drug or a cognitive enhancer, but believe me, whatever DARPA was calling it back then, there's no smart drug or cognitive enhancer on the market today that comes even close to what MDT reputedly does. And there's a reason for that. They don't want you or me or John Q. Citizen getting within a mile of the stuff. Why? Because it's too dangerous. And I mean dangerous as in a threat to *them*, to the establishment."

"How so?"

This elicits the inevitable, pitying *tsk*. Am I really that naive?

"I could give you a list of at least five Nobel Prize winners in the last thirty years where if you go back and look at their résumés, if you dig deep, in each case you'll be able to chart a point where, I don't know . . . *something* happened, where suddenly all their careers started to skyrocket, and consistently. I mean, I'm not saying these people were dumb beforehand, but they were nothing special, they were average. Then *boom*. There's a bunch of examples out in Silicon Valley, too. And that's not to mention some of the big hedge funds, the ones you don't hear much about that have annual returns north of sixty and seventy percent. Who runs *those*? I'm telling you, this stuff is out there. But it's very tightly controlled."

So give me the list, I think. Though I know that would be pointless—intriguing maybe, an invitation down a rabbit hole for sure, but far from proof of anything. Which is how this usually goes.

"What about Eiben?" I ask.

Kasper swirls the vodka in his glass, then takes a sip. "There are different theories about when and where MDT was first discovered, the depths of the Amazon jungle or a pristine lab in Switzerland, who knows where, but once DARPA got their hands on it, one of the pharmaceutical giants was never going to be far behind, because they have the resources and the time and the *money* to put into something like that."

"But the seventies, that was forty years ago, surely they would have developed it by now, got something out on the market, no? If it's such a powerful smart drug, wouldn't it be the biggest money-maker of all time?"

Tsk, tsk.

"You might assume so, Ray, but think about it: Why would they want people to be smart? That goes against every instinct and princi-ple of the free-market capitalist system."

"O-kay . . ." I feel this could do with a little unpacking, but maybe not right now. "What was in it for Eiben, then?"

"They broke open the compound. They repatterned it, adapted it. I mean, some of their blockbuster drugs from that period, like Phen-alex, and Triburbazine, and Narolet . . . these were game changers."

I look across the table. *Broke open the compound*? Is that even a thing? I'm no chemist, but this sounds like some high-grade bullshit to me.

"It's all documented," Kasper goes on. "Phenalex alone helped pull Eiben out of what was pretty much a slump in the seventies, then Triburbazine and Narolet came along and pushed it into the number three position worldwide."

"Yes, but they're not . . . these are not . . ." I stop myself. What was I going to say? They're not cognitive enhancers? They're . . . antipsychotics, or benzodiazepines maybe? Do I really want to start using words I don't fully understand? This is an area that it's clear neither of us is qualified to talk about, so why waste time on it? "Okay, look," I say, "just on MDT itself, they've what, kept it under wraps all this time? Is that what you're saying? I don't—"

"There *have* been leaks. Now and again stuff has gotten out. There was a guy in the late nineties, I can't remember his name, Eddie something, who ended up with a sizable batch. Spinola. Eddie Spinola. He lit a pretty big fire there for a couple of months, got into trading on the stock market and managed to do what these AI algorithms are doing for the big quant funds today. On his own. It was incredible. He made a killing, but then he disappeared. No one ever heard from him again."

Of course.

I'm getting tired of this. "How do I know that any of what you're telling me is true?"

"It's on record," Kasper says calmly. "Eiben almost went under at the time. They were being sold by their parent company, the Oberon Capital Group, and then these rumors started going around about protocol breaches at a lab in New Jersey."

So? That proves nothing. I don't know what I expected to hear by coming out this evening, but it certainly wasn't rumors.

"Also," Kasper goes on, "at different times over the last fifteen years there's been talk of 'bootleg' MDT being in circulation, watered-down versions, some kind of MDT Lite."

"Oh for fuck's sake," I say. "MDT Lite? What is that? A joke? A new brand of soda?"

"No, not exactly," Kasper says, a little defensively, "and I don't think it's *called* that, but what I've heard—and I talk to these guys all the time—is that Eiben has been anxious for a while now to get ahead of the curve, to develop a product before a competitor or some rogue operation with a bootleg stash comes along and beats them to it."

I have a hard time not rolling my eyes at this. "There's nothing *out* there, Kasper. There isn't even anything on the dark Web about it. It'd be easier to buy plutonium. Does this shit even exist?"

I pick up my glass and knock back the last of my vodka.

Time to go.

Kasper sighs. "I know you're skeptical, Ray, but you're not going to *find* something like this on the dark Web. We're not talking dime bags or tabs of acid. We're not talking smack or E or khat."

"I'm not looking to buy it. I just want to know that it's real, that it isn't some bullshit story."

"Oh, it's real, all right."

"How do you know that, Kasper? You haven't told me a single thing that would stand up to scrutiny."

Kasper gives a slow shake of his head, as if to imply that I am sadly deluded, that I'm missing the bigger picture here.

It's an impasse we've arrived at before. It's also usually the point at which Kasper, unwilling to concede, digs his heels in.

"Okay, I can't actually prove this, Ray, not to *your* high standards anyway, but I'm going to tell you something that I heard—it was maybe a year ago, two at the outside—from a guy who knows a guy who works at Eiben."

He actually uses the phrase "a guy who knows a guy." In my head, I have already moved on. I start sliding to the edge of the booth. "Yeah?"

"One of the reasons they're so desperate to develop a new product is that in the next couple of years the patents for both Triburbazine and Narolet will expire. That means Eiben is going to have to come up with fresh revenue streams and the word is that they've been working for nearly a decade now on a new drug for geriatrics."

I stop.

"It's a derivative of MDT that supposedly reverses dementia, that fast-tracks neurogenesis."

"What?"

"And apparently that's just for starters."

"Holy shit."

"Yeah, and I mean if you're talking about the biggest money-maker of all time, *that's* your target demographic right there, surely, the eighty-is-the-new-thirty crowd. They have all the fucking money in the world and boy, are they willing to spend it, because when you—"

I hold up a hand to stop him. "This is in development now?"

"Yep." Kasper is clearly gratified by this new urgency in my voice. "That's my understanding."

"Have they done any trials?"

"I don't know." Having reeled me in, to some degree, he can now afford to dial things back a little. "We'd have to assume."

I put my hand on the table, poised to leave. I look at the drinks and the untouched plate of pickled green tomatoes. "Let me get this."

"You're not leaving?"

"I have to. But listen, thanks." As I'm standing up, I pull out my wallet.

"Oh, put your money away," Kasper says. "I've got an account here. I don't understand, though. What's going on? What did I say?" He pauses. "What did I *tell* you?"

I shake my head. "Nothing." I turn to go.

"Come on. What is it? You can't leave me in the *dark*."

I glance back. "You just connected a couple of dots for me, Kasper, that's all."

11

The next morning, Sweeney doesn't even consider not taking another dose. He uses the same method, the one with the safety pin, but maybe he goes a little heavier this time, on account of how tired he is, on account of how he needs a boost. It still seems like an infinitesimal amount, because it's barely visible, but at the same time he's not under any illusions here.

He gets out of the house as fast as he can. On the train, he doesn't read the newspaper, but instead looks out the window. The vibrant green of Long Island soon morphs into the dirty gray of Manhattan, and before he knows it the train is pulling into Penn Station. Instead of taking the subway on to Forty-Second, as he usually would, Sweeney skips up to the street and starts walking. He goes south. Any anxiety he may have felt about simply not showing up for work today has already lifted.

There's a lot of noise and bustle and traffic on the streets, and the air is dense with smells—from exhaust pipes, ventilation grilles, papaya stands, hot dog carts, from *people*. These last are the most intense, the various body odors and perfumes all appearing in the atmosphere before him as colored streaks, endlessly swirling, looping, intertwining.

He really needs to tamp this down.

Ditto the cacophony of car horns, sirens, jackhammers, creaking steel frames in nearby buildings. Ditto the relentless chatter of innumerable human voices.

The weird thing is, though, he *can* tamp it down. It feels like a skill, but one he continually has to remind himself he has. Because a barrage of sense impressions like this could easily induce a feeling of panic. The key is to redirect his attention, and now he finds it landing somewhere around his feet, or beneath his feet, on the very sidewalk he's pounding. As he moves along, down Seventh Avenue, unexpected time-lapse images flash before him of Manhattan's layered history . . . of its once-pristine salt marshes and streams, of its unspoiled valleys and woods. He sees the great leveling, then the etching out of the grid, the wide north–south avenues, the narrow east–west cross streets, followed by the buildings themselves, the mansions, the brownstones, the apartment houses, and finally, the skyscrapers. These burst through the sidewalks, and with their steel frames and hoisting cables, stack up, story by story, decade by decade.

He needs to tamp this down, too.

What he really needs is to talk to someone, to engage. It's how he felt that first night. He looks around, but who is he going to talk to? That guy at the stand on the corner turning hot dogs? This movie barker behind him under the marquee, in the epaulets and braided great coat? The traffic cop over there on horseback? The bangled crone in the doorway next to the jewelry store? Fine. Why not? Why not any one of them? But how does he propose modulating the out-of-control dynamo that's currently running inside his brain? Because what if the only thing anyone wants to talk about is the game or the weather or what's showing at the Roxy? And why shouldn't they? Did you see *Stalag 17*? Is it going to rain? What about that Roy Campanella?

He just doesn't know if he'd be able to cope. Or if they'd be able to cope with *him*.

As he walks on, block after block, he scans the ever-approaching tide of new faces for any flicker of light or connection. But they're all preoccupied, all caught up in their own affairs—as he would be. At Twenty-Third Street, he looks right and sees the sign for the Hotel Chelsea. He crosses the street at an angle and walks alongside the mammoth building, gazing up at its redbrick façade and wrought-iron balconies. This place is a regular dive by all accounts, home to vagrants and countesses, anarchists and poets, and was built—he somehow finds himself knowing—by an architect called Philip Hubert in the 1880s. Originally an apartment house, it was later converted into a residential hotel. More recently, the place has been run by a couple of Hungarian émigrés.

Sweeney reckons there'd definitely be a few people in here he could talk to, or that he could get to listen to him, at least—if it weren't for the fact that they were all probably still asleep, being night owls and vampires and such, by reputation, at any rate. As he gets closer to the hotel entrance, he eyes it with curiosity. What is he going to do, though? Storm past the desk, head up the central staircase, and knock on someone's door?

Hey, wake up, TALK to me!

He might not have a choice. But then, weaving slightly and approaching from the opposite direction, comes a smallish man with round eyes and matted curly hair. He's wearing a tweed jacket and a polka-dot bow tie. He seems to be muttering, or cursing, and is making gargoyle-like faces into the air.

Sweeney slows his pace.

The man slows down, too. He's at the entrance to the hotel, clearly about to turn and go inside, but he has noticed Sweeney looking at him.

They stare at each other for a few seconds.

Sweeney knows who this man is, but can't remember his name. Then it comes to him, along with random fragments of poetry.

"Mr. Thomas, please," he says. "Do not go—"

"What? Gentle into that good hotel? Ha! I'm afraid I must. Or would you have me shit myself here on the pavement?" He waves a dismissive hand in the air. "The *sidewalk*." He sniffs loudly. "Do I know you?"

"We haven't met." Sweeney steps forward and extends his hand. "My name is Ned Sweeney."

They shake.

"Sweeney? The mad king, the mad, lost, wandering king, flying from tree to tree. Are you mad, Mr. Sweeney? Are you a *king*?"

"No, Mr. Thomas, I'm afraid I'm not. I work in advertising."

"Ah, then you will no doubt be able to lend me twenty dollars. And please, call me Dylan."

"Sure." Sweeney pats his jacket pocket. "I could write you a check?"

"A check? With a *q-u-e*? Why, that would be splendid."

Sweeney reaches for his pocket.

"But not here in the street, surely." Beckoning Sweeney to follow him, the man turns and heads for the entrance to the hotel. "Besides, my need for the lavatory is more pressing—temporarily, I assure you—than my need for the filth of your lucre."

Sweeney follows him inside and they make their way up to the second floor.

Dylan Thomas's room is a mess. There is dirty laundry strewn about the place, as well as empty liquor bottles and discarded candy wrappers. The poet disappears at once into the bathroom and shortly afterward Sweeney is treated to a symphony of farting and sphincteral spluttering. As this plays out, Sweeney stands by the window, gazing down at Twenty-Third Street, trying to retrieve whatever information is stored inside his brain about this curious little man. More fragments of poetry come to him, although he has no recollection of ever having read them. He recalls facts a little more clearly, stuff he must have absorbed, details: the wife, bad-tempered, fiery-haired Caitlin; the extensive reading tours; the endless, Benzedrine-fueled boozing. And isn't there a libel case?

Didn't the Welsh bard threaten to sue *Time* magazine for calling him "a trial to his friends and a worry to his family"?

Good luck with that.

And there's more, much more. It's just that Sweeney feels dizzy all of a sudden, woozy, as the room starts to melt around him, shapes losing their definition, colors dripping like wax . . .

Shit.

He shuts his eyes, as tight as he can, and keeps them closed. After a few seconds, maybe longer, he opens them again. To his relief, everything has pulled back into focus. But then he turns around to find that at the very least several minutes must have passed. Dylan is on the bed now, propped up with pillows, and looking extremely unwell. A dark-haired young woman is sitting on the edge of the bed, talking on the telephone.

"Yes, I'm holding for Dr. Feltenstein, and please hurry."

Elsewhere in the room, a man and a woman are seated at a small table, smoking cigarettes. They're in their forties, well groomed and elegantly dressed. They look like money.

Sweeney wonders if he wrote that check.

"Oh, but Ned, really," the woman is saying, as she looks up at him, "what are we supposed to make of it all? Wasn't this Mossadegh character *Time*'s Man of the Year for 1951?"

"Yes, but that's not necessarily a tribute," Sweeney says, continuing a conversation he doesn't recall starting. "They gave it to Hitler, after all—it's more an indication of someone's impact on the national or international scene, and Mossadegh certainly ruffled a lot of feathers when he nationalized the Anglo-Iranian Oil Company."

"But the fellow's a damn Communist," the man says.

"Not exactly. He's a populist, which makes him singularly *un*-popular over here."

"And what does that mean?"

"Well . . ." Sweeney turns and glances over at Dylan. He seems to be in distress now, his breathing slow and irregular. The woman on the telephone is sitting very still, staring at the floor, waiting. Sweeney turns back. "What it means is, we don't like popular uprisings because they're bad for business, they're bad for the big corporations, so I wouldn't be surprised to see something like this happening again, somewhere else—"

The woman on the phone sits up. "Dr. Feltenstein? Yes, it's Liz Reitell. Can you get here right away?"

"—in Guatemala, say, because I don't imagine the United Fruit Company can be too happy with that agrarian reform program Arbenz is currently implementing."

"But—"

"Yes, thank you, Dr. Feltenstein, *thank* you."

"But hang on, Ned, are you suggesting—"

Liz puts the receiver back on the cradle. "Come on, everybody," she says, clapping her hands. "We need to clear the room."

The man and the woman stub out their cigarettes. "Poor Liz," the woman says. "Come along, Jack. And Ned, darling, you're coming to lunch with us, I insist." She faces the bed. "Dylan, Dylan, what can—"

"*No.*"

"What?"

"Ned stays here. *I* insist." The poet's voice, both stentorian and mellifluous, brooks no argument.

Liz seems a little put out by this, but says nothing.

Once the others have left, Sweeney stands at the end of the bed. As Dylan talks, his voice subdued now—"I have seen the gates of hell"—Sweeney is busy finishing an earlier thought . . . Shukri al-Quwatli in Syria, 1949, another coup d'état . . . is there a pattern here? Even the Italian elections in '48, in retrospect, seem a little, well, convenient. He's not sure. There's *something* here, though—he senses it, a complex subterranean web of cause and effect, but it's ill-defined at the moment, it's elusive. His mind on MDT-48 is a sort of looping combination of information and intuition—and on this particular question he simply needs more information, more data. It's a little different looking at Dylan, however. Sweeney's got all the data he needs, and has, in any case, seen this before, or something like it, with Marilyn—he's felt it, the unbearable, raw-nerved intolerance of the very business of being alive, and especially being alive in those moments that aren't acutely heightened in some way, by acting or alcohol or adulation.

And even those moments—all of them, sooner or later—can wear pretty thin.

"You know, Ned, I haven't written a bloody poem in over two years."

"I believe it," Sweeney says. "I do. And you've obviously convinced yourself that you'll never write another one."

"Who *else* would convince me . . . ?" He closes his eyes, his voice trailing away. "Someone had to do it."

"Oh, enough of this," Liz says, steel in her voice. She has the demeanor and brusque efficiency of a physician herself, though it's clear that she's emotionally invested in what's going on.

Sweeney feels as if he's gazing down at the scene from a great height now, observing these people, seeing their confusion and pain but helpless to intervene. Then the doctor arrives. It seems like seconds later, but Sweeney is learning to accept that his perception of time is elastic. Feltenstein is tall and rangy, with a professional manner verging on the sacerdotal. As he administers to Dylan, with Liz close by, Sweeney hovers in the background. Words are said, about cutting down on alcohol, about eating three square meals a day, and about getting a proper night's sleep. It all sounds a bit cursory, but as he's speaking, Feltenstein expertly prepares a syringe and needle, turns Dylan on his side, and gives him an injection. He then takes a prescription pad from his leather bag, fills out a page, and hands it to Liz.

"You know the drill," he says.

Liz folds the prescription in half.

The doctor leaves and almost immediately Dylan is sitting up in the bed. His breathing is more regular and his eyes are alert. He declares that he's hungry and wants to go out.

"Only *beer*," Liz says, a little too fast.

"Of course, my dear. Or water, even." He looks at Sweeney and winks. "Let's go to Lüchow's."

Liz says she has work to do back at the office, but will join them later. While Dylan is putting his shoes on, she makes a face at Sweeney, one that he interprets as a plea. *I don't know who you are*, it says, *a hanger-on, or a genuine friend, I can't keep track, but please, please, look after him.*

Lüchow's is a German place on Fourteenth Street, and in the cab on the way there, Sweeney asks Dylan what was in that injection the doctor gave him.

"Cortisone. Wonderful stuff. It's a miracle drug. One shot and I'm free of the shackles of anxiety. Death takes a holiday, so to speak. From *my* mind, at any rate." He taps out an impatient drumbeat on his legs. *"La morte in vacanza."*

But in the movie, and in the Casella original, Sweeney thinks— and resists pointing out—it's Death who falls in love with a mortal.

Not the other way around.

Sweeney looks out at the passing liquor stores and delicatessens on Seventh Avenue. He has read about this miracle drug. It's a hormone—17-hydroxy-11-dehydrocorticosterone—first synthesized for commercial use a few years ago by someone at Merck and initially thought to be effective in the treatment of rheumatoid arthritis. But subsequent reports showed it to have a dramatic analgesic impact on a host of other conditions—Addison's disease, Hodgkin's disease, Cushing's syndrome, asthma, retinitis pigmentosa, even on gout and hay fever.

This was in an article he saw in the *Journal of the American Medical Association*. He was in a waiting room somewhere, as he remembers, a clinic. He didn't actually read the article, though. His eyes barely passed over the page. And yet he somehow managed to retain the whole thing. Just as he must have flicked through a volume of Dylan's poetry one time, perhaps in the Strand or the Gotham Book Mart, and could now, if he chose to, recite some of it back to him.

"And death shall have no dominion . . ."

"Ha! Quite so, Ned. Even on his holidays. But this afternoon, I am afraid, it is *beer* that shall have no dominion. I have a sudden thirst for whiskey." He leans forward in the cab. "Driver, let's take a detour to Hudson Street, shall we?"

They arrive at the White Horse Tavern, where Sweeney came with Matt Drake and Mike Sutton that night.

This time it's a little different. As Dylan slowly becomes embalmed in whiskey, shot after shot of Old Grand-Dad, it occurs to Sweeney that cortisone is no match for hard liquor, whereas the smallest tincture of MDT-48 would probably be enough to cure a whole roomful of alcoholics. Hangers-on soon arrive, and some genuine friends, too. Sweeney has no difficulty telling the difference, or keeping track, but what he can't help himself from doing is losing interest and tuning out of various channels of conversation. The atmosphere in the Horse is thick with cigarette smoke and alcohol fumes, but there's something else spiraling around in it as well—a desperate plume of longing for the finality of defeat.

Sweeney finds he has no patience for this.

So, when he sees a chance, he slips away.

12

I go to work the next morning and try to wade through some of the stuff that's been piling up on my desk, but I find it hard to concentrate. I've been in a sort of trance since my drink with Kasper Higgs.

I slip out of the office the first chance I get. I wander around for a while but inevitably find myself back at Proctor's apartment building on Beekman Place. There's a different doorman on duty and he eyes me suspiciously as I approach the desk.

"Ray Sweeney to see Mr. Proctor."

"Do you have an appointment?"

I shake my head.

We both know how this will end, but he goes through the motions anyway.

"I'm sorry, sir, but Mr. Proctor . . ."

Yeah, yeah.

I decide to head over to Peter Detmold Park. Proctor said he goes there every day. Maybe he'll eventually show up and talk to me for five minutes while he waits for his dog to take a dump.

It's all I want from him. Five minutes, a few answers.

It's not much.

But of course it is. And while I'm sitting on a bench, alone, staring across the river, I have plenty of time to figure out why. Incredible as it seems, Clay Proctor may well be a test subject in an unofficial drug trial, and as far as I can make out, it's a trial of the same drug that was used on my grandfather over sixty years ago. The thing is, Proctor originally approached *me* about this, through his daughter, and he seemed eager to talk the other day . . . but could it also be that he's operating, in some way, off-label? And that certain people in positions of influence—and many decades his junior—might regard the way he's currently behaving as reckless? If that is the case, then I'm probably wasting my time sitting here expecting him to put in an appearance.

I get my phone out and call Stephanie Proctor's office. Unfortunately, the congresswoman isn't available. She's in a meeting. I leave a message. Can she call me back ASAP? Before I get off the phone, I consider asking if I can speak to Molly Boyd. But I hesitate. Then I don't do it. And I'm not sure why.

I stay sitting in Peter Detmold Park for about an hour. People come and go with their dogs. I see a few King Charles Spaniels, but no Mitzi. Eventually, it starts to rain and I leave.

I spend the rest of the day in my apartment, reading. I can't focus on work, and I can't seem to make any headway on Proctor (two further calls to the congresswoman's office get me nowhere). By early evening I've had enough and I decide to go outside to get some air. I walk the few blocks to Fifth Avenue, and make my way down the side of Central Park to Fifty-Ninth Street. I'm not far from where Stephanie Proctor lives, and it occurs to me that I could drop by her building and see if she's home. She's likely not in. She's probably out at dinner, or at a fund-raiser. But if she is home, what will she make of me showing up like this? I've already left three voice messages and sent her two texts and an email.

I enter the lobby—another blaze of pink-flecked marble surfaces and gilt-edged mirrors—and get another suspicious look from another suspicious doorman. He's keying something in at his terminal and is about to ask if he can help me when I hear someone call my name. I turn and see Molly Boyd approaching from a bank of elevators over to the left. She's carrying a briefcase.

"Hey there," I say.

"Hi."

She stops directly in front of me. The doorman goes back to his screen.

"What are you doing here, Ray?"

"I need to speak to Stephanie. I've been trying to reach her all day."

"You and me both."

"But . . ." I look over at the elevators. "I thought—"

"I know." Her voice drops to a whisper. "She's up there, all right, but it's like trying to talk to a—" She stops, shakes her head. "Sorry."

"For what?" I wait. "What were you going to say?"

"Nothing. I have a big mouth. I should learn to keep it shut."

"Huh. Can I go and talk to her, then?"

"It's not up to me." Molly nods at the desk. "You can ask, but I wouldn't hold out much hope."

"No, I guess not. Well . . ." I look at her for a moment. "Can I buy you a drink instead?"

"Me?"

"Yeah, you."

She shrugs. "Why?"

"So I can pick your brain."

"Ha. There's nothing left to pick," she says, pointing to her head. "It's fried, burned to a crisp."

She looks pale and I notice a few freckles around her nose. Her blue eyes are tired, but they still have a brightness to them.

"How about this?" she says. "*I* buy *you* a drink. For the other day."

"Sure." I pause. "How'd that work out, by the way?"

"Pretty good. Thank you. Though it feels like longer than just the other day. So much more shit has happened since then." She glances down at her briefcase, then back up. "Where do you want to go?"

I suggest the Orpheus Room, which is nearby, but she groans.

"This is an *after*-work drink, right?"

"Yes."

"So let's go somewhere dark, somewhere dingy."

We find a place on Lexington. It's nearly empty and we sit at the bar. I order a Bushmills and she gets a Goose Island. We swap war stories and start bemoaning the current state of politics. By our third drink, I'm realizing a couple of things. One, I like her, and two, it feels inevitable that I'm going to blow any chance I might have with her by bringing the conversation back to the congresswoman. But weirdly, Molly seems to understand this and she does it for me.

"Look, that thing I was going to say earlier, about Stephanie?"

"You don't have to—"

"Shut up. You're dying to know."

I make a face, relieved, partly because I might find something out, but also because I'm under a bit of a spell now. It's the physical closeness, the bar-stool intimacy of it all.

"See?" she says. "But you first. Tell me why you want to talk to her."

"I thought this was an *after*-work drink."

"I really don't know if there is such a thing."

I peer into my glass before taking a sip from it. "It's actually her father I want to talk to. He told me something at that book launch and I need to follow up on it."

"Did you not find him at Beekman Place?"

"I did. But now he seems to be avoiding me."

"What was this thing he told you?"

Either that question was the next in a logical sequence of them, or she's playing me. And on behalf of the congresswoman.

I look at her. "What were *you* going to tell *me*?"

"Oh, come on. What is this, quid pro quo?" She laughs. "Have the lambs stopped screaming, Clarice?"

She started it, but I'm hardly going to say that, am I? Besides, I don't have to tell her everything. "He claimed to know my grandfather back in the fifties, when they were both young guys, and it made me curious."

"Oh wow." She mulls this over. "That's cool. Did you know your grandfather?"

"No, he died long before I was born."

She holds my gaze but doesn't say anything. A little pulse ripples through the air between us. I certainly don't feel like she's playing me. What I do feel like is leaning across and kissing her.

But the moment passes.

"Now, *my* turn," she says, and straightens up on her stool. "So, the simple fact is, Congresswoman Proctor's hit the sauce and pretty hard."

"Shit."

I wasn't expecting that.

"It seems she's been sober for over twenty-five years. Or had been."

"I didn't know."

"Have you ever noticed, she'll order a glass of wine but never actually drink it?"

I think about this and nod.

"Apparently, it's a thing, a control mechanism. But not anymore."

I shift on my stool. "What set her off?"

Molly shakes her head. "I don't know. I thought it was maybe the Rise & Unite bullshit, that she'd gotten a heads-up on it or something, but . . . that couldn't have been the reason, because it wasn't even true, as it turns out. Like you said."

"What kind of a state is she in now?"

Molly lifts her bottle and tips it in my direction. "She's way ahead of us, my friend. I was up there trying to get her to sign some papers"—she taps the side of her briefcase with her shoe—"but it was no use. She's incoherent."

"Man. Where does that leave *you*?"

"I guess we'll see. Either it's a blip, and she'll get her shit together, or it all falls apart. I don't know. She has plenty of people around her, but we're all so *young . . .*"

"Oh, come on."

"Seriously." She jabs me in the arm. "This is old-school stuff, empty whiskey bottles and overflowing ashtrays. Abusive language. We're snowflakes. None of us has ever seen anything *like* it."

"Yeah, I guess."

Stephanie is obviously in a bad way and I can't help wondering what's behind it. But what I'm really thinking about right now, to be honest—*all* I'm thinking about—is how I want Molly to jab me in the arm again.

"And you know what the weird thing is?" she says, stifling a yawn. "A part of me is looking at this as an opportunity. If Stephanie crashes and burns and I'm out of a job, then maybe that's great, because . . . I mean, is this what I want? This life? There was a time when I thought it was, but I don't know anymore."

"Maybe you just got hitched to the wrong candidate."

She considers this. "Maybe. Steph's a strange old bird, that's for sure."

There's a pause and then we both laugh.

"Where do you live?" she asks.

"Where do *you* live?"

"Queens," she says. "Astoria."

"I live ten blocks from here."

I open my eyes, immediately conscious of the fact that things are a little different—that the air in my bedroom has an unfamiliar fragrance to it, that I'm not wearing anything, that parts of me ache, that I'm not alone.

But also that my mind is as still and calm as a reflecting pool in a shaded garden.

I turn and look around. Molly is sitting over by the window, wearing one of my T-shirts, her briefcase open in her lap.

"What's up?" I say quietly. I know that we're on the other side here . . . the other side of an after-work drink, the other side of a whole night, and that nothing can be taken for granted.

That climates change.

She looks over at me and smiles, then goes back to whatever she's doing.

"*That* was nice," I say after a moment.

She looks up again. "Very."

"I'll put on some coffee," I say, rolling off the bed, scrambling for a pair of boxers. At the door, I glance back. "You already at work?"

"No, I . . . I remembered something," she says, throwing me a distracted look over the rim of her glasses. "There's a pile of stuff here, and I . . . I'm pretty sure . . ."

She goes back to it.

As I get to the counter, I hear a small yelp from the bedroom. "Found it!"

I put on the coffee and when I turn around, Molly is leaning against the doorway. She has a sheet of paper in her hand.

"What would you think of a trip to the Russian baths on Thirty-Ninth Street?"

"What?"

She waves the sheet of paper in the air. "The Russian baths on Thirty-Ninth Street. Clay Proctor goes there three mornings a week."

"You're kidding."

"No. I knew I'd seen a reference to it in there somewhere." She motions back at her briefcase. "It was in an email. Steph likes her emails printed out."

I shake my head, still a little confused.

"It was a few weeks ago, she was going over her schedule, and she mentioned it in relation to fitting in a block of time to see him."

I stare at her. "Which three mornings?"

She looks at the sheet of paper again, then back over at me. "What day is it today?"

13

Outside the White Horse Tavern, Sweeney asks himself what all of this is for. Could he be running Ridley Rogan Blanford within a couple of weeks? Sure, he guesses—if he *wanted* to. Could he take over the New York City Parks Commission from Robert Moses and do a better job? Absurd as it may sound, yes, he feels he could. He feels he could do anything. Because if information and intuition are two corners of this triangle, confidence is the third—the kind you're supposed to get from drinking alcohol, only multiplied by a thousand and minus any debilitating side effects. It's how he was able to confront Robert Moses in the first place. It's how he ended up in a suite in the Waldorf Towers lecturing Marilyn Monroe on the nature of fame and celebrity. It's how he got Dylan Thomas to confide in him.

And these were extraordinary experiences.

Sweeney doesn't know what they mean, though.

He wanders aimlessly for a while, torrents of information coming at him, unbidden and unfiltered, but when he finds himself back in Midtown at one point, on Broadway, in the low Forties, something occurs to him, and he slows down. Maybe the wandering hasn't been aimless after all, because wasn't it up here, a few blocks on, that Matt Drake was killed? Sweeney is still unclear about what happened that night, about what led up to the accident, but it strikes him now that he should try to figure it out.

He picks up the pace again.

First, it was an accident. Some unfortunate guy ran Matt over with his car. But that was only the final link in a chain of events that started back in Mike Sutton's apartment in Greenwich Village. As far as the cops are concerned, the case is now closed, because whatever drove Matt to run out into traffic may have been bizarre, and may have piqued departmental curiosity, but it was effectively irrelevant. There was no crime and therefore no perp.

But there *was* the question of Matt's possible double-life to consider.

The whip marks and the rouge.

Not that this makes any difference to Sweeney. His initial reaction to the news, as relayed by Dick Blanford, may have been one of shock, but that's not what he feels now. Matt Drake liked to wear makeup and be dominated? Big deal. Presumably he knew what he was doing. So fine. But what if he *didn't* know? That's the point. What if he'd never done anything like it before? What if the stuff Mike Sutton put in his drink caused Drake to flip out completely?

That's what Sweeney wants to find out.

He starts by asking around. He goes into a drugstore and sits at the lunch counter. He orders coffee and gets a conversation going—with the waitress, with the person on the stool next to him. That accident the other week? Fellow was run over? Late at night? You hear about that? He talks to a cop outside on the street and to a guy at a newsstand on the corner. To his surprise, people engage with him. They answer his questions and seem eager to offer up anything they know, which in most cases turns out to be nothing. Nevertheless, by aggregating the snippets of information he does get, Sweeney establishes two things: one, exactly where the accident happened, and two, the direction Matt was coming from when he ran out into traffic. This leads him, in turn, to a stretch along West Forty-Eighth Street, where he suspects he might find one or more of those underground clubs that Dick Blanford said the police had been interested in looking at. It's the afternoon, so nowhere like that is going to be open, but he sticks around anyway, pacing the sidewalk. Eventually, he settles on what strikes him as a likely spot—an unmarked entrance between an Italian restaurant and a movie theater that in the space of a half hour has two delivery trucks stop in front of it, one unloading cases of liquor and the other kitchen supplies.

Sweeney hovers around, waiting for the unmarked, metal door to open again, for someone to emerge. Instead, a dapper guy in a suit comes along, from the direction of Seventh Avenue. When he gets to the metal door, he raps on it with his knuckles. As he's waiting for it to open, he notices Sweeney.

"Hey, bub?" he says, a little suspiciously. "Can I help you with something?"

Sweeney steps forward. "This place here, I just had a couple of questions."

"What are you, a cop? A private dick?"

"No." Sweeney holds his palms up. "Nothing like that. A guy I know died. It was in this neighborhood. He got run over by a car. About a week and a half ago. On Broadway, early hours of the morning."

"Oh." The guy looks down, at his shoes. "I'm sorry to hear that." He raps on the door again. "But what's that got—"

"I think he was in your club that night."

"*My* club?"

Sweeney doesn't know why he's so sure about this. But he is. There's a loud clicking sound and the door opens.

"Hey, boss."

The guy rolls his eyes. He puts a hand on the door and looks at Sweeney. Then it happens, this *thing*. It was the same earlier, with the other people Sweeney spoke to—a subtle shift in attitude, like a small light bulb going on.

The guy tilts his head. "What's your name?"

"Ned Sweeney."

"I'm Billy Kline." There's a pause. "Come on in."

The place is called the Lemon Club and its main attraction is a drag act featuring a chorus of what Kline calls "all-singing, all-dancing pansies." The interior is dark but richly decorated in red and purple brocade, with a central bar, tables and booths, and an array of fake palm trees. In the twenty minutes or so that Sweeney is there, sitting at one of the tables with Kline, he glimpses a couple of the "exotic" performers, moving back and forth in a room to the side. They're in various states of undress. Kline is efficient and business-like, but he seems reluctant to break eye contact with Sweeney, and three times during the conversation he says, "I don't know why I'm telling you this." What he does tell Sweeney—against his better judgment, because apparently he somehow managed not to tell any of it to the cops when they came calling—is that yes, Matt Drake *was* up here that night, that he came with another guy, they were pretty hammered, Drake particularly, and things got out of hand.

"Was he a regular?"

"No, he'd never been here before."

"What about the guy he came with?"

Kline puts a hand on the table and drums his fingers. Then he looks to his left and shouts, "Lulu?"

After a moment, a tall, elegant drag queen appears from the room at the side. He's got dazzling eyes, full, pouty lips, and flaming red hair. He needs a shave.

"Mr. Sweeney," Kline says with a weary flourish, "Lulu."

"Hey there, Mr. Sweeney."

"Hello, Lulu."

Kline asks him to sit down and tell Sweeney about the guy who brought Matt Drake to the Lemon Club that night. Lulu is hesitant at first, continually glancing at Kline to check that what he's saying is okay, but pretty soon that thing kicks in again and Lulu requires no further prodding. What he reveals is that the guy, whose name is Mike Sutton, regularly shows up at the Lemon Club and hangs out backstage whenever he does, causing nothing but trouble. The reason they can't just kick him out is that he's a federal narcotics agent and corrupt as fuck, excuse the French. He deals drugs and he blackmails anyone in the chorus whom he finds out is a married guy with kids—which is a good number of them. "So this poor guy he dragged along that night," Lulu says, "was high as a kite on something. He didn't know where he was, and when Mike forced him to play dress-up, the guy went along with it, or didn't object, not at first anyway. Then it got crazy back there, really messy—and meanwhile we're trying to put on a show. But in the end the guy just couldn't take it anymore and he literally ran screaming out into the street." Lulu throws his hands up. "And the rest, as they say . . ."

Sweeney nods along. Poor Matt Drake, he thinks, what a way to go, effectively the victim of a sadistic bully. But wasn't he also, like Sweeney himself, the unwitting test subject of a drug experiment? That's the part Sweeney is now more curious about, the nature of the experiment, and the nature of the different drugs involved—what they're for, who manufactures them, who controls them, who *has* them. "So, this Mike Sutton," he says, "you haven't seen him back here since?"

Kline and Lulu shoot each other a look.

"No, we haven't," Kline says. "And maybe that's not such a surprise. But I wouldn't go looking for him either, Mr. Sweeney. He's a *very* dangerous man."

"I think I got that impression, all right," Sweeney says. Then he decides it's time to leave. But when he goes to stand up from the table, that woozy feeling returns. It hits him hard, like a rush of blood to the head, and as he's falling backward, without ever seeming to land, the richly patterned walls of the glamorous Lemon Club start dissolving all around him, Kline and Lulu receding to a blur . . .

Then he's back out on Forty-Eighth Street.

Or—

Is it Fifty-Second?

He's walking but needs to slow down, needs to catch his breath. He stops at a fire hydrant.

"You okay, mister?"

He tries to steady himself, then turns slightly. A young guy is standing there, thin, sallow-skinned, dark-eyed.

"Yeah, thanks," Sweeney says. "I'm fine."

"Looked like you were having a seizure, man."

"No, really, I'm . . . I'm fine."

"Solid. Because this really isn't the best part of town to be having a seizure."

"No."

Sweeney looks around. They're outside Hanson's Drugstore. He remembers reading about this place somewhere. It's a second-tier hangout joint for comics and actors and showbiz types.

"Stay cool," the guy says, and heads inside.

Sweeney follows him, and before he knows it he's at the counter, spritzing with the late-afternoon crowd, absorbing the jokes and impressions, the voices, the lingo, and transmuting it all as rapidly as he can into a routine, a shtick of his own—a competitive streak he didn't know he had driving him to push the envelope, to get more laughs than Joe Ancis here, or this Lenny, or Don, or whoever. Maybe that really was a seizure he had out there on the street, or a coronary, or a stroke, who knows, but Sweeney doesn't care, because this new thing he has, this ability to draw people in and gain their confidence, to make them want to engage with him, is causing both his heart and his brain to pulsate. But fuse that with his ability to process huge amounts of information and all of a sudden a place like Hanson's Drugstore, with its schleppers and dopers, its agents and pimps, is just no longer stimulating enough. He needs to keep moving, and he does—somehow ending up hours later in the lounge of the Copacabana nightclub on Fifty-Ninth Street chatting loudly with Dorothy Kilgallen and Porfirio Rubirosa about the recent coronation of the young Queen Elizabeth II of England. Sweeney's own view that the very notion of royalty at this midpoint of the twentieth century is absurd not only meets with considerable resistance, but also provokes a degree of irritation in a gentleman sitting at a nearby table.

"Hey you, knock that shit off, you hear?"

Sweeney turns. "Excuse me?"

The gentleman shakes his head. "What are you, some kind of Communist?" He's at a table with three other men, all burly, all in silk suits.

Sweeney does a double take. "Am I a *what*?"

Rubirosa nudges him with his elbow, and whispers, "You don't recognize—"

"Sure I do, Rubi," Sweeney whispers back, but it's loud, a cartoon whisper. "I certainly recognize his *hands*. I saw them on TV last year."

"What was that, you little punk?"

Frank Costello doesn't get out of his chair, but he motions to one of his associates, who leaps up and lunges toward Sweeney.

"What did you say again?"

"I refuse to answer," Sweeney shouts, backing away, "on the grounds that I might incriminate myself."

At this point, the other two guys at Costello's table get up and move forward. Rubirosa slips behind Dorothy Kilgallen, pushing her and another young woman directly into the path of the oncoming heavies. Panic erupts and in the ensuing confusion Sweeney turns and retreats.

Outside, there's a line of waiting taxis. He jumps into one of them and tells the driver Penn Station and to make it quick.

It's after midnight as he approaches the house on Greenlake Avenue. Physically, he's a little tired, the edge on this thing somewhat blunted now, but his mind is still racing. He shouldn't be apprehensive about seeing Laura—especially not after the day he's had, but he can't help it, and when he opens the door he feels the tension immediately, feels it rushing toward him like backdraft from a raging fire.

"Ned, oh my God, where were you, I've been worried sick all day, the office called this morning, three times, and again this afternoon . . . I've been going out of my mind . . ."

He should have called, that's pretty obvious. But what would he have said? What's he going to say now? *Laura, don't you see that all of these social conventions we live by are mere illusions? That ideas like authority and fame are nothing more than mental constructs? That our*—It takes Sweeney a moment to realize that he actually is saying these things, and that Laura is staring at him as if he's unhinged. Then it strikes him that Laura looks awful—she's got bags under her eyes and she reeks of cigarette smoke, the residue of which surrounds her like a miasma of cold despair. He knows she's been distraught all day, and that it's entirely his fault . . . but still, there's a barrier of some kind between them now, and it's not an illusion. He also remembers that he hasn't eaten since yesterday and that maybe that explains why he's feeling light-headed again.

"Ned!"

He reaches out for the bottom of the banister to steady himself. "I'm fine."

"You're *drunk*, or . . . or something."

"No, Laura, I've never been more sober in my life." He looks at her. "And in fact I've only just . . . I've . . . ." But there doesn't seem to be much point in continuing. Whatever magic he was able to work earlier in the day has deserted him. Or perhaps it's that Laura is immune to it. He doesn't know. Either way, he turns his gaze upward, tracing the line of the banister to the floor above. "You know what, Laura?" he says. "I'm tired. Can we talk about this tomorrow?"

When he opens his eyes the next morning, after a swampful of dreams, Sweeney feels terrible—nauseous, and racked with guilt. It takes him a few moments to register where he is—that he's *on* the bed, not in it, and also that he's stretched out across it.

And that he's fully clothed.

He sits up, turns around, surveys the room. Where did Laura sleep? And what time is it? He looks at the clock on the nightstand. Just after *ten*?

"Laura!"

He gets off the bed. He goes out into the hallway and then downstairs.

"Laura?"

He heads straight for the kitchen. There's a piece of paper on the table—nothing else, no cups or dishes or cutlery. He picks it up. It's a handwritten note. The message is clear and concise. Laura has gone to stay with her sister in Philadelphia for a few days and has taken Tommy with her. Ned's behavior has been so strange and unpredictable of late that she was actually afraid for her and Tommy's safety, and yesterday proved to be too much. She's sorry. But he knows where to reach her.

Sweeney places the note back on the table and stares into space for a while. On reflection, she did the right thing, given the circumstances. What else was she going to do?

And what's *he* going to do?

Have some breakfast, maybe. Orange juice, two eggs, toast. A pot of coffee. Then he takes a shower and shaves. As he's getting dressed, the telephone rings, but he ignores it. Who would it be anyway? Probably someone from the office again—his secretary, or Dick Blanford, or Jack Rogan.

The idea of having to talk to either of those guys hits Sweeney right in the solar plexus. It also serves as a reminder of just where that supreme confidence he enjoyed yesterday came from.

And with that, he sees his future laid out in front of him. He's had a taste of what MDT-48 can do, and it's been amazing, but he also knows it's been a bit random, a bit chaotic, and he blames himself for that. Next time he resolves to be more focused, more purposeful. He gets the shoe box down from the top of the wardrobe and prepares a dose, making it as small as he possibly can. He mixes it up and knocks the whole thing back in one go.

Then he pulls a travel bag out from under the bed and packs it with a change of clothes, some toiletries, his shaving kit, and the vial of MDT. Ready to leave, he goes downstairs, but lingers for a while at the door. As the effects of the drug start to creep up on him, he glances around. There's Tommy's train set on the floor of the living room, and Laura's camel-hair coat on the stand by the door . . . objects he suddenly perceives to be alive.

They're probably at Penn Station by now, or already on their way to Philadelphia, depending on what time they left this morning. Sweeney hates the thought of Laura's hurried, anxious departure, of how she must have bundled Tommy out of bed, getting him dressed and shushing him. *Daddy's asleep, we don't want to make any noise.* Sweeney loves them both, but he doesn't know how to be with them, not in his current state, at least not yet—though standing alone now in this empty house, MDT coursing through his system, he doesn't know if he ever will.

He steps outside and shuts the door behind him. It's a bright day, sunny and fresh. The train station is a ten-minute walk from the house, but Sweeney isn't taking the train today. He's decided he's going to drive instead. There's just one problem with this.

He doesn't have a car.

Only a few remain in the vicinity after the morning's exodus of commuters. Most of them are sitting in carports, and as Sweeney walks along Greenlake Avenue, he sizes these up. At the same time, he reviews in his head a conversation he once overheard in a bar about how to hot-wire an automobile. As it turns out, he doesn't need to do this, because the candidate he chooses—a Corsair Deluxe sedan—still has its key in the ignition. He can see it through the window on the driver's side. Before he opens the door, he surveys the area, but there's no one to be seen, there's no movement and no sound, save for occasional birdsong and the faint, lonesome hum of a vacuum cleaner.

Sweeney slides into the driver's seat. He turns the key and gently pulls out of the carport.

14

An hour later Molly and I are sitting in a coffee shop on West Thirty-Ninth Street across from the Hudson Baths. I've never heard of this place, but apparently it's been here for over fifty years. I know about the baths in the East Village, and about some of the fancier spots you see ads for in glossy magazines, with their jade soaking ponds and black-mud healing treatments, but this joint never made it onto my radar. And that's what it looks like, a low-rent joint—because from the entrance and the signage I can't imagine it being anything other than cheap and fairly sleazy inside.

As I keep an eye on anyone entering or leaving the place, Molly deals with some of the countless texts and emails she's received this morning. Apparently, suspicions are mounting around the congresswoman. Is she sick? Is there something going on? Where *is* she? For her part, Molly is happy to steer clear of the office, at least for the moment. They *are* working on an official statement, but—

I look at her. "What?"

"Over there." Molly is pointing across the street. "That car pulling up? I think it's Proctor's."

It's a black Lincoln MKS.

"What do you want to do?" she says.

There's no real plan here.

"I don't know. Try and see him before he goes in, I guess."

I pay and we head outside. We cross the street, weaving through traffic, and position ourselves a couple of doors up from the Hudson. The driver of the car gets out and comes around to open the rear door. Proctor emerges, wearing old-man sweats and a hoodie. He's carrying a small gym bag.

Sensing hesitation on my part, Molly steps forward. "Mr. Proctor?"

The driver—who could easily be Dean's kid brother—spins around. He's ready to raise an arm to block Molly's approach.

"Hello," Proctor says. "Molly, isn't it?"

Dean's kid brother stands down.

"Yes, Mr. Proctor, it is. Can I speak to you for a second?"

"Certainly," he says.

Then he sees me.

I come level with Molly and stand next to her.

"Ray, what a surprise."

"Is it?" I say. "I've tried to contact you several times."

"Really? I thought you might." He looks at Molly, then back at me. "*This* is interesting."

Molly exhales. "Listen, whatever Ray wants to talk to you about is none of my business, but *I* just thought you should know something."

"Oh, and you both just happened to arrive here at the same time, is that it?"

"No, but—"

"Don't worry. I think it's cute."

"I'm not worried," she says. "About *that*. I am worried about Stephanie, Mr. Proctor. She's in a bad way at the moment. The situation is . . . getting critical."

"Yes, I heard. She'll be all right."

"I don't think she—"

"She *will*, believe me." He turns to his driver. "It's okay, Karl."
Then back at us. "So, are you coming in?"

"Excuse me?" I say.

"Come on. Have a shvitz. We'll talk. You'll feel better. Both of you."
He turns toward the entrance.

Molly and I exchange looks, then follow him inside.

The lobby area is small, but clean. There's a reception desk, a wall
with noticeboards, and a window with blinds that looks out onto
the street. A young woman at the desk greets Proctor warmly. As
she turns her attention to us, he says, "These are my guests, Anna.
Make sure they're looked after."

Anna smiles and beckons us over.

She gives us each a pair of rubber clogs and a locker combination. We follow Proctor down a set of stairs where a tall guy named
Janek hands out terry-cloth robes and towels and directs us to the
changing rooms. Proctor wanders off to what I assume is a private
members area. As I change, and stash my clothes, phone, and wallet in the locker, I find it hard to believe that this is really happening. The bath area features a couple of steam rooms, a sauna, and a
cold-water plunge pool, as well as a row of showers and massage
booths. A few people are moving around, but there's a quiet, sleepy
air to the place. Molly appears from the women's side. She's wearing a towel, expertly wrapped. Her hair is tied back and she doesn't
have her glasses on. She seems perfectly comfortable. I'm just in
boxers and feel like I'm starring in a big-budget anxiety dream. After
a moment, Proctor himself shows up, small and wizened, a towel
around his waist. He's still wearing that thick black band on his
wrist. He stops and has a word with Janek.

Molly catches my eye, and whispers, "This is pretty wild for an
after-work drink."

Proctor then comes over and leads us into one of the steam
rooms. It's tiled in blue and aquamarine mosaics. It has two levels
of seating but is quite small. It's also empty.

"We won't be disturbed in here," he says and sits on the lower level. He holds out a hand. "Please, sit."

I put myself directly opposite Proctor. Molly sits further in and a level up.

It's hot, and I'm already sweating profusely. We all are. Which I know is the point, but—

"So, Ray Sweeney," Proctor says, "we should talk all of this out, am I right? We may not get another chance. And we have a witness." He does a half bow in Molly's direction. "This charming young lady here."

My head is spinning now, but I manage to zero in. "Why would we not get another chance to talk? I don't understand."

"Oh, let's park that for the moment. It's not so important. I'm sure you have much more interesting questions to put to me."

I do.

But am I willing to just blurt them out in front of Molly Boyd? Who I barely knew this time yesterday? I turn to look at her for a second—and yes, it would appear that I am. There's nothing rational about this, or calculated. It's her pale skin, glistening now with sweat, that I can still taste, and her blue eyes, closer to sapphire without the glasses, that I don't want to look away from.

"Mr. Proctor," I say, "Eiben-Chemcorp has been developing a drug for geriatrics, a derivative of MDT-48, for some years now. Are you . . . *taking* it?"

"Ha. You've done your homework. But no, not exactly. That's been abandoned. It was never going to work. They couldn't control it. They couldn't ratchet it *down* sufficiently."

I'm puzzled, and must look it.

"So what am I taking?" he says. "Because I'm clearly taking something, right? Well, I'm taking MDT-48 itself. The real thing. The original."

I sit back. Even though I want to, I don't so much as glance at Molly.

"Now, you have to remember," Proctor goes on, "I was starting from a very low base. I was what, eighty-nine at the time, or ninety, and I had dementia. Or at least it had started. Then, boom, one dose, and the fog lifted. It was incredible. And let me tell you, for one reason or another, I'd been putting off taking that one dose for nearly sixty years." He slaps his right hand on the tiled surface. "Carpe diem. That may be a cliché, but believe me, they're the wisest goddamned words you'll ever hear." He shakes his head slowly. "Anyway. Next day the fog was back, so I guess I was hooked." He smiles. "Luckily, I had a permanent supply."

"Eiben?" I say, my voice sounding brittle, even to me.

"Yes. They've been sitting on this thing for decades and they don't know what to do with it. They never have."

"*They?*"

"Very well, Counselor, *we*."

"So why not sell it," I say. "Or *give* it to the hundreds of thousands of people, the millions of people, suffering from Alzheimer's?"

Proctor shrugs. "Say you do that, fine, but how long you think before people start getting curious about what's in that little bottle in the medicine cabinet? Suddenly Grandpa's all focused and knows where he left his keys? Well, damn, you think—maybe *I'll* try a little of that, and before you know it you're speaking five languages, contradicting Stephen Hawking and dating Jessica Chastain. Then it gets out there, it's on the street, and there's no way to control it."

I'm sweating so hard now and my head is throbbing, but again I have to ask him the obvious question.

"So what? Why does it have to be controlled?"

It's a while before he answers. "You know what, Ray? After all these years, I'm not sure I can tell you. But it's always been the operating principle—as in, don't let this stuff get into the hands of ordinary people. I mean, look what happened with LSD, right?"

"But some ordinary people, as you call them, *have* gotten their hands on it. Eddie Spinola, for instance."

"Yeah, okay. Deke Tauber, too. And there have been others." He pauses. "Spinola was a wake-up call, that's for sure."

"What do you mean?"

"The guy was extraordinary." He pauses. "You see, not everyone reacts the same way to it, so a few more like him, a few more Eddie Spinolas, and the entire fabric of society would start to mutate and bend in ways we can't even imagine."

I stare across at this little old man, with his tanned and mottled skin, his bony frame, his searching eyes, and I wonder what he's up to. Why is he talking to me?

At this point, Molly clears her throat.

We both turn.

"I have a question," she says. "What the *fuck* are you guys talking about?"

Proctor looks at me. "You didn't explain any of this to her?"

What does he think? "No, Mr. *Secretary*, I didn't get around to it."

"Ha. Is the heat getting to you, son? I can see you're not used to it."

Molly clears her throat again.

"Okay, listen," the old man says, "you've heard of smart drugs, right? Well, this is a smart drug on steroids. MDT-48. It was discovered in 1912 in the Amazon jungle. It was extracted from a fungus that grew on the bark of the Bawari tree. The compound was later synthesized by a Swiss chemist and it first showed up in the U.S. around 1932 or 1933. But no one seemed to know what to do with it, so it languished in an Eiben Laboratories test tube until the early 1950s. That was when MDT and dozens of other compounds were tried out as potential weapons for use against our enemies in the Cold War. LSD was the front-runner, but it didn't take in the end, and most of the others were just forgotten about, including MDT."

"*Forgotten* about?" I say. "How is that possible?"

"Wait, wait, wait." Molly leans forward. "What *is* this stuff? You said it's some kind of a smart drug, and I get that, but—"

"No, listen," Proctor says, holding up a hand to stop her. "I know that's what I called it, but I meant the phrase as a kind of shorthand, because actually 'smart drug' is a hopelessly inadequate name for what this is."

Lowering his hand, he goes silent for a moment.

Then Molly says, "And that would *be* . . . ?"

"It's like . . . an entheogen. I suppose that's what you'd call it." He stops and looks down at the steaming wooden slats on the floor. He seems confused, or maybe embarrassed. I turn to Molly. Her eyes widen.

I widen my own in response.

Proctor looks up. "You know what that is, right, an entheogen? It's a psychoactive substance used in religious or shamanic rituals. It can be obtained from natural sources or it can be synthesized. It's like . . . peyote or ayahuasca. There's a ton of them—fly agaric, African dream root, Bolivian torch cactus. The food of the gods." He looks at me. "See, I've done my homework, too, Ray. I haven't had much else to do these last couple of years. So here's the thing, MDT is different from all of these other substances. Entheogen literally translates as 'generating the divine within,' which means you go off on a *trip,* you get lost inside yourself, and then you come back, maybe with a different understanding or insight on things. You learn, and you put what you learned into practice. Fine, but there's this binary aspect to it—here, there, inside, outside. If you're on ayahuasca, you're not going to be able to sit down and do your taxes, or go into a store and buy a pair of shoes, or teach a class on Lacanian semiotics. But on MDT, you could not only do all of that stuff, and exceptionally well, you could simultaneously observe and record every flutter of every atom in the space around you, see the patterns and understand them, trace their paths of origin and extrapolate their forward trajectories. And in that class you're teaching on Lacan? Or in the mall where you're buying those shoes? You could read the face of every single person you encounter and know them all as intimately as you know yourself. And it would feel so natural. It's not binary, it's integrated. It's the essence of maximal human intelligence."

As I look down at the floor, licks of sweat drip from my forehead. I've done LSD a few times in my life and it can certainly turn weird—oppressive, threatening, unending. A bit like this. I'm also anxious about Molly, but I can't look at her. If I'm clinging to anything here, anything fact-based, it's the anomaly of this man sitting in front of me set against his diagnosis of Alzheimer's from a couple of years ago.

But *she* doesn't know that.

"Now," Proctor goes on, "those aren't things that I can do, because strictly speaking I should be six feet under the fucking ground at this stage. So believe me, I'm good." He looks at Molly. "But that's what MDT is."

She shakes her head. "I don't believe this. You're a ninety-year-old hippy."

"Ninety-*two*. And it's a little different."

I stare at the floor again and repeat my earlier question. "So if people knew it was that powerful back in the fifties, how did it get forgotten?"

"Maybe not forgotten, then," Proctor says. "*Suppressed* is a better word."

This immediately raises so many questions that I'm unable to formulate a single one.

Proctor continues, "Later, in the mid-sixties, there was an attempt to revive interest in it. They tried to make tweaks, you know, to water it down. Because they figured it had to be a gold mine, right? Something that powerful."

"Who's *they*?"

"The guy that biography was about—you remember, Raoul Fursten? His whole crew. But they couldn't do it, because as these next-generation versions were developed and tested, it quickly became apparent that the drug simply couldn't be tamed, that its charisma, so to speak, couldn't be routinized. Then Eiben developed Phenalex and Triburbazine, and later Narolet, and MDT just sort of got put on the back burner again."

"Were those drugs derivatives of MDT in some way? Did Fursten, I don't know . . . break open the compound and—"

"What? Break it open? No. That's not how it works. Though maybe old Raoul was *taking* MDT, who knows. It wouldn't surprise me. In any case, he died in '73 and it wasn't until well after the Church Committee Hearings that MDT resurfaced—that was Operation Mandrake, but *it* didn't go anywhere, either. Then Jerome Hale came along in the mid-eighties and it was under him that things got a little . . . well, *leaky*, let's call it. So you get Deke Tauber, Vernon Gant, and then Spinola."

"Isn't that when *you* were CEO?"

"For a time, yes, but I was busy with other stuff. Narolet had taken off, and there were a couple of high-profile liability trials going on."

"And then?"

"Then Arnie Tisch took over R&D in the early 2000s, and with our big patents due to expire in the next couple of decades, a lot of money was poured into looking for something new, maybe something with a splash of MDT in the mix? Maybe." He exhales. "But so far no dice."

I think about this for a second.

"So how come *you* get a supply? What's that about?"

Proctor leans forward and rubs a hand over his moist head. "I've been around MDT for more than half a century," he says. "But I'd never taken it, not once. Never even considered it. Then I'm faced with literally losing my mind. I made a fool of myself on TV, and I could see it happening." He pauses, breathing slowly, staring at the floor. "In fact, Arnie Tisch approached *me*. It was his suggestion. Having tried everything else, Eiben was now interested in exploring MDT's potential as a life-extension drug." He laughs. "Can you believe it? It was all unofficial, of course, but I said sure, sign me up." He displays his wrist with the black band around it. "That was two years ago."

"Oh my God," Molly says. "I had no idea."

"I'm being monitored all the time, because it's clearly working. I mean, look at me. I'm alive. I'm healthier than I've been in fifteen or twenty years." He points to his head. "But what they're not monitoring, what they're not even aware of—at least I don't think they have been until recently—is the extension that's going on up here. The *expansion*."

I wipe my brow again, loose droplets of sweat hitting the tiles. "Are they worried?"

"I think they're beginning to worry—that I might go rogue, that is. And they're right, they should worry."

I don't know what to say to this. I just stare at him.

"You see, I'm almost ashamed to admit it, but I only really opened my eyes for the first time in my life two years ago. When I was ninety. Isn't that something?" He smiles. "And once I understood what MDT was," he continues, "you know what I did next, Ray?"

"No."

"I came looking for *you*."

15

Sweeney drives to Washington, D.C. It takes him about six hours, and when he gets there, he abandons his neighbor's car on Connecticut Avenue. He checks into a room at the Mayflower Hotel and has dinner at the Colony restaurant, where he gets talking to a Rhode Island Republican on the Senate Foreign Relations Committee. This fellow confesses to Sweeney that over the course of twenty years he reckons he's attended more than eight thousand cocktail parties and he doesn't think he can face another one. Later, Sweeney finds himself at a Georgetown soirée where he receives three separate but very different job offers: an advisory position with the Federal Communications Commission, deputy Washington bureau chief at *Newsweek* magazine, and the part of a Roman general in an upcoming sword-and-sandals epic at MGM.

Lying awake that night in his hotel room, the MDT wearing off, Sweeney has a sort of panic reaction—sweating, shortness of breath, accelerated heart rate.

What is he doing?

He has a family, a house, a job. He has a *future*. This is madness and he should put a stop to it immediately, or at least cut back. There's one problem, though. Whatever this is, it feels more real to him now, more vivid and intense, than anything in his normal life, anything in what he's increasingly coming to regard as his old life. It's just that he's already spent most of the money he had with him (on the hotel room, on dinner, on drinks), so how is he supposed to move forward? Does he look for a job, one he has an actual prospect of holding down? Why did he come to Washington in the first place?

As he stares up at the ceiling, Sweeney realizes he can't answer any of these questions. But he knows someone who *will* be able to.

In a few hours' time.

That other guy.

The one he becomes when he takes MDT.

Solving the money problem—where and how to get some—proves to be fairly straightforward. The "where" part is easy. It's in other people's pockets, in their wallets, in their bank accounts. The "how" part is a little more complicated. As he strolls through the lobby of the Mayflower, Sweeney recalls an article he read a few months ago in *Reader's Digest* about "confidence tricksters." The piece described common techniques these people use and it advised members of the public to be on their guard against them. At the time, Sweeney was horrified by the article. But now he needs money, and he needs it in a hurry.

So how hard can it be?

Not very, as it turns out.

In a quiet part of the lobby, Sweeney carefully drops his wallet and immediately becomes engaged in an activity, checking a number in the telephone directory or selecting a magazine at the newsstand. A concerned citizen sees what has happened, picks up the wallet, and brings it to Sweeney. During the brief dialogue that ensues, Sweeney takes a casual look inside his wallet and stops cold.

"What is the meaning of this?" he says.

"Come again?" the mark responds, flustered.

"This is outrageous," Sweeney says, raising his voice slightly. "I had sixty dollars in my wallet, three twenties . . . and now there is only *one*." Glancing around, surveying the lobby, he mutters the words "house detective" and "manager."

"But—"

Apply enough psychological pressure and the whole transaction can be over in a couple of minutes.

Or he goes into a nearby Western Union office, where, in a state of apparent agitation, he repeatedly asks the clerk at the counter if his money has arrived. Identifying a likely mark, Sweeney then starts up a conversation—stories are exchanged, a bond is forged, and eventually a pact is entered into: whoever's money arrives first will see right by the other fellow.

In this way, and in the space of a couple of hours, he pulls off a few of these so-called "short cons" and amasses over two hundred dollars in cash.

The second issue Sweeney faces is D.C. itself. Why here? He remembers a feeling he had on the road yesterday, a sense of purpose, of moving toward the center of things, and he liked it. But does he want to get involved in politics? Is that it? He doesn't think so. He suspects his purpose here may be larger than that. He may want to *understand* politics. Everyone he met last night, the senator at the Colony, and the others later, the lobbyists and diplomats and businessmen, these were all pieces in the mosaic, each interesting in their own way. But Sweeney is aware that MDT demands more, that it seeks out clarity and strives to make connections, that it hungers after the bigger picture, the whole equation. At the same time, he's not *un*aware that it can also induce a certain degree of impatience in the user, not to mention a tendency toward grandiose thought patterns. But these are things he can temper—in the same way, depending on circumstances, that he can now regulate the sharpness and intensity of his sensory perceptions. If he chooses to, and without losing his train of thought, he can surrender himself momentarily to the mystery and richness of a color—the cerulean blue, say, of the late-afternoon D.C. sky, or the purple dye of an individual strand of carpet fiber in the corridor of his hotel. He can lose himself in the thousand sounds on K Street—shoe leather on asphalt, the rattle of streetcars, the symphony of human voices. Or he can simply dial these things down to zero and focus exclusively on some interior concern, the unspooling of a childhood memory, the retrieval of submerged data, the calculation of a looming risk.

So, on reflection, no, he won't be putting a stop to this, or even cutting back. In any case, each dose is so impossibly tiny that it still seems as if nothing has come out of the bottle at all. In fact, at this rate, Sweeney suspects that his supply of MDT might just last forever.

In the meantime, though, he keeps busy. He buys some new clothes and moves to a less expensive hotel, choosing the Rutherford on Seventeenth Street. During the day he walks around, familiarizing himself with the city's streets, with its architecture and its monuments. He also spends a good deal of time in the main reading room of the Library of Congress, burning through material at a rate he would have previously found unimaginable. Sweeney graduated with a BA from Atherton College in upstate New York. Then he was busy working. Then he was married. Then he was a father. But he has read more in his three days here than he did in the entire time he spent at Atherton.

In the evenings, he goes out and meets people, striking up casual conversations in bars. During one such encounter, with a dentist from Cleveland, he decides that he's going to start playing cards. The dentist is in town for a poker game at a club out on Route 301, over the Maryland state line, and when he mentions the sums of money that are routinely involved, Sweeney figures he should give it a shot. He can play poker, just about, and gin rummy, but he doesn't see why he couldn't up his game considerably with minimum effort. It would be an easier way of making money than tricking innocent punters in hotel lobbies—though making money per se is not his motivation here. It's a question of convenience. He needs walking-around money. He also wants to send some home to Laura.

Despite how it looks, he hasn't actually walked out on Laura. Or Tommy.

Obviously.

So he tags along with the dentist. It takes them forty-five minutes to get to the neon-lit strip of 301 somewhere between the town of Waldorf and the Potomac River Bridge. When they arrive at the "club," which is one of many, it's very different from what Sweeney had imagined. There's no mahogany bar, no thick carpets, no dress code. The front section is two long rows of slot machines, with a clientele comprised mainly of hicks and locals who are out to have a little fun. At the back, there are a few smaller rooms with tables set up for various card games, and the dentist retreats to one of these. Casing out the rest of the joint, Sweeney soon finds himself standing at a blackjack table, and although it's not a game he's ever played before, twenty minutes watching the dealer is enough to convince him that he could play it.

But not only that. He reckons he could beat the odds as well.

The goal for both the dealer and the player in blackjack is to draw cards that get as close to a total of twenty-one as possible without going over. Aces count as either one or eleven, and this is decided by the player. Jacks, Queens, and Kings all count as ten, and each numbered card counts as its face value. Now, if you weren't thinking about it, you would probably assume that during play one card has the same chance of being dealt as any other. But as Sweeney stands there, watching closely, it strikes him that in fact the odds on this depend on which cards are in play and which are still in the deck—and that the advantage can therefore shift, sometimes in the dealer's favor, sometimes in the player's. So if he could keep track of the cards—of which ones were in play and which had yet to be dealt—and if he varied his bets accordingly, wouldn't that give him a competitive edge?

After a while, he manages to get a spot at one of the tables and starts playing.

It takes a great deal of concentration, and the first few times he busts, but soon enough he gets a handle on things and his initial thirty-dollar stake increases to seventy-five dollars. This isn't a lot, but he sees the potential. He returns over the next few nights—to a different club each time—and sees his winnings slowly climb into the hundreds. Then into the thousands.

With his pockets now bulging, Sweeney buys a black Pontiac sedan at a police auction for 750 dollars in cash and a used Remington portable typewriter for ninety dollars.

He wires five hundred dollars to Laura. Then he decides to open a bank account.

But before he does that, he reckons there's something else he should probably do, and that is to adopt—or acquire—a new identity. Given his circumstances, Sweeney doesn't feel comfortable revealing information about himself, and since he's finding it increasingly difficult to remain anonymous, or even get away with just being cagey, he makes arrangements through a guy at one of the mob-run clubs he's been playing at to get a fake driver's license and a social security card.

But he's not sure what name to give himself.

He mulls it over for a while and in the end he settles on Tom Monroe.

Over the next few weeks, there's a lot of talk around town about a dynamic young man who keeps showing up at Georgetown cocktail parties and expounding ideas that people find either disturbing or exciting. He has views on everything—from the McCarthy hearings to segregation to nuclear weapons—and he is refreshingly fearless about expressing them.

But just who is he?

He's from New York and his name, it appears, is Tom Monroe.

Everyone assumes he's a writer of some kind, or a professor. He has an easy charm about him and a compelling manner that people find irresistible. But is there a particular reason he's appeared on the scene now? Rumor has it that he might be angling for a job at the State Department or the Treasury, or that he might be eyeing a Senate seat in next year's midterms.

But is he a Republican or a Democrat?

No one seems to know.

And that's how Sweeney would like to keep it.

It's difficult, though. He has a hard time containing himself in conversation, reining in the impulse to share every thought that crosses his mind. Certain people have a higher tolerance for this than others, and these are the people he needs to seek out. Because it's not just intelligence that counts, or intuition, or empathy. What shapes and informs the personality of a charismatic individual more than anything else is the power they have to influence others.

Sweeney has experienced this for himself recently, albeit in small doses. He certainly knows it when he sees it—or, rather, when he doesn't quite see it, he knows why. At newspaper columnist Joe Alsop's house, for example, he has met various characters who would generally be considered exceptional, but there's usually something holding them back, and it never takes Sweeney long to identify what that is.

His closest brush with the real thing—apart, obviously, from his brief encounter with Marilyn—comes after nearly a month in D.C. By this stage, having attended committee hearings, sat in the public galleries of both houses, and devoured the *Congressional Record,* he's thoroughly bored with the entire political process—though, to be fair, it's not so much the process as the people. And they're not *all* boring. He has a morbid fascination, for example, with Joe McCarthy. The tail-gunner wields considerable power, it has to be said—even if it's less the result of charisma than of a certain deftness at pulling off what is essentially a parlor trick. *I have here in my hand a list of names.* Fred Lawson, another newspaper columnist

Sweeney has befriended, introduces him to McCarthy one day at La Salle du Bois on M Street. The senator, with his chief counsel Roy Cohn in tow, is passing their table on the way out and he stops to chat for a moment. Sweeney can tell right away that McCarthy is sizing him up.

"Where you from, Mr. Monroe?" he asks.

Sweeney looks at the senator, at his hooded eyes, at the beads of perspiration on his brow.

"Oh, I think I'm going to plead the fifth on that one."

McCarthy frowns and then pretends he didn't hear correctly. Cohn's eyes widen in disbelief.

Fred and the senator make small talk for a moment, agreeing that a poker game is long overdue.

As they leave, Cohn leans in to McCarthy and whispers something. It strikes Sweeney that a whiff of desperation has worked its way into their little double-act. If this is D.C. politics, he thinks, it belongs in the schoolyard. But then, a couple of days later, on the sidewalk outside the same restaurant, Sweeney is talking to Joe Alsop's brother, Stewart, when a car pulls up and out get three men— one of them a tall, jug-eared, bug-eyed tornado of a fellow that Sweeney takes a moment to place as the new Senate minority leader, forty-five-year-old Lyndon Johnson from Texas.

This, he thinks, is an entirely different ball game.

"Stew, you old son of a gun," Johnson booms, stopping directly in front of Alsop, towering over both of them. "What's going on?" He looks at Sweeney. "And who's your buddy here?"

Alsop does the honors. "Senator Johnson, Tom Monroe."

Sweeney surrenders his hand. "Pleased to meet you, Senator."

"Oh, call me Lyndon, son. It's easier." He pulls his head back slightly, examining Sweeney for a second. "So, are you another one of these journalist fellas like this bow-tie-wearing reprobate here?"

"Not exactly, sir, no," Sweeney says, and then, feeling a strange compulsion to engage, announces something that he didn't know himself until this very moment. "But I *am* writing a book. It's going to include a chapter on McCarthy."

Johnson doesn't seem particularly impressed by this and asks Monroe if he couldn't find something more productive to be doing with his time.

Sweeney smiles. "I have to say, sir, and with all due respect . . . but if the Democratic leadership were a little more aggressive in taking a stand against McCarthy, there might not *be* a need for that chapter in my book."

"Hold on a damned second—"

"I can see why you wouldn't have much of a stomach for the fight, he's a dangerous man, but surely if anyone is going to bring him down, sir, it should be you."

"Now don't you go bringing my stomach into this," Johnson says, and pats his belly. "But let me tell you, Mr. Monroe"—he pokes Sweeney in the chest with his finger—"that son of a bitch *is* dangerous, you're right, but if you want to kill a snake, you got to get it in one blow, there ain't no second chance. McCarthy is riding high, sure, but as soon as the fever cools a little, that's the time to act." He nods his head, in full agreement with himself.

In the background, Johnson's two-man entourage seem anxious to get moving. Alsop is also clearly uncomfortable.

This is more important, though.

"Yes, I understand that, sir," Sweeney says, "but I reckon the fever *is* cooling and that McCarthy has more or less exhausted his inventory of exposable Communists. I mean, as I hear it, the joke going around now is that Party membership is declining to such a degree that cells are mainly made up of government double-agents."

Johnson stares at him, a flicker of bewilderment crossing his face. "Ha," he says. "Is that a fact?"

"Yes. And as you know, McCarthy is not going to stop, so what *that* means is he's going to overreach, he's going to attack someone or some institution so revered that it'll all backfire on him and there'll be no route home."

"Well, exactly," Johnson says, patting his belly again. "But he hasn't done it yet, has he? And as I explained to you, son, that's what we have to wait for. We've got to be patient."

Sweeney stops, realizing he's just been making Johnson's argument for him.

How did that happen?

"Stew, give my best to your brother," Johnson says, turning to go.

"You want to know the way to get him?" Sweeney says.

"*Tom,*" Alsop mutters under his breath.

Johnson turns back. "Oh, and you're going to tell me, is that it? Why don't I just go ahead and make you my chief of staff, get this over with?"

"You couldn't afford me, Senator."

Johnson laughs, but it has an edge to it. He approaches Sweeney, puts a hand on his shoulder and grips it tightly. Sweeney feels a surge of energy run through his body. Johnson's face is inches away now and he can smell his hungry breath, see the telltale lines in his skin—the decades of bending everyone to his will, of cajoling and browbeating his way to one victory after the next.

"Let's hear it, son," Johnson says, "but make it quick—there's a sixteen-ounce sirloin steak in there with my name on it."

Sweeney doesn't blink. "TV, sir."

"What?"

"TV. Get him in front of the TV cameras. Whoever his next target is, or whenever the next hearings are, arrange it somehow for one of the networks to do a live telecast. And forget those nightly round-ups they edit from kinescope recordings, do all of it, gavel to gavel. You remember the Kefauver hearings a couple of years back? People ate that stuff up, and they loved Kefauver, but do you really think they're going to love Joe McCarthy? I mean, hour after hour of the guy? *That's* how you destroy him."

Johnson relaxes his grip on Sweeney's shoulder. "Oh my Lord."

"Let people see what a bully he is. Let him do the work."

"Right," Johnson whispers, withdrawing his hand slowly.

"TV, Senator. It's the thing this year. Don't take it from me. Ask Dinah Washington."

"That's pretty fucking smart, son. Why didn't *I* think of that? You hungry? You want a sirloin steak?"

In the split second before Sweeney shakes his head and says no, he sees this man's political career stretching out in front of him like strands of multicolored bubble gum—sticky, relentless, entangling everyone, but in the end a mess, a waste.

And he doesn't want any part of it.

"No."

"*No?*"

He also feels dizzy under the hot afternoon sun.

"No, Senator, but thank you all the same." He starts backing away. "Now, if you'll excuse me, I'm . . . I'm late . . ."

"All right, son, no problem," Johnson says. "I'll just get your telephone number off of Stewie here."

Back in his hotel room, Sweeney gets out the typewriter he bought and sets it up on a small table at the end of the bed. He puts in a new ribbon, feeds in a sheet of paper, and starts clacking away.

16

"Why me?"

"It wasn't you specifically, Ray. I knew Ned had a son. I thought about him periodically over the years." He shrugs. "I wanted to see if he was still alive, or . . . if there was anyone else."

"Why? What for?"

"I didn't get it back then, Ray. None of us did, really. We were Company men, or corporate men, in *suits*. There was nothing you could tell us. We knew everything." He pauses. "And look how that turned out."

I wait for him to say more, but he just stares down at the wooden slats.

"That's not much of an answer, Mr. Proctor."

"I know, Ray. But what do you want me to tell you?"

"Some *facts*?" I glance up at Molly, expecting bewilderment and irritation. I definitely see bewilderment. I also see a fleeting smile, and I'm grateful for it. I look back at Proctor. "You told me my grandfather's death wasn't a suicide. Let's start there."

Proctor clears his throat and shifts his position on the bench. "I also told you he was one of the most extraordinary men I'd ever met. And when I first met him, by the way, he wasn't Ned Sweeney, he was Tom Monroe."

"What? I don't—"

"That was the name he was going by, Tom Monroe. This was out in California, Santa Monica—"

"*What?* Are you—"

"Listen to me, Ray. I know what I'm talking about. *You* don't. Now, 1953, Santa Monica, the RAND Corporation. This guy Tom Monroe shows up looking to speak with John von Neumann. Tell me you know who *that* is, right? Smartest guy who ever lived. Game theory, computers, the hydrogen bomb, artificial intelligence? Johnny set the whole show on the road." He pauses. "So he and Monroe meet, they get talking, they become friends. What are they talking about? Who knows. Certain people are interested, though. Because even then, as far as the Pentagon was concerned, and the defense department, and the Joint Chiefs, von Neumann was infallible, he was *it*. So they started paying attention."

"You mean the CIA?"

Proctor holds his hands up, palms out. "Look, Ray, everything was murky in the fifties. What do you want me to tell you? But yeah, it was because Monroe came out of nowhere and suddenly he's hanging out with with John von fucking Neumann. I mean, please. Word is also filtering out that someone with the same name was causing a stir back in D.C., and that Lyndon Johnson of all people was going crazy trying to track him down."

"LBJ? That's ridiculous."

"Apparently they'd met, I don't know how, and there was a series of phone calls—Johnson wanted Monroe to come and work for him, Monroe refused and then disappeared. A couple of weeks later, he shows up in California."

I want to stand up and leave at this point, but I can't bring myself to do it.

"This makes no sense," I say. "I thought it was the CIA who gave him the MDT in the first place. You're making it sound like he was already on it."

"He was. It's a long story."

"*Well, fucking tell it to me, then.*"

This is pretty loud. Molly jumps, but Proctor doesn't react. Janek comes to the door. He opens it and looks in.

"It's okay, Janek," Proctor says. "We're fine."

Janek doesn't seem convinced, but he withdraws.

Proctor looks at me. "I was on the RAND campus at the time and I was assigned to keep an eye on Tom Monroe, and in the course of doing that, I met him a few times. I had a few conversations with him. And I'll say it again, he was extraordinary."

"How so?"

"Look, it's an overused word, but he had charisma. It was like electricity, just talking to him. I was originally at RAND to do statistical analysis of data relating to mental illness and he knew all about the field, he understood the new psychodynamic approach, he'd *read* the DSM, the first edition that had just come out. But it wasn't only that, he'd loop and spin a conversation in ways you couldn't even imagine."

"So what happened?"

Proctor looks up at Molly, then back at me. "Someone recognized him. Someone who knew him as Ned Sweeney. It was a few months later, but—"

"Who recognized him?"

"It was an Agency guy. He saw a photograph in the newspaper. There was some event, a big dinner in a hotel, a lot of the RAND people were there, and so was Monroe. This guy followed up on it. He later claimed that Ned had stolen a quantity of MDT back in New York."

"*Stolen* it?"

"Yes, it was—"

Janek reappears at the door. He's got a cell phone in his hand. "Mr. Proctor?" he says, and holds out the phone. Proctor takes it.

I lean forward and bury my face in my hands, ready to scream.

"Fine, fine," Proctor says into the phone. He hands it back to Janek. "I have to go."

I look up. "No *fucking* way."

"Hey!" Janek points a finger at me. "Watch the language. Not in here."

"It's okay," Proctor says, waving Janek away. He stands up.

"You can't do this to me again, Mr. Proctor."

"There's a medical unit outside. They think I'm going to have a heart attack. *I* think I'm going to have a heart attack."

"What happened to Ned?" I say. "Tell me."

"We didn't treat him well, Ray. We didn't. We were afraid of him. That's the truth. We didn't understand what MDT was, what it could do. We just wanted to shut it down. We wanted it to *stop*."

"But—"

"And the fact is, I wasn't there, because they took him back to New York from Santa Monica, so I didn't see what they did to him, and I never asked. But I could guess." He turns to leave. "Meet me upstairs in fifteen minutes, Ray. There's something I want to give you."

He walks out the door.

I'm too dumbfounded to say anything or to try to stop him. I look up at Molly. We stare at each other in silence. Then she slides off the upper bench, comes over, and sits next to me.

I get back upstairs first. I wait by reception and pretend to read something on one of the noticeboards.

Tom Monroe? Santa Monica?

This is all new to me. I don't even know if I believe any of it. Instead I'm back to thinking that old man Proctor is fucking nuts. Molly appears. She walks over to where I'm standing in front of the noticeboard. She takes my hand and squeezes it.

"You've got some explaining to do," she whispers.

"Yes."

"Maybe over a drink? After work?"

"Sounds good."

Proctor's head appears at the top of the stairs. He's back in his old-man sweats and hoodie, and is carrying his small gym bag.

"Thanks, Anna," he says, and waves at the girl behind the reception desk. He comes over and stops a few feet away from us.

"I'm sorry about all of this, Ray." He looks at his watch and takes a deep breath. "I wish I could be more specific about what happened to Ned, I really do. But that's not why I wanted to find you. It wasn't to get into the details. What does any of that stuff matter now anyway?" He glances out the window. There's a black van parked where his Lincoln was earlier. He looks at me again and comes a step closer. "Besides, I'm running out of time."

"What?"

"You remember in the park I told you that I thought we might have blown it, that humanity might have blown it?"

I nod.

"Well, if we have, I believe it's a process that dates back to 1953. Because that was one hell of a year, Ray." He takes another deep breath and starts talking really fast. "Look, two essential things happened that year—one, we started figuring out how to build a digital universe, and two, we started figuring out how to decode our own genetics. And we did it ourselves, using *these*"—he points to his head—"our brains, our wetware, but since then there's been a tug of war between the two sides, and now we're losing the fight, because it seems like we're bending over backward to outsource to technology the one thing we can't afford to give up, our *intelligence*. Twenty, thirty years from now, and that'll be gone. It's not the rise of the machines, Ray, it's the rise of the goddamned algorithms, it's the rise of big data. And the so-called hard problem? The one about the nature of consciousness—where it comes from, where it's located, what it means, the *mystery* of it? Well, that gets left behind, it gets forgotten in the relentless and infinite expansion of ones and zeroes. It really will be artificial intelligence . . ."

Molly is still squeezing my hand.

". . . unless we push back," he goes on, "unless we expand our idea of what intelligence is, or can be, unless we realize that human intelligence simply can't be separated from human consciousness."

Outside, a car door slams shut. We all turn and look out the window. A man—it looks like Dean—has left the van and is approaching the entrance to the Hudson.

Proctor rummages for something in his gym bag.

"Ray," he says. *"Here."*

He tosses something at me and Molly releases my hand. The object is small. I catch it. It rattles.

The door opens and Dean enters, removing his sunglasses. Street sounds flood in.

"That's organic," Proctor whispers, nodding at my hand. "It comes from a plant, a *living* thing." His eyes widen into a broad smile.

Molly nudges my hand and guides it behind my back.

"I think it's time there was another leak," Proctor whispers. "Ned did his best. So did Eddie Spinola. See what you can do." He looks at Molly. "The two of you."

"Mr. Proctor," Dean says, "they're waiting for you." He glances over at me, his face expressionless.

"Okay, Dean, I'm coming. Take my bag, will you."

As he passes the bag to Dean with one hand, he turns back to me and Molly and makes a flapping gesture with his other, indicating that we should wait till he's gone.

"Anna, my dear," he then says in a loud voice, turning to the desk this time, "see you soon."

"Goodbye, Mr. Proctor," Anna says, looking up from her phone.

Dean gets the door and holds it open for the old man. They leave.

Molly and I stand watching through the window as they get into the black van. It pulls away and disappears into traffic.

We go back to the coffee shop across the street.

"I didn't know that was going to get so weird," I say. "I'm sorry. I should have warned you."

She shakes her head. "I probably shouldn't have been there."

"No." I lean forward. "I'm glad you were. Otherwise I might have strangled him. Besides, it was thanks to you that it happened in the first place."

A waitress comes over and we order coffees.

"I'm not sure where to begin."

"You don't have to begin at all. You don't have to say anything if you don't want to."

"I know, but I do want to." I pause. "He came across as pretty close to insane there, right?"

"I guess, but in an interesting way."

"Sure. But here are two things I know for a fact. He did work for the CIA in the fifties and he *was* diagnosed with Alzheimer's two years ago."

"Shit."

"That's why I've been pursuing this."

"And to find out about your grandfather."

"Yeah. But Proctor wasn't too helpful on that score." I reach into my pocket and take out the bottle of pills that he tossed at me. It's unmarked and I reckon it contains about fifty or sixty of them. They're small, white, also unmarked. I give the bottle a gentle shake and place it on the table between us. "He seemed more interested in these."

She hesitates, then picks up the bottle, examines it, and puts it down again. "They look like homeopathic pills to me."

"Let's hope they're a little more effective."

"Do you really think these are—"

"MDT? I don't know. Why else would he give them to me?"

The waitress approaches. I pick up the bottle and put it back in my pocket.

We sip our coffees in silence. After a while, I'm about to say something, but Molly's phone pings. She checks it.

"Shit, Ray, I have to stop pretending I don't have a job."

"Tell me about it."

"We've put a statement out saying Steph has pneumonia. So I need to get back to the office." She makes a face.

There's another silence, an awkward one.

"Look, why don't you send one of those pills to a lab," she says eventually, "and have it tested. See exactly what it is."

"Maybe."

"*Don't* take one."

I look at her.

"Or *do*. Who am I to tell you? But . . ." She leans forward. "I know this has all been weirdly intense, and also confusing, but . . . I like you, Ray, and I don't want anything awful or stupid to happen to you."

"I like you, too, Molly."

She taps the table gently with her hand. "Good."

We make an arrangement to meet later, then head our separate ways. I walk to Seventh Avenue, my heart pounding to a rhythm of names, a sequence of syllables—Clay Proctor, Tom Monroe, John von Neumann, Molly Boyd.

I hail a passing cab and tell the driver Sixty-Fourth and Lex.

As the cab moves off, I take the bottle of pills out of my pocket and examine it again. Despite what Molly said, I know I'm going to take one of these sooner or later, and as I consider the various ways that that could go horribly wrong, I also detect an unmistakable hint of anticipation.

17

It's during the third, rambling, hour-long telephone call to his hotel room from Senator Johnson that Sweeney realizes he's had enough. The senator wants Tom Monroe to come and work for him and won't take no for an answer. For his part, Sweeney can think of few things he'd like less. But in this third call he makes the mistake of getting Johnson all fired up. He starts by telling him that he's too Machiavellian, that it's an instinct he needs to rein in, and that sooner or later he's going to have to commit to something, to take on a fight or an issue that will either destroy him or catapult him into contention for the White House—something like, say, civil rights.

"Go on."

"Okay, since you entered Congress, Senator, you've voted against every civil rights bill that's come up, and it was probably the pragmatic thing to do each time, I'm not saying it wasn't, but history, or rather the future, is on the other side of that argument now, and if you want to make yourself acceptable to liberals and Northerners for '56 or '60, which you'll *have to*, you need to do something this bold. I mean, you could single-handedly turn the whole civil rights thing around, send it in a different direction."

Johnson considers this, clicks his tongue a couple of times, then says, "Fuck me, son, that's just brilliant. Now I've *got* to have you on my team."

Sweeney can feel the pull of Johnson's personality here, the insatiable need for attention, for loyalty, and he knows it won't stop. Also, Sweeney has spent the best part of a week huddled over his Remington typewriter, getting ideas down on paper, and he's concluded that this is a much more productive way to spend his time than simply talking to people—or, increasingly, *at* them. He told Johnson he was writing a book, and now that he actually is, he likes it, and wants to continue.

But there are too many distractions to contend with. Besides, it was clearly a mistake to think that the nation's capital was where he was going to find the nation's best minds. Now that he's had some time to mull it over, he reckons he knows where that is—or, at any rate, where it's more likely to be. So he decides to move on. He packs up all of his stuff, checks out of the Rutherford, and gets behind the wheel of his car.

Leaving D.C. behind, he heads west.

There's a freedom in driving, and in being out on the open road, that helps him to order his thoughts. He doesn't know what he's going to call this book yet, but it's shaping up to be an examination of human history—not so much the familiar succession of personalities, governments, conflicts, and fluctuating powers, but rather a study of how and why whole civilizations rise and fall, the hidden forces, the larger patterns. But it could also—he's not sure—be a book about the future, an elaborate extrapolation of the dynamics he sees at work in the world today. The scale of it worries him, though—he already has a couple of hundred typed pages in the trunk of the car, and he sees no end to the flood of ideas.

He stops at motels along the way, making sure that he eats properly and gets at least four or five hours' sleep a night. It's been a while since he had one of those incidents where he gets dizzy and blacks out for seconds or even minutes at a time, and he's not sure why this should be. Maybe he's finally got the dosage right, maybe it's a cumulative thing, he doesn't know. But his energy levels are extraordinary, as is his ability to focus, and up and down the sensory scale—so whether it's a vast tableau of billowing clouds in the sky ahead or the single flick of an insect wing on the edge of his vision, a crack of thunder or the barely audible squeak of a loose V belt, it doesn't matter, he's paying close attention and taking it all in.

Over the course of three or four days, he makes his way through West Virginia, Kentucky, and into Missouri. At Springfield, he joins Route 66, and keeps on going for another four or five days. He passes mining districts, cattle ranges, woodlands, flatlands, factories, oil derricks, hundreds of gas stations, and countless towns—a few big, many small, some abandoned. He drives, bleary-eyed and sun-baked, through the Texas Panhandle, the Staked Plains, the Mojave Desert, and on, finally, to the cool orange groves and vineyards leading to Pasadena and then Los Angeles itself. Driving west through Beverly Hills, he stays with Route 66 for its last seventeen-mile stretch, to the shore of the Pacific Ocean at Santa Monica.

The end of the road.

Except, of course, it's nothing of the kind.

Sweeney finds a studio apartment to rent in the Sausalito Arms, a three-storey, oceanfront stucco building with double windows and Moorish columns. His room is on the second floor and he sets his typewriter up at the end of the bed, exactly as he had it in the hotel in D.C.

The RAND Corporation campus is on Fourth and Broadway, a block from the ocean—just opposite city hall at the edge of Santa Monica's business district. The building is brand-new. It has two stories and is in a modernist style. That's from the outside. Sweeney has only heard about what it's like on the inside. Apparently, it has a dense, lattice-like structure that was mathematically designed to maximize the number of connection points in the hallways and corridors, the idea being to promote chance interactions between employees. But the problem is, he can't get any farther into the building than the lobby area. This is a heavily guarded facility, and Sweeney doesn't have a security clearance.

He doesn't care, though. He's not looking for work. He's not looking for a contract. He just wants to *talk* to people.

The thing is, D.C. is for politicians, and what politicians do is compromise. The successful ones do it with art and cunning and patience, but at the end of the day it's still compromise. Out here, by contrast—in Santa Monica, at RAND—none of that applies. Scientists, mathematicians, and economists are all encouraged to dream and innovate, and if one of them has an idea at three o'clock in the morning . . . well then, fine, let him come on in, because the place is always open. (This is something Sweeney read about in *Fortune* magazine. They also wear short-sleeved shirts, apparently. And no one wears a tie.) But what really interests him about RAND is what they do there.

It's a think tank.

So they *think*.

Under contract to the Pentagon and the Atomic Energy Commission, RAND's stable of eggheads are essentially using theoretical and applied mathematics to game U.S. nuclear defense strategy. Sweeney is not much of a math guy—not yet—but this really appeals to him. It's not the military stuff so much as the idea of solving complex problems using systematic thought and quantification. It's something he brings up in conversation with John von Neumann the first time they meet.

Sweeney arrives at the entrance asking to speak with von Neumann and is basically told to take a hike. But he persists and von Neumann's curiosity is eventually piqued. It's a little awkward at first, but Sweeney manages to press the right buttons and within half an hour they're deep into a discussion about rational choice theory. They meet again a few days later for coffee, and the following week Sweeney goes to dinner at Johnny and Klara's house.

Each time they meet, Sweeney has done his homework, so he's

able to keep up. But it's not just about that. Von Neumann is warm and sociable. He loves a drink, and a bad pun. He has an astonishing memory and is insatiably curious. He's deeply empathetic. In fact, he operates at a level of intellectual and emotional clarity that is exhausting for most people to be in the presence of. So when Sweeney is leaving their house after dinner that night, he finds himself wondering—and he has to accept that this is what drew him to the guy in the first place—if von Neumann isn't somehow on MDT. Sweeney has met other RAND people around Santa Monica. At one event in particular, a gala dinner at the Hotel Casa Del Mar, he met quite a few of them, and while they're all extremely smart, geniuses in some cases, the intelligence gradient seems to curve upward to a peak that is undisputedly occupied by von Neumann.

Plus, he always wears a jacket and tie.

So he *is* different.

Nevertheless, the idea that he is on MDT is absurd. There's no question that Sweeney finds von Neumann's company massively stimulating, but as the weeks go by, and as 1953 gives way to 1954, things do begin to change. It's not so much that Sweeney disagrees with positions von Neumann is taking, it's more that he feels himself moving beyond those positions—being able to extrapolate so much farther into a matrix of real-world outcomes than von Neumann could possibly imagine. When Sweeney talks about the "limits of rationality," von Neumann bristles. But von Neumann's understanding of behavior comes, in the main, from theoretical models formulated in the intellectual hothouse of a government-funded think tank. Sweeney's, on the other hand—most recently, at any rate—comes from observing the heat and desperation at the card tables in the clubs and casinos over in Gardena. This is human nature in the raw, he points out to von Neumann—visceral, irrational, often delusional—and it's really all he or anyone else needs to know.

"You can make predictions," he goes on, "and fairly elaborate ones, but they can never just be based on the numbers."

They're strolling in Palisades Park in late January and von Neumann is about to make a rejoinder when someone calls out his name.

They stop and turn around. A young man approaches, a colleague of von Neumann's from RAND. He's short and slim, with thick curly black hair.

"Ahh," von Neumann says, and then adds, under his breath, for Sweeney's benefit, "shoot me now."

"Johnny, listen," the young man says, "I meant to mention it yesterday, but I forgot. Will you come for lunch this Sunday? Sally and I are having some people over and we'd love to see you and Klara."

"Well, uh—"

"And, of course"—the young man turns to Sweeney—"any friend of Johnny's is welcome, too."

Von Neumann suppresses a weary sigh.

Sweeney extends his hand. "Tom Monroe, pleased to make your acquaintance."

"Likewise," the young man says, smiling broadly. "The name's Clay Proctor."

Sweeney accepts the invitation, but is disappointed when Johnny and Klara don't show. They send their apologies, saying something has come up. The afternoon with Clay Proctor and his wife, Sally, and their little newborn, Stephanie, along with various people Sweeney has never met, is perfectly pleasant, but Sweeney has a slightly uncomfortable feeling about it all. It's as though he is being observed, assessed, even. The feeling is exacerbated over the next week or two when he finds himself continually bumping into this Clay Proctor. It seems casual enough—Santa Monica isn't that big—but he doubts these encounters would pass even the most basic statistics-and-probability smell test.

At RAND, Proctor appears to be fairly low-level in terms of the work he's doing, but he lets it be known that he has a top-secret security clearance. He also makes a point of talking up his various business and political connections—he does work for Eiben Laboratories, he's had lunch with Senator Karl Mundt. Sweeney doesn't care about any of this, or about the fact that he himself may well be under surveillance. If, as seems likely, Proctor is the person actually conducting the surveillance, then Sweeney reckons there isn't much to worry about. Besides, what dark secrets or shady affiliations do the people Proctor is working for expect him to uncover?

Tom Monroe doesn't *have* a past. It's his future they should be more concerned about.

Or *all* of their futures, really.

Because if there's one argument Sweeney can't get away from in the countless pages he has typed and left neatly stacked on the floor of his room in the Sausalito Arms, it's that the higher your level of natural intelligence, the closer you'll inevitably come to devising—or helping devise, or being co-opted in to devising—a technology that will become, sooner or later, a direct threat to human civilization. It's happening here at RAND—and at Stanford, at Princeton, at MIT. The generals want bombs, the eggheads want computers. Numerical simulations are essential to the design of the bombs, and computers are essential to the execution of the numerical simulations.

Money is essential for both. So it's checkmate to the generals, because they have the money.

It's a long game, though. At least that's how Sweeney sees it. Because as far as the bombs are concerned, once they're developed and tested, yes, they may well proliferate—but a single device is all it would take, which means that the very first one could easily be the last. However, with the computers (assuming anyone survives the bombs), increases in processing power will necessarily be a slow-burn affair, taking decades probably, but at *some* point a line will be crossed and these coded sequences will then surprise everyone by doing two things: thinking for themselves and reproducing. In all likelihood, that will be the end of *Homo sapiens*—at least in any currently recognizable form.

These dark extrapolations fill Sweeney's mind and he does his best to get them down on paper. He can only go so far with them in conversation, because pretty much everything he says now, to some degree, is heretical. He engages with Clay Proctor, and others, and enjoys twisting them into intellectual knots, but there's no doubt that it's all becoming increasingly difficult for him.

Sweeney has no problem talking to nuclear physicists, however, and in late February he accepts an offer to join a group of them on a trip to Bikini Atoll in the Marshall Islands, two and a half thousand miles west of Hawaii. The purpose of the trip is to witness the detonation of a thermonuclear, or hydrogen, bomb. A few telephone calls are made to high-level officials and an interim security clearance is arranged. Sweeney and the group fly Pan American from Los Angeles to Honolulu, then on to an air force base in the South Pacific. From there they are transported to the USNS *Ainsworth*, which is docked a couple of hundred miles east of the test site.

The nuclear device, code-named Castle Bravo, was designed using complex mathematical simulations and is supposedly small enough to load onto a U.S. Air Force bomber, which could deliver it to the skies above an enemy city such as Moscow within minutes. With a projected yield of six megatons, Castle Bravo is expected to explode with several hundred times the force of the atomic bomb that was dropped on Hiroshima.

In a minority report to the AEC, Enrico Fermi, an alumnus of the Manhattan Project, has already called the hydrogen bomb an "evil thing." Sweeney doesn't disagree with this, but he wasn't going to pass up an opportunity to be present at what will either be a critical turning point in history, or simply the end of it.

For the duration of the trip, he slightly increases his morning dose of MDT. While this adds another sensory dimension to the experience, it also means he can keep up intellectually with his fellow "observers" and distract them from the fact that he's not actually a physicist.

In the early morning hours before the test, huddled in one of the bunkrooms of the ship, they drink Chivas Regal and swap predictions. Two of them are extremely nervous, convinced that the explosion will be so powerful that the hydrogen in the earth's atmosphere will catch fire and burn the planet to a crisp. Two of them are fairly relaxed, convinced that the calculations and projections made at Los Alamos are unassailable.

Then there's Tom Monroe.

With that extra kick of MDT in his system, Sweeney finds that he can talk fluently and comprehensibly with these guys—take in new information on the fly and respond to it, even though he doesn't necessarily understand everything he's saying. It's as if the knowledge is self-aware, and in charge, and happy to use him as a conduit.

"Tom? You get the deciding vote."

"Ha." He peers into his glass of Chivas. "The strange thing is, I think you're *both* going to be proven wrong."

"What?"

"Look, as I see it, the yield we're expecting—six megatons or so?—that's way off. It's going to be a lot more than that, two or three times more, and—"

"That's ridiculous, Tom. How do—"

"It's the isotopes in the lithium deuteride, they've enriched it to forty percent lithium-6, right? But they're not taking into account all the lithium-7 in there. That's going to release additional fission power, which means a much bigger explosion and a *lot* more fallout."

They all stare at him, their brows furrowed, calculating in furious silence.

"So the mushroom cloud," he goes on, "you'll see it expand to maybe . . . seventy miles? And it'll reach fifty thousand feet."

This elicits a collective gasp.

"But at that point—I think—it'll slow down. It has to."

No one says anything.

"It's the lithium-7. It's *there*. You can't discount it." Sweeney shrugs. It seems so obvious.

At 5:15 a.m. they all trudge up to the deck and wait for the countdown. Even though the sun hasn't come up yet, every person assembled there—observers, engineers, crew members—puts on their high-density goggles. As he stares out into the darkness, Sweeney can smell the fear—it's in the air around him, mingling like pollen with the residue of last night's tropical rainfall. He doesn't feel it himself, because he knows what's going to happen—or, rather, he knows that the worst *isn't* going to happen, at least not today. What he does feel is a profound, cellular-level queasiness.

Nausea.

This is the evil thing, after all, and it shouldn't be happening—less than a minute to go now—especially not as a result of mere calculations, the head-scratching doodles of some very clever men.

Thirty seconds.

Mild-mannered, pipe-smoking men.

Ten, nine, eight . . .

And they *are* all men.

. . . three, two, one.

There is a flash of thermonuclear light and then a flood of gamma radiation fills the air. Deciding to let the mushroom cloud form and rise up behind him, Ned Sweeney quickly turns around. What he sees instead—X-rays laying everything bare—is a gallery of faces that have glimmered and bleached into skeletal negatives . . . eye sockets, jawbones, rows of teeth.

18

I place the bottle of pills Proctor gave me on the top shelf of my medicine cabinet and try not to think about them.

But it's difficult.

It reminds me of that last tiny envelope of smack I managed to keep in my wallet for a whole month before I convinced myself to throw it out. There's a thin line between anticipating something and being tormented by it.

I have another thought. If these pills are mine now, where does that leave Proctor? Does *he* have any left?

I don't know.

I putter around for a while and send a few work-related emails. But it's no use.

I actually hate that this is the stuff I'm thinking about, when what I should be thinking about is Ned Sweeney.

The situation as sketched out by Proctor was annoyingly light on detail, but some of what he had to say was intriguing—the stuff about Ned calling himself Tom Monroe, for instance, and about his being in Santa Monica, and meeting John von Neumann.

What's frustrating is that my only "source" here is Clay Proctor himself. But then I remember something Jill said to me when I spoke to her on the phone that first night. *And then before Mom died I had a few conversations with her about it all. Actually she said a lot of stuff, which I'll have to tell you about some day . . .*

I never knew this, and I wouldn't have cared anyway. But I do now. And there was also Dad's old stuff—boxes and boxes of shit he'd accumulated over the years, the detritus of a life. I remember going through some of it in the basement of the old house in West- chester. But that was years ago. And I wasn't looking for anything in particular. Whatever became of all that?

Only one way to find out.

"Twice in the space of a week, Ray, what's the matter with you?"

"I love you, too, Jill. I'm . . . I'm working on something, and you know how I get, I'm obsessive. So indulge me."

I ask her what became of Dad's old stuff.

"My God, what exactly are you working on?"

I'm going to have to tell her sooner or later, but not right now. "Just answer my question, Jill, and I promise I'll explain."

"It's all in storage, everything. His stuff, Mom's, decades' worth of garbage. I wanted to get rid of it, but Jim wouldn't let me. You think *you're* obsessive? He's clinically insane. It's, 'Oh, you never know'—and about everything! My God, talk about a hoarder. We've still got unused packs of diapers from seven, eight years ago."

"In storage where?"

"It's a unit. I don't know. Out on Route 35 somewhere. Empire Self-Storage. We have *three* of them. It's embarrassing."

"I'm coming up there."

"*What?*"

"I'll get a flight, it'll be . . . tonight or tomorrow morning."

"Ray!"

"I'll explain when I see you. It's just that I heard something. It was about Ned. Maybe things happened differently than we thought."

Silence.

"Jill?"

"I'm here."

"You okay?"

"Let me know when you're getting in."

I go to meet Molly for a drink at six o'clock at a place on Third Avenue. I get there first, sit at the bar, and order a Bushmills. I'm anxious to share my plan about paying a visit to Jill's with her. I also want to hear any news there might be about the congresswoman.

She walks into the bar a few minutes later, glances around, and spots where I am.

"Hey there," she says and leans in for a kiss. She looks different. She's wearing jeans and a short leather jacket.

"So, how was your day?" I ask.

She plants herself on the stool next to mine, puts her phone on the bar, sighs, and looks around for the bartender. He appears and she orders a Goose Island.

"How was my day?" she says. "Well, it started out *great,* then it got a little weird, then it got kind of awful. But I think it's heading back to great again."

"And the awful bit?"

"Stephanie. She's sobered up, at least for the moment, but there's something bugging her and I don't know what it is, no one does. She seems depressed."

"Could it be something to do with her dad?"

"I was thinking that, but . . . I couldn't say it to anyone. The mood in the office is pretty grim. It's as if we're looking into the abyss. Everything is kind of on hold at the moment."

"Maybe I could talk to her. She listens to me for some reason."

"Yes." Molly pokes me in the arm. "I've noticed."

"You always thought I was an interfering jerk, didn't you?"

She makes a face. "Come on, you know how it is. Message control is a delicate business."

"That's one way of putting it."

The bartender arrives with her drink.

"So, did you pop one of those, what are they called . . . Dr. Proctor's Astounding Pep Pills?"

"No," I say, taking a sip of Bushmills. "I wanted to."

I tell her about Empire Self-Storage and my plan to head up to Boston tomorrow. I explain how I really need to understand what's going on.

"That makes sense," she says. "How long are you going for?"

"I don't know. Tomorrow's what, Saturday? Just the day, I guess. Back tomorrow night."

"You want company?"

At the airport the next morning, Molly gets a text saying that Clay Proctor has just been taken to the hospital. She sees the concern on my face and immediately texts back for more.

"He's in a coma."

"Shit."

We look at each other.

"Oh, Ray."

"Is this because he doesn't have his pills?"

"He gave them to you. He knew what he was doing."

"I know."

We say nothing for a while, airport stuff going on around us.

"What do you want to do?" she says eventually.

"What do you mean?"

"Do you still want to go?"

I think about it. "There's no point in staying here if he's in a coma. In fact, it's all the more reason to go and find out what I can." I pause. "You don't have to come, though."

"I want to."

During the flight, I fill her in on some details about my father. Not long ago, if the subject of Tom ever came up, I would have dismissed him as an asshole and moved on. But I can't really do that anymore. He *was* an asshole, but now it all feels a bit more complicated than that. I barely know anything about his early life—or about our mom's, for that matter—just the stuff you pick up along the way. He was from Long Island. He did two tours in Vietnam. When he came back, he got a degree in engineering, then worked as some kind of a technician—I think. By the time Jill and I came along, he was running a small construction business. The main thing I remember about him from when I was small is the shouting—the raw face, red with rage, the open mouth, the spittle, the door slamming.

Stop it.

Shut up.

Get out.

Fuck you.

Drop dead.

He never hit us, or our mom, but his presence in the house was toxic. When I was older, I realized he was a big drinker and that this was part of the problem. But it wasn't everything, by any means. He was angry and bitter, and in the end I basically had no relationship with him at all. I didn't know him. I didn't get anything from him. He made our mom miserable and I hated him.

"Jesus."

"Yeah. And at the back of all this was a vague, whispered story about *his* father jumping out a fourteenth-story window in Manhattan when Tom was only six or seven years old. I never thought of it as an excuse, or even an explanation. It always just confused me."

"When did he die?"

"Dad? About ten years ago."

She's leaning her head on my shoulder. I stare straight ahead. My eyes sting and my throat feels a little raw. If I wasn't sitting on a fucking plane right now, I'm not sure I'd be able to keep this under control.

At Logan, we rent a car and head out to West Roxbury. Jill is an actuary and does a lot of work from home. When we get there, she has lunch ready, some pasta and a salad. I texted her earlier to say that I was coming with a friend, so when she sees Molly, her interest skyrockets. But I don't want her giving Molly the third degree, so I remind her that we're only here for a few hours.

"Aw, Ray." She drags the syllable out. "Josh and Ellie won't be here until this evening. They'll be so disappointed."

I can see her clocking Molly's reaction.

Who are Josh and Ellie?

But there's no time for this.

"We'll come back, I promise. We'll stay for a week. Won't we, Molly?" I don't even look at her when I say this. "Now, Jill, we need to *talk*."

How our mom, Sara, put up with Tom for so long has always been a mystery to me—or not even a mystery, because that implies I spent time thinking about it. It certainly never occurred to me that she loved him, or that she stuck around for our sakes.

That both of these things were true comes as a shock to me now. When Dad died, Jill and I were both really still kids, resplendently dumb in our respective levels of self-absorption. But by the time Mom died, five years later, Jill already had two kids of her own. I was still dumb, but it seems that Jill had somehow managed to move on, grow up a bit, and maybe find some common ground with Mom. Naturally, I wasn't around for any of this. The funeral was a somber, quiet affair and the opportunity to talk or ask questions never arose.

"She opened up a lot to me in those last couple of months," Jill says. "I knew I'd get around to telling you about it some day, but you know how time slips by . . ."

Anyway, according to Sara's account of things, our dad's entire life was dominated by his own father's suicide—trying to understand it, to interpret it, to forgive it, even. But he never succeeded at any of these. If it had just been "straight suicide" (whatever that even means), things might have been different. But there were certain peculiar circumstances surrounding Ned's death, and preceding it, that Tom found out about from our grandmother, Laura, when he was in his late teens.

Apparently, before he killed himself, Ned went missing for about six months—a period of absence that remains unaccounted for. When he reappeared, he was a changed man: he seemed twenty years older and more than a little disturbed. But the strange thing was that during his absence he sent money home, regularly and in increasingly large amounts—so much money, in fact, that after he died, Laura was financially secure for years to come.

This, too, was never explained.

"So Tom was tormented by these weird, isolated bits of information," Jill says. "Throw in his two tours in Vietnam, in '69 and '70, some PTSD, a perforated eardrum, and I don't know what the hell you end up with. But the thing that really twisted him came in the mid-seventies."

As Jill is talking, I glance at Molly. I barely know her and here she is knee-deep in my family history. I wonder what she makes of it all.

"So, late one night," Jill goes on, "he gets a phone call. It's from someone who won't identify himself. Mom always wondered if this person was drunk, or deranged, but whatever they said that night shook Tom to his core. It was around the time of . . . what was it . . . ?" She clicks her fingers. "You'd know more about this than I would, Ray, the Rockefeller Commission, and the . . . Something Committee?"

"The Church Committee."

"Yes."

Molly looks at me.

"It was 1975," I say. "They were hearings about the CIA's involvement in illegal wiretapping and domestic surveillance, assassination plots, all sorts of weird shit."

"Fucking incredible," Jill continues, "but anyway this guy led Tom to believe that in the early fifties his father had been the victim of a medical experiment, that it was some kind of government-sponsored program, and that he should look into it. Dad believed him, of course." She throws her hands up. "It was something to cling to. Then in the late seventies, early eighties there was a lot of high-profile litigation, class-action suits, whatever, by people who had been victims of this thing. He followed all of these cases, and even tried to get involved. But there was nothing for him in any of it, no medical records like these other people had, nothing, not a single thread linking Ned with anything. He spent ten, fifteen years chasing his tail, and by the time you and I were hitting our teens, he was wasted most of the time and pretty much gone."

We sit in silence for a moment.

"Mom put up with it all because she felt bad for him, and she loved him, I guess, but she didn't buy any of it for a second. Or she realized it was pointless to pursue it."

There is another silence.

"So, Ray," Jill then says, an almost accusatory tone in her voice, "what is this thing that you heard?"

"It's sort of . . . what you just described. All of it."

"Oh God. Are you going to lose your mind now, too? I mean, who *cares*? It was sixty fucking years ago."

"I know, don't worry. I've already been in and out of the rabbit hole." I pause. "But I do need to go through Dad's stuff."

She looks at Molly, then back at me.

"I get it. Just one more hit off the crack pipe, right? We all know how *that* goes."

Empire Self-Storage is a vast, indoor affair, and Jill's units are at the end of a long, brightly lit aisle. She opens the lock, raises the steel roll-up door, and flicks on a light switch. The unit is about fifty square feet. Looking in, I get an immediate and unexpected sensory blast from my childhood. That armchair, the coffee table, the metal filing cabinet, the framed mirror—these are all items yanked from my memory and repositioned here in this dream-skewed tableau.

There is a row of stacked boxes at the back. I head straight for these, skirting around the furniture, and choose one at random from the top. I lay it on the ground and bend down to open it. I remove the lid. The box contains old documents, letters, subpoenas, writs, newspaper cuttings. I open a second box and it's the same. I pretty quickly discern a pattern. A lot of this material relates to class-action suits filed in the early eighties by victims' groups looking to extract compensation from the government.

Choosing another box, I glance back at Jill and Molly. They're standing out in the aisle, chatting quietly. I remove the lid. The box contains three large brown envelopes—thick, padded ones. I lift out the first one. Inside is a wad of typed pages. It looks like a manuscript of some kind. I do a quick check of the other two envelopes, and they're the same. I extract the wad of pages from the first one and flick through it quickly. Some of the pages are torn, or dog-eared, or have stains on them. The paper is old and dry, and the print is faded. It has that classic typewritten look.

I don't know what this is, but I have an intuition that it's the only thing of significance I'm going to find here.

I flick through the wad of pages again and stop at one randomly, a solid block of type with no paragraph breaks. I try to focus on a few lines.

. . . a global convergence of interdependent organisms, a collective mindscape of data expressways, a living skein, a rippling membrane stretched out over the entire surface of the planet . . .

I don't know what this means exactly, but I find it astonishing that it was written when I think it was written. In the early 1950s. Tom had this all along? What did he make of it, if he even read it?

I gather up the three envelopes and lay them to the side. I feel that I have to check out the rest of this stuff, even though my gut tells me to just leave. I open a few more boxes. A couple contain more recent material, from the nineties, medical records, insurance claims, tax forms. Another one has documents relating to Tom's construction business. A few more are filled with personal stuff—those old books, magazines, and LPs.

After a few minutes, I've had enough. I close up the boxes and carefully place them in their original positions. Then I put the three bulky envelopes in their box, lift it up, and turn around. Jill is still standing out in the aisle, her arms folded, but she's alone. Carrying the box, I make my way gingerly back through the dusty labyrinth of eerily familiar objects.

Jill seems bored now. "What have you got there?"

I ignore this. "Where's Molly?"

She nods back toward the other end of the aisle, where Molly is pacing up and down. She's on her phone.

I turn back to Jill. "I need to take this stuff with me. I'm not sure what it is, to be honest, but I want to check through it carefully."

"Sure you don't want to take all of it?" she says, glancing over my shoulder. "That old armchair, the mirror? We're paying two hundred dollars a month for the climate-controlled privilege of not throwing this crap out."

"Maybe next time."

"Funny."

Molly is off the phone and walking back toward us. I can tell that something is up. I wait until she's close. "Anything wrong?"

"He's gone," she says, shaking her head in disbelief and holding up her phone. "Clay Proctor."

"Dead?"

She nods.

I put the box down. "Fuck."

"What?" Jill says. "Who's Clay Proctor?"

I wait a moment, then turn to her. "That thing I heard? Clay Proctor is the man who told me."

19

On the return flights, to Honolulu, and then Los Angeles, there is endless discussion among the scientists about what happened at Bikini Atoll—about how they could have gotten it so wrong and yet still be so lucky. The yield was an incredible fifteen megatons, and the radioactive contamination, as a result, is much more widespread than expected.

Sweeney has been getting a lot of curious glances, but no one has approached him with the obvious question. *Hey Monroe, how did you do that? How did you work it all out so accurately?* At the same time, he finds it remarkable how quickly these guys can put what they've seen out of their minds and get back to fiddling with their slide rules.

By the time they land in Los Angeles, Sweeney is also beginning to understand why his nausea hasn't lifted yet. He's not physically sick—though that may come, and not just to him; it may come to any or all of them in this group returning from the Marshall Islands, and sooner than they think. It's more that he has lost his bearings. Because how is it that a mere thirty-six or forty-eight hours earlier he was so sanguine about the prospect of witnessing what could have been, quite literally, the end of the world? It was a real prospect. Until he worked out that it probably wasn't. But before that? He had no thought for his wife and six-year-old son, no feelings of separation or loss, no desperate urge to make contact with them. How is that possible? Because if not with them, where else does he think there's even the remotest chance that he's going to find any meaning in life? In Santa Monica? In the South Pacific? How about he goes to the moon?

All he'd need for that is a slide rule and a few hundred million dollars.

Sweeney is not blaming the MDT for any of this. *He's* the one holding back and resisting. *He's* the one with a six-year-old son on the other side of the country. Crucially, Tommy won't always be six. He'll grow up and become a man. He'll do things, forge a career, make decisions. Maybe he'll have a kid of his own someday. It'll all be beautiful. But what is Sweeney saying here? That apart from sending regular checks home, he's prepared to forego any involvement in Tommy's life?

MDT can't make you smart, not if you choose to be stupid—not if you choose to close your eyes while standing in a field of flamered California poppies at sunrise. Sweeney knows that. So when it eventually comes, the decision is quick and unequivocal. He'll return to New York, to Laura and Tommy. It won't be easy at first, he'll have to learn how to pace himself, but it'll be worth it, because whatever path he's going to take in the coming years, it really has to be with them.

On the drive back to Santa Monica, Sweeney decides that one thing he should do before leaving town is gather up the hundreds of typed pages that are distributed all around the apartment now and start organizing them into a coherent manuscript. At least that way, when he reappears in New York, he'll have something to show for the six months he's been AWOL. The ambitious scale of the book, and the prodigious amount of work he's already done, will provide him with considerable cover when he shops it around to some of the big publishing houses.

It's late evening when he arrives at the Sausalito Arms. He gets to the door of his apartment, puts his travel bag down, and is just reaching into his pocket to take his key out when he senses that something isn't right—and it's ten different things at once. He turns around, intending to go back down the stairs, when a man appears from the shadows to his left.

"Mr. Monroe?"

Sweeney stops. "Yes?"

"George Blair, Federal Bureau of Investigation." The man has a badge and flips it open. "Can I have a word?"

Sweeney remains still. Then he turns back around and points at the door. "There's someone in there, isn't there?"

"Think of it as a welcoming party."

"That's illegal entry."

"Nah, I don't think so. Not when it's a *party*." Blair takes a step closer and taps on the door with his left hand. It opens immediately. The room is in darkness, but standing there, framed in the doorway, is Clay Proctor.

Sweeney is simultaneously surprised and not surprised. He walks around Proctor, drops his travel bag to the floor, and flicks on the light switch. The place has been overturned. The furniture he doesn't care about, but his typewriter is on its side at the foot of the bed, and the pages of his manuscript are strewn everywhere. His initial thought out in the hallway was that the interim security clearance he'd gotten for the trip might have raised some red flags and that this was a follow-up investigation of some kind. But that doesn't explain Proctor. It doesn't explain the illegal entry.

"Hey, Tom," Proctor says with a smirk. "Sorry about the mess."

"Then why don't you clean it up?" Sweeney says.

He knows that isn't going to happen.

Behind him, he hears George Blair enter the room and close the door. If this isn't about his security clearance, Sweeney thinks, then what is it about? He casts an eye over the blizzard of manuscript pages. Some are facedown, some fanned out. From this distance, he recognizes occasional paragraphs, either by their shape or from certain stand-out words—*convergence . . . plurality . . . cybernetic . . . multidimensional*. If he had to, Sweeney could retype this whole thing from memory—maybe not syllable for syllable, but close enough.

"What do you want?" he says.

Blair steps around to face him. "You're quite an interesting character, Mr. Monroe."

"What's that got to do with anything?"

Blair seems puzzled by this. He's clearly an idiot. Sweeney looks at Proctor, who goes out of his way to avoid making eye contact with him. He's clearly an idiot, too.

But Sweeney already knew that. There's something else going on. He surveys the chaos again and the open window catches his eye. This has nothing to do with his manuscript. That was going to be disturbed no matter what went on in here. This was more deliberate. This was a *search*.

Which can mean only one thing.

Sweeney's stomach turns and he feels weak all of a sudden. He's reached the limits of today's dose and is already exhausted from the traveling.

"What do you *want*?" he repeats, though now he's fairly certain he knows. He just doesn't understand where this is coming from or where it's headed.

He glances over at the bathroom door. He sees that it's ajar and that there's a light on inside.

"We want to know who the hell you are," Blair says.

"Why don't you ask *him*?" Sweeney whispers, nodding toward the bathroom.

There is silence. Then the bathroom door creaks open and a man in a cheap suit and a homburg emerges.

"Hello, Ned."

Sweeney half gulps, swallowing back some reflux.

"Huh?" Proctor says. "Who's Ned?"

"Ned Sweeney." Mike Sutton gestures toward him. "Advertising executive from New York."

"But I thought—"

"Shut up, Clay."

Proctor opens his mouth, but doesn't say anything. Blair just stands there. Sutton reaches into his pocket and takes out his cigarettes and lighter. He holds the pack up, offering one to Sweeney.

Sweeney shakes his head.

"I knew it," Sutton says. He lights one up for himself. "So, Ned, they tell me you're something of a big shot out here. You care to explain?"

Sweeney's mind is racing. "Look, I really don't know what—"

"Yeah, yeah." Sutton blows smoke out of his nostrils. "I was reading some of this stuff you've been writing here." He moves a couple of typed pages around with his foot. "You know what I thought? This guy's got to be hopped up on *something*. That's what I thought. And then I remembered." After a pause, he stretches his hand out, wiggles it. "Come on, hand it over."

Sweeney just stares at him. "How did you find me?"

"What makes you think I lost you?"

"Nothing," Sweeney says, defeated. "What do you want me to say? You're the best?"

"It was a photograph. I saw it in the *Chronicle*. In the social pages. You and some of those brainy fucks from RAND. At a gala event. It was in the . . . what's the name of that hotel?"

"The Casa del Mar," Blair says.

"That's the one. There was a little group, and then you were off to the side." He clicks his tongue. "The image was grainy, but it was unmistakably you. So I made inquiries. Came all the way down from Frisco just to see you."

Sweeney remembers the event. There were a lot of photographers there. And some TV people as well, conducting interviews. He even said a few words himself.

But now he shrugs. "Why do you care about this?"

"Why do I *care*? Holy shit. You stole something from me. Right out of my goddamn apartment." He flicks ash from his cigarette onto the floor. "Now hand it over or I'll break your legs."

"I don't have it."

"Not *this* again." He rolls his eyes. "Clay, do me a favor, search his bag, would you?"

As Proctor reaches down to pick up the travel bag, Sweeney lunges forward to try to grab it first. But in that same moment Blair cuts in, blocks Sweeney, and pushes him back. When Sweeney straightens up again, he sees that Blair is pointing a gun at him.

"Easy, soldier."

This is escalating fast, and as it becomes clear to Sweeney just how far it's likely to go, a second wave of exhaustion hits him.

"What am I looking for?" Proctor asks. He's got the bag open now and is rummaging through it.

"I don't know," Sutton says. "A bag for shaving gear, I guess, or toiletries, something like that."

Proctor pulls out a shirt, drops it to the floor—some socks, the same—and then a small leather bag with a zip.

"Yep," Sutton says, doing another hand wiggle.

Proctor tosses it to him.

Sweeney can still feel the MDT in his system, but only just. He can picture the final sparks and embers of it dimming to ash.

Sutton opens the small leather bag and quickly extracts the tiny bottle of MDT. He discards the bag, throwing it onto the bed. He holds the bottle up to the light and examines it.

"There's quite a bit left."

As Sweeney stares at the bottle now with a combination of longing and incredulity, he is tormented by a series of very obvious questions. Why wasn't he more careful? Why didn't he divide the MDT up? Why didn't he analyze it—*learn* how to analyze it—synthesize it, reproduce it? Why didn't he find out what it *was*? It was always his intention to do these things, and more—to share his experience of MDT with the world. He planned to do this through the book he's been writing, in which he explicitly mentions MDT, and then later, who knows, he'd do it through some other, more practical means. He thinks of the way that recent psychiatric drugs—tranquilizers such as Equanil and Miltown, for example—have become as widely available and irresistible to people as a cigarette or an ice-cold soda. Why couldn't there be an MDT pill that would be just as widely available, he wondered, and not only to the patient with a doctor's prescription, but to everybody, and for free?

"So Ned, you lied to me."

"Huh?"

"You lied to me. You told me you'd dropped this on your kitchen floor, that it all spilled out and you had to clean it up. Tsk, tsk."

Sweeney doesn't say anything.

With his foot, Sutton moves some of the loose pages to one side, clearing a space on the parquet floor.

"No," Sweeney says, leaning slightly forward, but all too aware of the gun Blair is still pointing at him. "Don't. *Please.*"

Sutton holds the bottle up between his thumb and index finger. Then, with a thin smile, he releases it.

Sweeney groans, barely able to watch.

The bottle lands on the shiny wooden floor, but doesn't smash. It bounces a couple of times before settling on its side.

Intact.

Sweeney feels a surge of, what . . . ? Relief, hope?

"I guess you must have a harder floor in your kitchen," Sutton says, and then steps on the bottle with his heavy brown leather shoe, crushing it. The glass and liquid make a crunchy, squelching sound.

Sweeney gets a little sick in his mouth again. "What have you done?" he says, gulping it back down.

Sutton gestures at Blair to put his gun away. "What have I done?" he says. "I just destroyed the evidence, that's what. And of a federal crime, I might add. But at least now we don't have to arrest you."

Feeling woozy, Sweeney takes a step backward and slowly lowers himself onto the edge of the bed.

Crouching down to the same level, Sutton clicks his fingers to get Sweeney's attention, to make eye contact with him.

"On the other hand," he says, "there *are* some people back in New York who'd like to ask you a few questions."

This time, when Sweeney gets sick, it doesn't stop at his mouth.

20

We get back to my place after midnight. Molly roots around in the fridge and cupboards. As she's chopping parsley and mint, she talks about how weird it is to meet someone like Clay Proctor, so briefly, in such an intense way, and then to hear he's died. I open a bottle of wine and put on some Tomasz Stanko. Five seconds in and Molly asks me if I'm fucking serious. She scrolls through my iTunes library for another five seconds, and then finds a radio station on her phone that plays Lorde and Lana Del Rey.

The three bulky envelopes are stuffed in the duffel bag I had to buy at the airport, which is still on the floor. I really want to break it open, but something is making me wait. With Clay Proctor gone, it's all I have left. What if it's nothing? What if it's unrelated?

I'm not sure I can stomach the thought.

After we've eaten, Molly gets lost in her phone for a while. I stare at my bookshelves.

Maybe Jill is right, though. It *was* sixty years ago—and it ruined Tom's life. Am I going to let it ruin mine?

As I'm thinking about this, a message alert pings on my phone. I extract it from my pocket and look at the screen.

"That's odd."

Molly looks up. "What?"

"I just got a text from Stephanie. She wants to know if I'll meet her tomorrow." I pause. "Her place, 10:00 a.m."

I can't tell if Molly is uncomfortable with this, but I wouldn't blame her if she were. I immediately give her a quick rundown of my interactions with the congresswoman, the advice I've given her, how mundane most of it was. "And besides," I say, "full disclosure, her father told me he was the one who set the whole thing up in the first place."

"Full disclosure?" Molly says. "What is this, *Meet the Press*?" She leans forward. "You think I give a fuck about this? Believe me, I don't." She waves a hand in the air. "I may be a little curious about what's going on between *us* right now, okay, but that's an entirely separate matter."

On the elevator ride up to Stephanie Proctor's apartment, I wonder what I'm going to say to her, what form of words I'll use. *Sorry for your loss?* I hate these situations.

The elevator opens onto a vestibule that leads directly into Stephanie's apartment. One of her staff accompanies me into a fairly fabulous *Architectural Digest*–style living room. I glance around. The empty whiskey bottles and overflowing ashtrays have been removed. The congresswoman is sitting in a floral chintz armchair and doesn't look too good. Her face is a little puffy and her eyes have a faraway expression. As I approach her, she stands up and we shake hands. It's oddly formal. Then I remember that that's appropriate.

"Sorry for your loss," I say.

"Thank you." She nods, and sits back down. "Please."

I take an armchair opposite hers.

"I expect you heard that I haven't been 'well,'" she says, throwing ironic air quotes around the last word.

"I heard something."

"Yes. It was glorious. For about an hour. Those first three glasses of Scotch, oh my God, a sensation that was twenty-five years in the making. And the first cigarette wasn't bad either." A sigh. "But then . . ."

She closes her eyes.

I sit there, waiting. Has she fallen asleep?

"What did he want from you?"

Her eyes are still closed.

It's a direct question and I suppose it deserves a direct answer. "That's really none of your business, Congresswoman."

She opens her eyes. "Oh, for Christ's sake, call me Stephanie, would you? I'm not going to be a congresswoman for much longer anyway."

"Okay. But the answer's the same."

"Yes, yes, and how *would* it be any of my business? But that's not the point. I still want to know."

"Why?"

"Because whatever this thing is he had with you, it seems to be the key to . . . to . . ."

She looks out over the room, exasperated, avoiding eye contact with me. Then she stands up and paces around.

"Two years ago," she says abruptly, "he changed. Fundamentally. He seemed to be getting sick, he was going downhill, we thought it was some form of dementia, but then he changed. He *changed*. There's no other word for it. He was put on various medications, and I know they can alter moods and so on, but this was more than that." She stops pacing and looks directly at me. "One thing is that in the midst of this change, for some reason, he developed a keen interest in you." She pauses. "Can you explain that to me, Ray?"

I don't answer.

"He pointed me in your direction, recommended you, *told* me to hire you." She waits for a response. "Did you know that?"

"Yes. He mentioned it."

"But for the longest time he seemed to be just circling around you." She shakes her head. "I had to report back every time we met. Eventually, he said he wanted to meet you himself."

I shift around in my armchair. This is extremely awkward. "How did he change?" I ask. "In what way?"

"Oh Lord." She sits down again. "He got . . . he got *nice*. Considerate. Reflective. I thought it was an act. I kept waiting for him to revert to type. Because let me tell you, Clay Proctor was a lot of things over the course of his life and his career, but *nice* was never one of them. He was a bully and a manipulator and a liar." She drums her fingers on the arm of the chair. "I've been a psychological wreck for the last two years waiting for him to take off the mask and go *boo*. And now he's gone. And I'm confused."

She's not the only one. Does she really not know anything?

What do I tell her?

"He knew my grandfather," I say. "In the early 1950s."

She looks at me. "And?"

"He wanted to talk about him. I figured it was old-man stuff . . . you know, looking back over the years."

She holds my stare. It's clear that she's unconvinced. "Look, the only reason he would do that," she says, "seek someone out from the past, would be if he had an outstanding score to settle."

"Or if he felt guilty about something?"

"*Guilty?*" She shakes her head and emits a mirthless laugh. "Clay didn't do guilt." She leans back in the chair, then immediately sits forward again. "But why did you say that? Why would he have a reason to feel guilty?"

Now I wish I hadn't said it. "Look, not long after they met, a few months . . . my grandfather committed suicide."

"Oh God."

It's as if I've just gently stabbed her in the heart.

I want to follow up by adding that the two things aren't necessarily connected. But of course I know they are. At least in some way. At some level. I try to anticipate her next question. Because how much can I tell her? How far can I go? It's actually puzzling to me that she doesn't know this stuff already.

But in the end it doesn't seem to matter.

"You know what," she says, "you're right, this isn't any of my business, and I'm sorry for pestering you about it."

"If it helps," I say, "I didn't get any satisfactory answers out of him."

"That doesn't surprise me."

We sit in silence for a while.

"You know," she says, "he kept trying to talk to me. Especially in recent months. But all I did was push him away. I didn't trust him. I couldn't. He sounded like a different person."

I feel bad for her. Because this clearly isn't an act. It's just more damage, more fallout.

"Maybe in some strange way he *was* a different person," I say. "Dementia can affect the brain in some very weird—"

"You're sweet, Ray, but this wasn't dementia." She throws her hands up in surrender. "He was in full control of his faculties."

"As a matter of interest," I say, "do you know what medications he *was* on?"

"Pffh. God knows. He had a team of doctors looking after him around the clock. I didn't get involved."

She really doesn't know. I change the subject. "What did you mean earlier when you said you wouldn't be a congresswoman for much longer?"

She looks at me. "Did I say that?"

I nod.

She smiles, her first. "I could insist that I misspoke, I suppose. Play the game. But that's the whole point. I'm tired of this." She lowers her voice. "I haven't told anyone officially yet, but I've decided I'm not running for reelection."

I'm surprised, and show it, but don't say anything.

"For some reason, I trust you, Ray, so please, hold on to this for a bit, will you? I'll announce something soon enough."

"A lot of people will be disappointed."

"I know. But my heart was never in it. This was his show from the very beginning. And the system is rigged anyway. Campaign funding these days is an unending flood of dark money from nonprofits and super PACs, and that only leads to one outcome: they own you. In my case, we're talking about Eiben-Chemcorp." She sighs. "And look, I know I'm not the only one, they collect us like baseball cards. That's how it works. But I *am* sick of it."

"It's a solid seat, and you're good at this, so won't they just keep hounding you to run again?"

"Oh, sure, and they have been, because let's face it, they have their agenda, which is, one: fight any increased regulation of drug pricing, and two: resist any relaxing of the rules governing generics. It's that simple." She laughs. "I mean, old drugs are coming off patent faster than new drugs are being developed, so it's like an existential crisis for these guys, and they're in a permanent state of anxiety about it. This won't be easy for me. They know how to pile on the pressure."

"So what will you do?"

"Ha. That'd be telling you." She studies me for a moment. "But you know what, I actually think I will tell you. I have to tell someone. The plan I have is sneaky, ingenious, and *very* dangerous." She pauses. "You know how I fell off the wagon the other day? That wasn't an accident. I knew what I was doing. It was a test. I wanted to see if I could still bring the crazy, and boy, you should have seen me. I think I scared a few people." She leans forward. "The thing is, if I go back on the sauce, I'm no good to anyone. They can badger me all they like, harangue me, twist my arm, they can even try to blackmail me, but if I'm shitfaced at ten in the morning, what difference does it make? A story or two in the *Post* or on BuzzFeed and then it's game over. They'll move on to someone else in time for November, and . . . I'll be free."

As I'm about to step into the elevator, the soon-to-be-former congresswoman puts a hand on my arm. "By the way, is it true what I'm hearing, Ray?"

"What's that?"

"About you and Molly?"

I feign surprise.

"Well, I hope it is," she says. "Because Molly's great. And she's smart. She deserved a better break than the one I gave her."

I can't help thinking that if anyone is catching a break here it's me. It's certainly not Stephanie.

"She's going to ask me how this went," I say. "Our little sit-down."

"Tell her the truth." She gives my arm a squeeze. "Always do that."

On my way home, I think back over everything Stephanie told me. I try to square up the two Clay Proctors—the one I met a handful of times and the one she knew all her life.

Could taking MDT have changed him that much? I guess I'll never know for sure. The only remaining link to that time is lying in a duffel bag on the floor of my apartment.

I send Molly a text about meeting up later on. She took the train out to her place in Astoria this morning. I promised her I'd keep her in the picture, and I will—but when I see her.

Back in the apartment, I take the three big envelopes out of the duffel bag and put them on the table. I gather all of the typed pages together into a single pile. It's a substantial manuscript.

I put on some coffee.

The first thing I do is try to establish if the pages are in any kind of order. They don't seem to be. Some of them are numbered, but not all, and as far as I can see the manuscript doesn't have a title page. So where does it begin or end? The whole thing is confusing.

I read random sentences here and there, but find it hard to place as a text. Some of the language is dry, some is technical, some flowery. So is it a scientific paper? A political tract? A *sermon*? I don't know. However, with each new fragment I read, I feel an increasing sense of curiosity and excitement. I glimpse ideas in passing that strike me as peculiarly modern. I pick up on what appear to be some fairly astounding predictions.

But aside from what it actually is, I can't help wondering who the author was—though given where the manuscript has been all these years, I don't think it's idle to speculate that the author might, in fact, have been my grandfather.

I flick through it again and come across a blank page I must have missed before. I flip it over. On it, centered and in bold type, is the following:

The Paradox of Emergence
by
Tom Monroe

And there it is, the name Clay Proctor said my grandfather was using out in Santa Monica.

Over the next few hours, I make a more concerted effort to get the pages into order, determining thematic sequence, working out if there are gaps and where they might be—solving the puzzle of how it all fits together.

Then I start reading from what I judge to be the beginning.

In the evening, after a long Sunday of laundry and podcasts, Molly comes back into the city.

As she walks through the door, I can tell that she's preoccupied about something and probably wants to talk. But when she sees me—sees the look on my face—she stops in her tracks.

"What happened?"

I point at the manuscript over on my desk.

"It's the most extraordinary thing I've ever read."

Her eyes widen.

She walks over to the desk. Sitting on top of the neat pile of manuscript pages is the bottle of pills that Proctor gave me. Next to the manuscript is a glass of water.

She looks around. "Did you . . . ?"

21

Mike Sutton looks down at his shoes in disbelief.

"Aw, Sweeney . . . *Jesus.*"

He rushes over to the bathroom in the corner.

Sweeney, for his part, gazes down at the small pool of vomit on the floor, any immediate relief he feels drowned out by the wider horror of what's happening.

He sits up straight and looks around. George Blair, the FBI agent, is standing guard by the door. Clay Proctor wears a look of disdain on his face and keeps his distance.

"Sorry about the mess, Clay," Sweeney says, mustering a grain of sarcasm from somewhere.

Proctor looks away.

Apart from the sound of running water in the bathroom, there is silence. Then Sutton reemerges. His shoes are clean again. He's carrying a towel, which he throws on the floor to cover the vomit.

"Okay, let's get moving," he says.

"But—"

"What?"

"My . . . my stuff."

"What stuff? You just came in, your bag is already packed."

Sweeney takes a moment. "My *work*."

"What?" Sutton indicates the loose pages strewn about the floor. "*This* crap? Are you kidding?"

Sweeney glares at him.

"All right." Sutton shakes his head. "Clay, George, gather this stuff up, would you?"

Sweeney reaches over to get his travel bag. He opens it and removes a few items.

When the other two have gotten all of the pages together into a single pile and placed it on the bed, Sweeney starts carefully transferring the pages into his bag. He zips the bag closed. A part of him realizes that this is utterly pointless, but then again, what has he got left? The MDT is gone. It's mingling there on the wooden floor with the crushed glass and the vomit, slowly being absorbed by that cheap towel he bought in Henshey's.

He can't believe it. The fucking *San Francisco Chronicle*.

He remembers the photographer that night, blowing flashbulbs like his life depended on it.

"Okay, come on." Sutton claps his hands together. "Let's go. We've got a train to catch."

Proctor disappears at the station.

Sutton and Blair take Sweeney on the *Super Chief* from Los Angeles to Chicago and then on the *20th Century Limited* from Chicago to New York.

The glamour of it all is lost on him. He spends most of his time handcuffed to a metal post in one of the sleeping cars. He feels awful in any case and has no interest in moving about the train, in visiting the observation lounge or even the diner. On the first day he's in a sort of daze and from then on he just feels weak. Blair hardly speaks a word and spends most of his time reading twenty-five-cent novels with titles like *Jealous Nights* and *Out of Nowhere*. Sutton talks now and again, usually to taunt or insult Sweeney, and he smokes incessantly.

Once in a while, it occurs to Sweeney that he should speak up and object. If he's not under arrest here, then what right have they got to . . . to . . .

Or is it that . . .

Or . . .

Doesn't he have a right? To walk away? To disembark when they get to Chicago, for instance? To go about his own business?

He's pretty sure he does.

He just can't ever quite summon the energy or focus to put the thought into words.

By the time they get to New York, Sweeney has regained a certain degree of equilibrium. He is able to acknowledge that MDT-enhanced levels of intelligence are now beyond his reach, but he also no longer feels as if he has just had a lobotomy.

Still, resisting Sutton seems futile.

"Where are we going?" he asks at one point.

Sutton ignores him.

A car is waiting for them outside Penn Station. Sweeney and Sutton get in the back and Blair takes the front passenger seat.

The driver remains silent. They head uptown and are soon leaving the city.

"Where are we going?" Sweeney asks again.

"Shut up."

He wonders about Laura and Tommy. He is physically closer to them now than he has been since late last year, which feels strange. He knows that he has sent a lot of money to Laura, in weekly or biweekly installments, though he doesn't know—or can't remember—exactly how much. He does remember going to casinos and attending private poker games in and around Santa Monica, and casually, effortlessly, amassing a small fortune. But the strange thing is, right now, although he can remember this stuff, he can't actually *imagine* it.

Back in Santa Monica, Sutton said that there were some people in New York who wanted to ask him a few questions. He wonders who these people are. And what they want to ask him. It's early evening when they approach what looks like some sort of an institution, a large gray building set in landscaped grounds.

They can't be far from Albany, he thinks. As the car pulls in through entrance gates, Sweeney—slumped back in his seat— glimpses a sign silhouetted against the darkening sky. They've arrived at the New York State Psychopathic Hospital.

When they get inside, to the reception area, Sutton and Blair disappear.

Sweeney hasn't been in a hospital since he was a kid, and he's never been in a hospital like this one. He is led to a room. It's bare and dank, with a cot and a stained washbasin in the corner.

The orderly is a lumbering man with ginger hair and enormous hands. He doesn't utter a word and when he leaves he locks the door behind him.

Sweeney can hear muffled voices talking and, occasionally, distant screams.

One good thing: he's able to sleep, and he wants to, pretty much more than anything else.

The door opens early the next morning and a man in a white coat enters. Tall and distinguished-looking, he's about sixty years of age and is wearing glasses. He seems kindly.

"Hello. I'm Dr. Bill Cordell."

They shake hands. Dr. Cordell offers Sweeney a cigarette.

"No, thank you."

"Don't you smoke, Ned?"

"No."

"Did you ever smoke?"

Sweeney has to think about this.

"Well yes, actually, I did. I smoked Camels. All the time."

"Good." Dr. Cordell takes a cigarette himself and lights it up. "Why did you stop smoking, Ned?"

"I don't know."

"I'd like you to think about it for a while."

He places the pack of cigarettes and the lighter on the little bed-side table and leaves.

Sweeney knows why he stopped smoking. And when. But he doesn't want to talk about it to Dr. Bill Cordell.

Later, he takes some of the typed pages out of his travel bag and looks at them. He recognizes individual words, but they're packed into long, convoluted sentences, and when he tries to read them, the whole thing becomes a blur. He gets a headache, so he gives up and puts the pages back in the bag. As he stuffs them in, a few rip, but he doesn't care. Or, rather, he's too angry.

What's happening to him?

It's bad enough that Sutton took back the MDT and then destroyed it, but this subsequent degrading of his cognitive abilities is alarming, even terrifying.

What do these people want?

Later on, Dr. Cordell comes back with a clipboard and a pen. Sweeney sits on the edge of the bed and Cordell sits facing him in a chair. He asks Sweeney a series of questions, most of them fairly standard. Where were you born? Where did you go to school? Do you have any known medical conditions? Have you ever used narcotics?

Sweeney answers the questions truthfully, except for the last one. Would MDT be classed as a narcotic anyway? He doesn't know. But he's not going to mention it. If it's going to be brought up, let them do it.

Cordell records all of the answers on his clipboard and at the end he points to the pack of cigarettes on the bedside table and asks Sweeney to take one out and smoke it.

"No." A pause. "I don't want to."

"Oh, come now, Ned."

Sweeney shakes his head.

"I'm afraid in that case," Cordell says, "I'm going to have to insist."

"How can you insist? That's ridic—"

Cordell slaps him hard across the face.

Sweeney reels backward, holding his head, glaring at Cordell in horror.

"That's it," he says, his voice trembling. "I've had enough. I want to leave this place. I want to go home. You can't detain me here."

"Oh really?"

"Who the hell *are* you?" Sweeney shouts, a surge of anger rising in him. He clambers off the bed and is about to lunge at Cordell when the door opens and two orderlies come rushing in. They quickly overpower Sweeney, holding him down on the bed. One of them, the ginger-haired guy, sticks a needle in his side. Seconds later, everything slows down, becomes heavy, and dissolves to black.

When he opens his eyes again, he feels groggy and has a headache. It's the middle of the night.

Cordell comes back in the morning and tells Sweeney to smoke a cigarette.

Numb and exhausted now, he lights one of them and smokes it. The whole experience is horrible, but he decides to get it over with as quickly as he can.

Cordell takes notes as Sweeney is smoking.

"Good work," Cordell says at the end. Standing up, he points at the pack of cigarettes, and then leaves.

Sweeney sits on the bed, waiting, but nothing else happens and the hours pass. The ginger-haired orderly brings him meals and escorts him to the bathroom. He hears distant screams again, sporadically, throughout the day. The place smells of disinfectant and boiled cabbage.

He wonders if he's allowed any visitors. Or phone calls.

Cordell is angry the next morning when he arrives and sees that Sweeney hasn't smoked any more of the cigarettes.

"What do you think they're there for?" he says. "Are you stupid?"

"Okay, Doc, okay, fine!"

He smokes five during the course of the day and nearly gets sick each time.

Cordell takes more notes the next morning, but doesn't say anything.

Sweeney finishes the pack, and it gets a little easier. Partly driven by boredom, he finishes another two packs over the course of the next three days. He spaces them out, as a way of breaking the days down into psychologically manageable chunks.

The next time Cordell visits, he doesn't bring any more cigarettes with him, and Sweeney is relieved. But he's also puzzled. Cordell inspects the full ashtray on the bedside table. Then he sits down and begins to chat.

"How are we feeling?" . . . "The weather's nice out there in that Santa Monica, I'd say." . . . "So how did you first get into the advertising game?"

Sweeney plays along. He doesn't know what else to do. Then it hits him—what's going on, what Cordell wants from him.

"Say, Doc," he says, at what seems like a natural break in the conversation, "do you happen to have any smokes on you?"

Cordell looks at his watch and makes a note on his clipboard. Without answering the question, he stands up and leaves.

Exhaling loudly, Sweeney falls back on the bed. He rolls over and groans. Is all of this really happening? How long is it going to last?

Ten minutes later, Cordell returns. He's carrying a small glass of clear liquid. It looks like water. He hands it to Sweeney. "Drink this, please."

"What is it?"

Cordell doesn't answer. He waits.

Sweeney considers flinging the liquid at Cordell and taking the consequences. But he's tired. He drinks it, knocking it back in one go. It *is* water, but it has a weird, vaguely familiar taste.

Cordell takes the glass back from Sweeney, turns, and leaves again.

Ten minutes go by before Sweeney's suspicion is confirmed.

He has just been given a dose of MDT-48.

As the room begins to pulsate, Sweeney's first reaction is to panic. He welcomes the rising flood of sensations, the widening field of perception, the lifting of the fog, the surge of energy . . . but the prospect of being confined to this awful space is intolerable to him. Agitated, he paces back and forth, trying to figure out if there is any way he can escape.

Panicking will only make things worse, though. He sits down on the edge of the bed.

Keeping his back straight, he regulates his breathing. He looks at the bag in the corner. Those pages inside—he remembers them now, the shape of what he wrote, the rhythm and scale of it all. But he doesn't need to take the manuscript out. He knows he could stand up and recite the whole thing from memory. Why would he, though? For whose benefit? So in the absence of any external stimuli—unless you count the dramatic, swirling daubs of thick beige paint on the walls, or the veined map of cracks that is the ceiling—Sweeney closes his eyes and retreats into a state of profound stillness.

After about an hour, he hears footsteps approaching along the hallway outside.

He opens his eyes.

Cordell enters the room.

"Hello, Doctor," Sweeney says, almost in a whisper.

Cordell closes the door behind him. He has the clipboard in his hand. He takes a pack of Camels from the pocket of his white coat and places it on the bedside table next to the lighter and the ashtray. Then he sits down in his usual position, opposite Sweeney.

"How are we feeling, Ned?"

"Interesting question. If you mean, how am *I* feeling, then fine, I guess, under the circumstances. But how are *we* feeling? That's a bit of an ontological conundrum, wouldn't you say, Doc? Because I don't think *you're* feeling that well at all."

Cordell looks at him, his brow furrowed.

"I mean, you're what, sixty, sixty-one, and look at you. You've got that gray complexion, those bags under your eyes. I don't think you've had a good night's sleep in—"

"Ned?"

"What?"

"Be quiet. You asked if I had any smokes." He nods at the bedside table. "There they are. Now smoke one."

"Uh-uh." Sweeney shakes his head. "I don't think so."

"Why not?"

"I don't want to. And besides, I don't like the odds."

"What does that mean?"

"In 1950 alone, five epidemiological studies were published that showed smokers of cigarettes were more likely to contract lung cancer than nonsmokers." He glances at the bedside table, then back at Cordell. "You know, Doc, you might consider quitting yourself."

Cordell sighs impatiently.

"Look, Ned," he says, "if you don't smoke one of those damn cigarettes, I'm going to call Glenn and Brad in here. They'll put you in a straitjacket and give you another injection. Then we'll start this whole thing over again tomorrow. Is that what you want?"

This time Sweeney sighs.

He reaches over for the pack of cigarettes and the lighter. The first thing he does is offer a cigarette to Cordell.

"*Ned.*"

"Fine."

He takes one out, puts it in his mouth, and flicks the lighter. He really doesn't want to do this. He brings the yellow flame to the tip of the cigarette, makes contact, and inhales. He immediately feels the black, chemical heat of the smoke enter his mouth, move through his trachea, his esophagus, and reach down into his lungs with its sticky, resinous coating.

"Oh shit." He starts coughing and spluttering.

Cordell glares at him before making a note on his clipboard. "Okay," he says, "again."

Sweeney hesitates, then takes another drag from the cigarette. He tenses up and puts a hand over his mouth. He gets off the bed, rushes over to the sink in the corner, and throws up in it.

"*Goddammit,*" Cordell yells. He stands up, stares at Sweeney for a moment. Then, muttering under his breath, he leaves.

The MDT effect lasts for the rest of the day and into the night. At a certain point, Sweeney feels that if given the opportunity he could easily talk his way out of the New York State Psychopathic Hospital—or even talk his way into a job running the damn place. But he never gets that opportunity. No one comes near him. On several occasions, he tries to get someone's attention by calling out, but he also decides early on that he isn't going to shout or bang on the door or act like a crazy person.

Eventually, he has to take a piss in the sink.

By the time Glenn or Brad, whichever one it is, comes in the following morning, Sweeney has slowed down at every level. He can barely even nod yes to an offer of food.

The day passes, and then more days pass. Dr. Bill Cordell never reappears. There are no more cigarettes, no more glasses of water.

Just long hours, sleepy ones, lonely ones, blank ones.

Eventually, after maybe a couple of weeks, someone does show up.

"My God, Ned," Mike Sutton says, "you look awful. Come on, pack your bag. You're leaving."

And just like that, he leaves. No fuss, no forms, no signing out. Sutton drives him back to the city and talks the whole way, about himself mainly—his early days under Harry Anslinger at the Federal Bureau of Narcotics, some of the big, high-profile busts he's made, his time with the Office of Strategic Services during the war, and the top-secret Agency stuff he's doing now, working with the likes of Eiben Laboratories and IBM. "Oh yeah, Ned, you picked the wrong guy to fuck with, let me tell you. But I'm going to let bygones be bygones. And you know why? Coz I got bigger fish to fry than some loser asshole like you."

Sutton lets him out near Penn Station.

Standing on the sidewalk with his travel bag in hand, Manhattan popping and fizzing all around him, Sweeney wants to say something to Mike Sutton, but he can't concentrate. He doesn't know where to begin.

"Ned? *Ned?*"

"What?"

"Are you going to be all right?"

Sweeney nods, then something occurs to him. "I don't have any money."

Sutton throws his eyes up. "Holy shit, you're a mess, you know that?" He digs into his pocket, takes out a roll of bills, peels off a twenty, and hands it to Sweeney. "Now, go on, get out of here."

Sweeney wanders off. He goes into Penn Station, gets change for the twenty, and finds a telephone booth.

Where else can he go except home?

He calls Laura.

But he doesn't know if she'll be there or not. She could have moved. Maybe she's still in Philadelphia with her sister.

He doesn't know what he'll do if she isn't there.

It rings. "Hello?"

"Laura? It's Ned."

There is silence.

"*Laura?*"

The silence continues, but out of it rises a low whimper. Then, "*Ned?*"

"Yes, it's me. I'll . . . I'll be home on the next train."

When he arrives, Laura is agitated and angry and possibly even a little drunk. She's clearly ready to slit his throat and ask questions later. But when she sees him standing in the doorway, she goes pale and has to fight back tears. The questions she's been carefully formulating for months, the arguments and the counterarguments, the case for the prosecution—it all evaporates, and within minutes she's running a bath and putting his clothes into the washing machine and heating up some dinner while hushing Tommy, who can barely contain his excitement.

Sweeney keeps offering to explain, but Laura just shakes her head at him, *no, no, no . . . be quiet, be still . . . there'll be time for that later.*

He's not aware of it himself, but it emerges soon enough that he has lost a lot of weight and looks gaunt. And he seems . . . *slow.*

That part he understands, that part he feels.

But damn, he thinks, you should have seen me a few weeks ago.

"Your father's not well." This is what he hears Laura telling Tommy. "But he's home now."

"Yes." Tommy snuffling, fighting back tears.

"And he'll be well again very soon."

"I know. He *will.*"

Sweeney almost believes it himself.

The days pass. He sleeps well and eats well. Looking around, he notices that a few changes have been made. The place has had a paint job. Some of the furniture is new. Laura's hair is different.

It's all nice.

He and Tommy spend lots of time together, playing in the yard, horsing around, and *talking*—about trains, about baseball, about the future. But he and Laura haven't really talked yet. It takes them about a week to work up to it.

Laura explains, finally, that when she came home from Philadelphia and Ned wasn't there, she got angry. She stayed that way for a while, but then she started to worry. She was on the point of contacting the police when the first payment came through. Someone from the bank got in touch and advised her that five hundred dollars had been transferred into their savings account. She didn't know what to make of it, but had to assume that it was from Ned, and that therefore he was okay. The second payment, a couple of weeks later, was for a thousand dollars. Where was he and what was he doing? At that point her imagination ran away with her and she began to picture all sorts of lurid possibilities. But once her anger reestablished itself, and the money kept coming, and in ever larger amounts, she just let it slide.

For his part, Sweeney doesn't have as coherent a story to tell.

"I went to California . . ."

This is how he starts, and more than once—but it's also as far as he ever gets. If he was going to tell the truth, he could talk for hours, but he's rehearsed telling the truth in his mind, over and over, and it doesn't sound good. He doesn't think Laura or anyone else would believe it.

"I went to California . . ."

And he wouldn't blame them.

So he goes with amnesia.

". . . and after that I really don't remember very much at all."

On several occasions, he takes out the typed manuscript he had in his travel bag and reads short sections from it. He knows he wrote this stuff himself, but it's as if he's seeing it for the first time, and he's intimidated by it, by the fluidity of its prose and the complexity of its ideas. When he's feeling stronger, he intends to read the whole thing, and maybe do something with it, but for the time being he decides to just store it away. The manuscript is about four or five hundred pages long, so he divides the pages up and fits them into three separate padded envelopes. He puts these into a bag, which he puts on a shelf in the garage.

The next morning over breakfast, Laura suggests that maybe he should make an appointment to go see a psychiatrist, that it might be of some benefit to him.

Sweeney's initial reaction to this is defensive, but he quickly backtracks. He sees that she's probably right.

"Wouldn't it be very expensive, though?"

"Yes, I'm sure it would, but . . ."

"But what?"

Laura seems surprised. "Ned, don't you know how much money there is in our savings account?"

He remembers his trips to the bank all right, but there were so *many* of them.

He shakes his head.

Laura looks around, as though someone—one of the neighbors, perhaps—might be within earshot. Then she leans toward him and whispers, "It's over two hundred and fifty thousand dollars."

Although he maintains the pretense of amnesia, Sweeney finds his sessions with Dr. Lazlo Rothmann very helpful. The weekly trips into the city are enjoyable—he's not on his way to work, he's not anxious, he's not under pressure.

But because he has so much time on his hands, he does a lot of thinking and reflecting. The one thing he keeps circling back to in his mind is what happened at the New York State Psychopathic Hospital with Dr. Bill Cordell and those fucking cigarettes. What was that all about? And who was Cordell working for anyway?

Sweeney is strolling along Park Avenue one morning, after a session with Dr. Rothmann, when something occurs to him. Mike Sutton once said in passing that he had occasional dealings with Eiben Laboratories. Maybe that was who he got his supply of MDT-48 from. And maybe Eiben Laboratories was also who Bill Cordell was working for.

In which case, Cordell probably heard from Sutton about how MDT kills the desire to smoke and was putting it to the test in a sort of limited clinical trial. Cordell got Sweeney into a pattern of regular smoking, administered some MDT, then checked to see if the pattern would be interrupted. Not only was it interrupted, Sweeney threw up and is unlikely to smoke again as long as he lives.

All of which is fine, as far as it goes. But what about MDT's many other and far more interesting properties? Cordell showed no interest in those whatsoever.

In fact, he showed no *awareness* of them.

Sweeney stops at the corner of Sixty-Fourth Street.

Is it possible that no one at Eiben Laboratories is actually aware of just what a powerful drug MDT is? More to the point—at least as far as Sweeney is concerned—do they still have a supply of the stuff?

He gazes down Park at the Helmsley Building.

But of course they *must*. Because even a drug that did nothing else but eliminate nicotine cravings would surely be worth millions, if not tens of millions, to a company like Eiben. So at the very least— Sweeney imagines—they have to have it in development, right? And with a view to launching it on the market as soon as they possibly can.

The very prospect stirs rapid, spiky changes in his body chemistry.

That evening, he and Laura are having cocktails at a neighbor's house across the street when Sweeney picks up a copy of *Time* magazine from a few months back. It has an article in it stating that "tars from cigarette smoke" have now been proven "beyond any doubt" to cause cancer in mice. Some of the big tobacco companies are pretty spooked and are starting to put a lot of money into medical research. The cancer cat, it seems, is now clawing its way out of the tobacco-industry bag. There's been a lick of panic on Wall Street, too, apparently, with stocks falling sharply in recent months— American Tobacco losing about 6 percent of its value and Reynolds closer to 10 percent.

As Jerry pours martinis and Samantha passes around canapés, Sweeney notices that everyone is smoking. No doubt this scene is being replicated in living rooms, bars, and hotels across the country. And that's when it hits him. *Dr. Bill Cordell doesn't work for Eiben Laboratories.* It's much more likely that he works for one of the big fucking tobacco companies. Or for all of them. Because Cordell was angry that day. He snarled at Sweeney and stormed out of the room. Why would he do that if he'd just had it confirmed that the substance he was testing actually worked, that it was the pharmaceutical equivalent of pure gold?

Sweeney feels weak. It seems so obvious now. Cordell works for American Tobacco or R. J. Reynolds or Philip Morris. And Sutton works for everyone. Or anyone. The FBI, the CIA, whoever.

He drains his martini and takes another one from a passing tray.

Mike Sutton had at least twenty different vials in his freezer— all supplied, presumably, by Eiben Laboratories. He also had that long list of abbreviated chemical names in his notebook, and when Sweeney lied to him about the effects of MDT, telling him that all it did was make him not want to smoke, Sutton immedi-

ately crossed it off his list. But if he then chose to take this information to Cordell, it's probably safe to assume that he said nothing
about it to Eiben, or to anyone else.

Which still means Eiben has a drug in its labs somewhere that
not only eliminates the craving for nicotine, but actually has the potential to transform society at a fundamental level. They just don't
know it. They don't know any of it.

Someone needs to tell them.

Sweeney's initial attempts are not encouraging. He finds the number for Eiben Laboratories at the local post office the next morning
and telephones them, but his request for a meeting is met with bewilderment. He tries a few more times over subsequent days and is
eventually told to stop calling them.

The next week, carrying a briefcase and wearing a new suit, he
takes a cab out to the Eiben Laboratories plant in Hoboken. The
irony is that if he were actually on MDT, this would be a whole lot
easier. Unannounced, he asks to see Lloyd Buntin, a vice president
of sales whose name was mentioned on one of the phone calls. There
is a little confusion and eventually Buntin appears, but things don't
go well. Sweeney plays his hand too soon and when he mentions
MDT-48 by name, alarm bells start ringing.

"I'm very sorry, Mr. Sweeney, I don't know who you are or what
you want, but I'm going to have to ask you to leave at once."

On his way back, Sweeney curses himself for his stupidity. How
did he *think* that was going to go?

Then he has an idea. That journalist fellow he once met—it was
on the very first night—what was his name? Vance Packard. He
writes for *American Magazine*. Surely a story like this would be right
up his alley—pharmaceutical company harbors drug that could help
millions kick the smoking habit?

A cure for alcoholism, even? Addiction?

That's Pulitzer Prize territory.

Sweeney gets on the phone with *American Magazine* at once and asks to speak with Packard. Again, there is a little confusion, but Packard eventually remembers Sweeney, and when he does, he gets excited.

"Why, yes . . . Ned Sweeney, right? I remember. That was a fascinating conversation we had—in fact I've been working on some of those ideas we discussed. Yes, I'd *love* to meet, so long as you don't disappear on me again."

They make an arrangement for the next day. Sweeney says he's free any time. Packard suggests early evening. He has a few appointments so, say, where they went before, Peacock Alley at the Waldorf, 7:00 p.m., is that good?

Absolutely.

And it is. Because Sweeney is excited, too. He sees this as a way of possibly extracting some MDT-48 from Eiben Laboratories. Or as a first step, at any rate. Sweeney's only worry is that Packard won't find him as convincing as before.

He arrives at the Waldorf early. He enters the vestibule, goes up the short flight of stairs, and crosses the main foyer. The last time he was here he remembers registering a flood of visual data—colors, textures, architectural details. It was effortless. This time he is oblivious to pretty much everything, except for the drumming in his ears and the thumping of his heart.

Peacock Alley is fairly busy, but he sees Packard immediately. He's not far away, standing over to the left, between a table and one of the glass display cabinets. He's talking to a tall man with slicked-back hair and a mustache. Beside this man is a small boy, maybe seven or eight years old. He's got wavy blond hair, a pudgy face, and a ruddy complexion. While continuing to listen intently to the man, Packard spots Sweeney, and with a deft movement of his eyebrows, indicates that he'll be with him in a minute.

Although there is a babble of voices in the room, Sweeney still manages to catch certain words and phrases from the conversation. "Luna Park . . . FHA . . . Capehart . . ."

But none of it means anything to him.

Seconds later, in any event, Packard is saying, "Okay, Fred, good, I'll talk to you again." Then the tall man and the boy turn away and move in Sweeney's direction.

As they pass around him, the boy sticks his tongue out at Sweeney, does a rapid pivot, and kicks him in the shin. The tall man just clips the boy on the side of the head and says, "Donnie, cut it out."

Sweeney does his best to ignore the sharp pain in his leg. Smiling, he takes a step toward Packard. They shake hands. Packard seems shocked.

"Did that kid just . . . ?"

Sweeney shakes his head. "It's nothing."

But the incident has definitely thrown him off balance, and as they sit at a table and start talking, he finds it hard to concentrate. Also, unlike the last time, he finds himself a little intimidated by Packard.

It's not a good start.

Packard listens, even asks a few questions, but Sweeney can soon tell that he's perplexed, and then losing interest. "I'm not sure what you're telling me, Ned, and honestly, without some kind of evidence, I don't see there's anything I can do."

Again, how did Sweeney think this was going to turn out? He manages to get away before things become too embarrassing and promises Packard that he'll follow up. But even as he's saying this he's not quite sure what he means by it himself.

A few minutes later, Sweeney is walking along Forty-Ninth Street toward Lexington Avenue when he hears a voice from behind call out his name. He stops and turns around. Mike Sutton is ten feet away and catching up.

"Hey, Ned, I thought it was you."

Sweeney's heart sinks. He's already demoralized from the meeting with Packard, and now this?

"Hello," he says.

"Where are you headed?"

"I don't know. I'm going home." He studies Sutton for a moment. "What are *you* doing here?"

"This and that, you know. I'm a busy guy. Between here and San Francisco I don't know where I am half the time."

Sweeney senses that something isn't right. "What do you want?"

"What do I *want*? Nothing. Can't a fella say hello?"

"A fella like you doesn't just pop up out of nowhere."

"Suspicious, aren't you?"

"Good night."

Sweeney turns and starts walking.

"Don't you want to hear what I have to say?"

"No."

"Not even if it involves a fresh batch of MDT? Ten of those little vials?" He makes a kissing sound with his lips. "I could maybe do a little business on the side, Ned. If you're interested."

Sweeney stops.

He knows something still isn't right, but he also knows he can no longer just walk away.

He turns around again.

"I have a couple of things to do," Sutton says, looking at his watch. "But meet me in an hour, say, at my hotel?"

"Maybe."

"I'm at the Fairbrook, on Forty-Third Street. Room 1406."

22

"No, not yet," I say.

But then I reach for the bottle. I take out one of the tiny pills and knock it back with some of the water.

Even as I'm doing this, it strikes me as reckless and irresponsible. For a guy in his late teens or early twenties, it might be liberating, or even thrilling, but it definitely carries a different weight when you're ten or fifteen years down the line, one that presses in on your chest, and presses hard. Because you realize there are only two possible outcomes from doing something this dangerous—either you get lucky and survive, or you don't, in which case the last thing in life you'll ever have to confront will be the immutable fact of your own stupidity.

Still, if this is actual MDT-48, then the irony here is that *not* doing it would feel just as irresponsible.

I can't speak for Molly.

She picks up the bottle and shakes one of the pills out into the palm of her hand. She reaches for the glass of water.

"Look, Molly, you don't ha—"

"Shut up."

She takes the pill.

And that's it. We wait to see what happens.

Molly reads the manuscript in twenty-five minutes. While she's turning the pages at flip-book speed, I deep-dive around the Web and quickly manage to locate a ten-second clip of my grandfather being interviewed at a gala event in some hotel.

"And you, sir, your name is . . . ?"

"Monroe, Tom Monroe."

The film is grainy and slightly blurred, and the sound is hard to make out. Camera flashbulbs are going off in the background. I reckon this must be in Santa Monica, probably late 1953.

"And are you a mathematician, sir, or a physicist?"

"No, I'm afraid I'm here on false pretenses, but it sure is a swell gathering this evening, isn't it? Throw a rock and you're bound to hit *someone* with a PhD."

"Well, I—"

The clip cuts off at that point. There are others from the same event, brief interviews with von Neumann and Herman Kahn, but the Monroe clip—the *Ned Sweeney* clip—is mesmerizing.

I watch it ten times on a loop. There's something electric about Ned's presence, something irresistible in his tone. I also see a clear resemblance to my father, to Tom, it's in his eyes, and after the fourth or fifth viewing of this thing, I can't help feeling that I could meld into the screen and *become* Ned Sweeney—there in that ballroom, on that balmy evening so long ago.

When Molly's done with the book, we come together in the middle of the room, and just stand there for a moment facing each other.

"Oh my God."

"Which?"

"Both. *This.* And the book." She shakes her head. "It's incredible."

"Which?"

"Shut up."

We start laughing.

Then we compare notes, on the lookout for anything unfamiliar or irregular. But basically I feel amazing. There is a heightened awareness of . . . *everything*, sense perceptions, intellectual clarity, intuition, emotions, and all in perfect proportion.

To which Molly goes, "Check, check, check."

Though maybe not *perfect* proportion, because I soon find that I'm consumed with an overwhelming, heart-quaking desire for every inch of her, and while I have to believe that this would be happening anyway, since it's happened before, there is a gathering rhythm and intensity to it now that is undeniably new.

And, luckily . . .

Check.

We fall into each other's arms. Spinning lightly, whispering, we trace a slow arc across the floor toward the bedroom.

"And then there's my kid sister," Molly is saying. "She missed out on the worst of the drama, so she's, I don't know, smoother, like a version 2.0 with all of the bugs removed. But then again she had to grow up without a dad, I suppose, and that's . . . that's . . . oh my God, I can practically *see* it now, if I picture her face, it's there, like a seam or a vein, it's always been a part of her."

She sits up straight now, her back against the pillows.

"Ray, you have to tell me to shut up. I could go on talking all night. I know you asked me about my family and stuff, but this has been like the equivalent of fifteen years of therapy, in what, twenty minutes?"

I stroke her arm. "I wouldn't yield the floor just yet, Mol, if I were you."

"Why? Coz then you'll start up?"

"It seems inevitable, doesn't it?"

"I wouldn't mind."

Eventually, though, we move on to talking about the manuscript on the table in the other room. Which we've both now read. Somehow, and with uncanny accuracy, Ned Sweeney—or Tom Monroe— managed to describe a scientific, technological, economic, and sociological paradigm that today we may only just be reaching the outer limits of, namely the great delusion of infinite expansion. He saw in Eisenhower's America what was happening with consumerism and how that could only ever go in one direction; he saw what was happening with the nerds at the RAND Corporation and how their hard-on for the exponential growth curve could only ever result in an infinite winter of automation; he saw what was happening in the university laboratories and how the exquisite flowering of learning and insight they'd achieved over the centuries could only ever lead, in the end, to the bleak realization that this supposedly grand dance humanity is caught up in is merely a mechanistic, ticktock interaction of chemical impulses.

And if he'd left things there, it would indeed be bleak—but he didn't. There's a whole final section where he proposed what was effectively a taxonomy of human intelligence, and at the apex of this he placed intuition, or unconscious intelligence. He defined this as the organic seat of disruption and creativity, and identified its source as some possible combination of the biological and the metaphysical.

"It's pretty scary, the amount of stuff he predicted," I say. "Under normal conditions, you can only extrapolate so far before things will go a little off course, and then, pretty fast, *way* off course. But he steers a clear line right through."

Molly sits up straight again. "My impulse is just to ask how he did this," she says. "But right now I almost feel as if I *know*, as if I could imagine doing something like it myself."

In the stillness of the room, I can't be sure if the insistent thump of our side-by-side heartbeats isn't actually audible.

"Let's go out," I say.

23

Sweeney wanders around for the next hour, tormented again by the irony that if he actually had MDT in his system, he wouldn't be doing this. More than likely, he'd already be on the train home.

But here he is.

The Fairbrook is a stately old redbrick pile, built in the 1890s. It probably has about fifteen hundred rooms. It's stuffy, dark, and oppressive.

Sweeney walks across the lobby to the elevators. He tells the operator which floor. Soon, he's stepping out onto a long, empty, thickly carpeted hallway.

He starts counting down the room numbers. 1412, 1411, 1410. He only has a few moments left to change his mind. 1409, 1408, 1407. The good outcome in this scenario is that Mike Sutton actually meant what he said. And, for him, what he said isn't all that implausible—that he's willing to siphon off some of the drugs that come his way and make a bit of extra money.

1406.

But how much of his own money is Sweeney willing to siphon off for a vial of MDT? That's the question. He guesses he'll find out in a minute.

He knocks.

Sutton holds the door open and Sweeney walks in. As hotel rooms go, it's dingier than most. The lighting is dim, coming from a single bedside lamp, and there's a musty smell in the air. It takes Sweeney a moment to realize they're not alone.

A man is standing over by the window. He's in a dark suit and is partly obscured by the heavy burgundy drapes.

Sweeney's heart sinks. "Hello, Clay."

"Hello," Proctor says. "So what are you going by now? Tom or Ned?"

Sweeney ignores this.

Sutton stays where he is, as if he's waiting for someone else. Then, on cue, there's a light rap on the door. Sutton opens it and George Blair slips in.

Sweeney throws Sutton a look. "Was he following me?"

"What do *you* think?"

Fixing his gaze now on the stained, olive-green carpet, Sweeney says, "Okay. I'm here. What do you want?"

Sutton doesn't answer.

Sweeney looks at him again. "I assume there are no ten vials of MDT."

"Not in *this* room."

"Well then, I should probably be on my way."

But he doesn't move.

"What do you want?" he repeats after a moment, this time in a whisper.

"Look," Sutton says, "people are upset. You make calls to Eiben Laboratories with some story? You show up out in Hoboken? Then you contact a journalist, a high-profile magazine writer like Vance fucking Packard? And tell him the same story? Christ."

"Except, the thing is," Clay Proctor says, taking a step forward, "it's *not* a story, is it? Bill Cordell can attest to that. Since you were up there with him, he's carried out a few more trials on individual patients, and it's definitive."

"What is?"

"That it works. MDT. Cordell's report has been making the rounds, and let me tell you, it's got a lot of people scared shitless."

"Why?"

"Come on, Ned. Why do you think? Tobacco is a multibillion-dollar industry. I mean, all the medical research into cancer these days is bad enough, but *this*?" He makes a snorting sound. "If this gets out, it could knock the industry stone-cold dead overnight."

Sweeney looks at him, puzzled. "Why do you care?"

Proctor shrugs and makes a face, but it's unclear what he means, and Sweeney feels a twitch of panic. "What about Eiben Laboratories?" he says. "Surely MDT is a huge opportunity for them?"

"Maybe. In theory. But things aren't that simple. Eiben is a small company and there are competing interests here. And questions of ownership. It's . . ." He waves it away. "Let's just say that a lot of very influential people are paying close attention to this."

"What people? I don't understand. The tobacco companies? The government? Who are you working for, Clay?"

Sutton clears his throat loudly. "Jesus, enough already."

Sweeney tries to regroup. "No, wait, listen to me. This isn't just about cigarettes or money—you do *know* that, right?" His hands are shaking. He takes a deep breath to steady himself. "I mean, let me ask you a question, Clay. Do I seem like a smart guy to you? Not particularly, right? Not smart like I was out in Santa Monica, that's for sure. So how do you think I was able to keep up a conversation with someone like John von Neumann? How did I second-guess all those nuclear physicists at that test site on Bikini Atoll?"

"When you were a kid you ate your greens. How do I know?"

"It was the MDT." Sweeney leans forward. "It *makes* you smart. It's like a nuclear explosion, only inside your brain." He throws his hands up. "It won't just eliminate the craving for nicotine, it'll eliminate the craving for all those things that make us anxious, and drive us insane, and push us over the edge—power, control, money."

Proctor stares at him, a flicker of uncertainty behind his eyes.

"Oh boy," Sutton says. "I bet that's just what all those CEOs are *dying* to hear." He clicks his tongue. "Right. Let's get this over with."

Sweeney turns around. "Get what over with?"

"You should have kept your mouth shut," Sutton says. "It's that simple. You were home and dry, but you couldn't leave it alone, could you?"

"Oh God." Sweeney turns back. His voice is shaking. "You don't understand."

Proctor is still staring at him.

"What I said is *true*, Clay. If you don't believe me, take some yourself."

Proctor swallows nervously.

"Come on!" Sutton shouts. "We haven't got all night."

"Seriously, Clay." Sweeney is pleading now. *"Try it."*

Proctor hesitates, then gives a quick, determined shake of his head. Taking a step back, he reaches up and pulls the heavy drapes to one side. He opens the window, letting in a stream of sounds— traffic, distant voices, a whispered breeze.

Sweeney's gaze moves beyond Proctor now, to something across the street, a neon sign flashing on a building. He stares at it in disbelief: on, off, on, off, it's like a pulse . . . his life as it could have been, his life as it is now, his life as it could have been, his life as it is now . . .

Behind him, there's a ripple of movement, and something new in the air: a smell, it's sweet, but it's also pungent. Before Sweeney can react to it, a hand—Sutton's or Blair's—reaches around and wraps a chloroform-soaked handkerchief over his mouth. Sweeney struggles, kicks, flails, but the sounds streaming into the room become muffled, and the throbbing light across the street settles into a blur.

He's sinking.

And soon, emerging briefly from the darkness, he knows he's falling.

24

Talking nonstop, we get up, put on some clothes, and head out into the night. The city is pulsating all around us, and we fall in with its rhythm of sounds, of light, of movement. I don't feel high, or drunk, or intoxicated. It's more a preternatural clarity of mind. Everything is quick and frictionless, every thought I have, every connection I make. But I can't help wondering what this must have been like for Ned—especially that first time, when he had no idea what was going on. He seemed to cope pretty well, though. Later, according to Clay Proctor, he stole a quantity of MDT before heading out to Santa Monica, but . . . who did he steal it from? And how? And why did he end up calling himself Tom Monroe?

These questions make me realize how little I still know about any of what happened back then. Clay Proctor was maddeningly selective in what he told me.

But maybe I'm beginning to understand why.

We're just coming out onto Lexington Avenue and I turn to Molly. "I think I want to go to Forty-Third Street."

Her brow furrows. "The hotel?"

"It's not there anymore, but still . . ."

Next thing I know, her arm is out and a yellow cab immediately pulls up. In the back, we retreat into our phones for a few minutes, burning through texts and emails, until Molly says to the driver without even looking up, "This is good." She pays and we get out.

We walk a couple of blocks to the spot where the Fairbrook Hotel once stood. So many of Manhattan's old hotels are gone now—long demolished and replaced by steel-and-glass office buildings. The Fairbrook came down in the late sixties after a fire and this thing was erected in its stead, an anonymous, international-style high-rise. As we stand in front of it, gazing up at its geometric lines, I try to calculate where the fourteenth-floor window of a stuffy Beaux Arts heap might reasonably have been located. It's unverifiable, so I just settle on a position and conjure up a tableau of flickering ghosts . . .

Again, there's no way of verifying this, but my intuitive sense is that Clay Proctor lied about not being in New York when Ned Sweeney came out of that window up there. I think Proctor was in the room and I think he knew exactly what happened.

It was the one thing he couldn't admit to.

I look down at the sidewalk now, and as with the building, it's different. These aren't the same paving slabs that were here sixty years ago. But I choose a spot anyway and then see it happen, *feel* it happen, the sudden whoosh of impact, the already misshapen body, limbs twisted, shards of broken bone protruding . . . eyes, nose, mouth, all oozing blood.

The final breath, so much of the story going with it.

I wish I could have learned more, a lot more. All of the facts. But when does that ever happen, really? The key thing I know now that I didn't know before is that Ned Sweeney didn't commit suicide—a fact that itself rewrites history. But would my father have been any less angry or tormented if he had known? Would his life have been any less miserable? Or just miserable in a different way? And how about Jill's life? How about mine? There are no answers here.

We walk on and get another cab. We head downtown. We flit

around for an hour or two, going to bars and clubs, weaving in and out of different conversations, different orbits, but always circling back to each other, where the engagement is sharper, denser, deeper. We end up walking home, back to my place, which is over sixty blocks, but this is nothing, each block passing like the mechanical flick of an old taxi meter.

And we talk the whole time. Mainly about the possibilities of MDT-48—where we could go with it, where we could take it.

"The biggest land grab in history is taking place right now," I say, "and it's for our data. Companies are silently amassing it, harvesting it, and storing it, and whoever owns it will end up owning the future. But so far, none of these companies has shown that they're capable of behaving any differently from Hertz or Philip Morris or Eiben or Nike, because they all end up having to do the same thing, turn a fucking profit—the same way all politicians end up having to sell themselves in order to get elected. MDT could short-circuit that whole system and rewire it."

But Molly is focused on the practicalities.

"That bottle has, what, maybe sixty pills in it? Split fifty-fifty, you, me—that's a month. Even if we cycle it out to one dose each a week, that's still not much more than six months. Say we cut each pill in two, and do the same, that's still only a year. So we need to determine what this stuff actually is. We need to put on our lab coats and go from Chemistry 101 to advanced chemistry, and fast . . ."

Our levels of excitement are at fever pitch now, but once we turn the corner at Sixty-Fourth, once we're within a few feet of my building, I can tell that something's not right. Molly puts a hand on my arm.

"What is it?"

"I don't know."

And I don't, not yet—but it feels like I'm doing some sort of rapid calculus based on factors I'm not even aware of. Temperature, maybe? Air density? I enter the lobby and immediately detect a slightly stronger note of whatever it is I'm picking up on. I hurry over to the elevator and tap impatiently on the panel. Once we're inside the car and moving up, I realize what it is.

"Shit."

Molly deflates, knowing now in essence what I know. The details aren't important. How could they be?

She doesn't even ask.

I have to say it anyway. "It's faint, but . . . do you get that?"

There's a trace of something in the air.

Molly pauses. "Cologne?"

"It's Dean's. Proctor's security guy. Maybe he wasn't Proctor's. Maybe he's Eiben." The elevator stops and the door opens. Stepping out, I release a heavy sigh, and whisper, "Of course he's fucking Eiben."

We move slowly down the hallway to my apartment. I can already see from here that the lock has been tampered with—hairline scratches from a bump key. I get my own key out and open the door. I flick on the light switch. A couple of pieces of furniture have been turned over, some drawers have been pulled out and shelves have been cleared, but all in a line to the bathroom, where—predictably—the contents of the medicine cabinet have been tossed and spilled on the floor.

I get down on my hands and knees and sift through the items. Needless to say, the MDT is gone.

I turn and lean my back against the toilet bowl. Through the doorframe I can see Molly in the living room. She's perched on the end of the sofa with her head down.

I close my eyes.

I left it in the fucking medicine cabinet? Why didn't I put more thought into this? There were signs I should have read—even Proctor was paranoid. He didn't say it in so many words, but it was obvious.

I open my eyes again and see Molly standing over by the desk.

I get up and slowly make my way back into the living room.

"They left this behind," she says, and points at the manuscript, which is still there, exactly as we left it. "And that's because they don't know what it is."

I take a step forward, my eyes on the neat stack of pages.

"They're idiots," she says.

"*I'm* an idiot."

"No." She pauses. "Well, not in their league." She leans over and rests her hand lightly on the title page. "This is a time bomb, Ray. Almost literally."

I look at her.

"Think about it," she says. "If someone wrote *The Paradox of Emergence* today, they'd probably be accused of plagiarizing the works of established thinkers, of neuroscientists and anthropologists, or at the very least they'd be accused of spending too much time reading *Wired* or watching TED Talks on YouTube. Right?"

"Probably."

"But it was written in 1953." She throws her hands up. "That's sixty years ago, and it effectively predicts everything that came after it—the internet, big data, nanotechnology, stem-cell therapy." She counts them off. "Facebook, VR, Bitcoin, even blockchain. It's incredible. But not only that, it was written under the influence of a *named* psychoactive substance. It's stated explicitly." She clicks her fingers. "I think it's on—"

"Page fifteen, second paragraph. *My initial dose was 75 mcg of MDT-48 . . .*"

"Exactly. So if we publish this, if we get it out there, and get people to read it, Eiben won't be able to sit on MDT for much longer." She pauses. "Besides, they don't own MDT. I mean, what did Proctor tell us? Doesn't it originally come from a fungus that grows on the bark of some tree?"

"Yeah, the Bawari tree. In the Amazon jungle."

"Right. He also said it was time for another leak. But you know what, Ray? I think it's time to break open the whole dam."

She's right. But I look ahead and all I can see are obstacles.

The document is not real.

It's a hoax.

It's *fake*.

Molly takes her phone out and starts scrolling.

"What are you doing?"

"None of this will be easy," she says, still focused on the screen, still scrolling. "So first I'm going to find someone who can analyze these pages—the paper stock, and then the ink from the typewriter ribbon. Obviously, we need to prove that the manuscript is as old as we think it is. Then we can establish copyright and ownership."

I keep staring at her. My heart is quaking again. "And second?"

She looks up and holds my gaze. "Well, the dating and legal stuff is probably going to take a while . . . so in the meantime I thought I'd find us a cheap flight to Brazil."

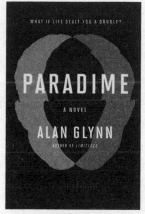

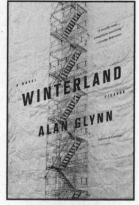